TALL, DARK, HANDSOME AND AVAILABLE

"No amount of money in the world is enough to make me marry you. Jordan, I'm leaving." She stepped toward the door. The taller man followed her out of the room.

He extended a hand toward her. "I think we met under the wrong circumstances. Let me introduce myself. I'm Kwabena Opoku."

Tamara accepted his extended hand. His hand was big and slightly rough. "Tamara Fontaine. And I am not marrying that idiot in there you call your friend."

He smiled in response. "Good." Tamara looked at him, puzzled. "Because I believe you are marrying me."

Tamara looked up at him, surprised. He was more handsome than she remembered. He exuded an aura of effortless virility and sensuality. And in spite of this stressful situation, he seemed calm and rational. He looked like the type of man women would fight over. Why would a man like him have to pay for a wife to get a green card? Was this some kind of scam?

A Marriage of Convenience

JEWEL AMETHYST

LEISURE BOOKS   NEW YORK CITY

This book would not be possible without the unwavering support of my sister and my husband. Thank you both.

A LEISURE BOOK®

August 2009

Published by

Dorchester Publishing Co., Inc.
200 Madison Avenue
New York, NY 10016

Copyright © 2009 by Jewel Daniel

ISBN 10: 0-8439-6298-4
ISBN 13: 978-0-8439-6298-7
E-ISBN: 978-1-4285-0723-4

Visit us online at www.dorchesterpub.com.

A Marriage of Convenience

Prologue

Chaos, utter chaos, was the only suitable description of Tamara Fontaine's bedroom suite. Hair, clothes and makeup adorned every surface. Tamara sat in front of the mirror, a professional beautician applying costly makeup to her face while her hairdresser added the finishing touches to her hairdo.

"Ok, there." The beautician swiveled the chair to face the full-length mirror, a satisfied smile on her lips.

"Wow," Tamara gasped. She had never looked or felt so beautiful. *It really is happening. I am getting married!*

Her unruly brown hair with added extensions and burgundy highlights was gelled and brushed into submission, then swept up in a French roll with fine curls hanging over her temples. The makeup was perfect, with eyelash extensions framing almond-shaped eyes made dark brown by contacts. Strawberry lipstick and dark lip liner gave her ordinarily thin lips a full appearance. Bronze blush accentuated her newly discovered cheekbones and blended well with her smooth light brown skin. She was still dressed in her strapless corset bra and her petticoat. The elegant satin gown with a form-fitting bodice and delicately embellished train laid across the king-size bed waiting to grace her new body. It accentuated the waistline she discovered after losing twenty-five pounds. The dress was a size sixteen, four dress sizes smaller than two months ago.

Tamara's divalike first cousins, Darlene and Ebony, hovered between the bedroom and the sitting room, laughing, teasing, getting hair and nails done, wriggling into tiny dresses. In the meantime, a professional photographer, determined to capture every moment of this fairy-tale wedding snapped photo after photo, while Aunt Leticia ran around shoving a video camera in their faces.

Tamara was elated, laughing at everything. Today she and Jared Turnbull would exchange vows in the gazebo on the back lawn of their new home, the swimming pool as their backdrop. The sky was clear and blue and the temperature a balmy eighty-two degrees. And tonight, oh tonight, she and Jared were going to fulfill their love in the most special of ways, right in this bedroom. During the ceremony, her wedding planner's crew would be in here preparing the bed with fresh linens and rose petals. They would fill the heated Jacuzzi just before the reception was over when Jared and Tamara would steal away to consummate their marriage.

Ebony removed a negligee from the nightstand and held it up. "Oooh, aren't we sexy," she teased and tossed it to Darlene, who motioned to the photographer to get a shot of it. As Tamara reached for it, she tossed it back to Ebony, laughing.

"Quit playing around. You'll make me late for my own wedding," Tamara scolded Darlene impatiently.

"Looks like somebody can't wait for that cherry to be picked," Ebony taunted, laughing as she removed her hot pink satin bridesmaid dress from the hanger.

"At twenty-five, don't you think I've waited long enough?" Tamara asked.

"That thing's probably so tight, you need a jackhammer to get inside," Ebony said.

They all burst out laughing. This was the first time in a long time Tamara and her first cousins, with whom she was raised, had been able to share such lighthearted banter. She had always envied her tall, slim, long-legged cousins with their smooth chocolate complexions and dark brown eyes framed by long eyelashes. At five-feet-four inches and yo-yoing between two hundred and two hundred and twenty pounds with light brown eyes and short curly lashes, Tamara always felt like the ugly duckling among them. Worst of all, her very light complexion quickly became as red as a vine-ripened tomato with the slightest embarrassment.

Darlene, a polished twenty-six-year-old legal secretary who spent most of her energy trying to snag a wealthy professional, was the most derisive when it came to Tamara's appearance. She criticized everything from her excess weight to her wavy, sometimes frizzy hair, except when she wanted a favor. Ebony, a twenty-five-year-old single mother of two who worked at McDonalds, was less derisive than Darlene, but used Tamara as her babysitter, often without prior arrangement. Their behavior toward Tamara eroded her confidence around men and made for a sometimes strained relationship with them. But today, they had put all differences aside and lent their full support to their cousin. This was, after all, Tamara's big day, the day she committed to the man she loved.

Tamara thought about her handsome fiancé, and her heart skipped a beat. They'd met barely three months ago at a career fair in San Francisco. He was six feet tall, athletically built, with a caramel complexion, whiskey eyes and a honey-coated tenor voice. Jared had solicited Tamara's help with his computer in the booth where he recruited for his financial services company. Then he surprised Tamara by asking her to dinner.

It was love at first sight. That night, they went back to his five-star hotel. He kissed her like there was no tomorrow and they struggled to contain themselves before they went too far. She was, after all, a virgin, and he was a deeply religious man. They spent the remainder of the career fair taking long walks and holding hands along the moonlit shores of San Francisco Bay, dining at elegant restaurants and sharing passionate kisses. Each kiss held a promise of the ecstasy and fireworks this wedding night would surely bring.

They parted sadly, he returning to Chicago and she to Baltimore. A few weeks later, he surprised her with a trip to Ocean City. There under the stars on the boardwalk, he proposed.

"Tammy?" Darlene's voice behind her brought her out of her starry-eyed reverie. "You need to get dressed."

Tamara smiled. "Sure," she said, carefully slipping into the heavy wedding gown.

She looked at the clock on the wall. It was a little past four. She heard the band playing outside. "Maybe we should start heading downstairs," she suggested.

Just before they stepped out of the bedroom, her best friend, Jordan, entered delivering Devon, his four-year-old son, the ring bearer. Tamara nervously adjusted the tie on his rented tuxedo.

"Tammy, you look absolutely stunning," he said.

"Thank you." Tamara gave him a hurried kiss on his cheek, leaving bright red lip marks. "Ok, guys, let's go."

"No need to rush. The groom's not here as yet," Jordan informed them and went downstairs ahead of the girls to take up his station as best man.

The bridal party entered the formal living room, laughing and chatting, trying to get a suitable position for more photos. Just then the door opened and Leyoca Novak, Tamara's mother, stepped into the living room. A hush came over the crowd, and Tamara's face turned deep crimson. Both Leyoca and Tamara observed each other while the others stared in silence, waiting for sparks to fly.

Tamara was the first to break the silence. "I thought you weren't coming," she said tensely. It had been two months since Tamara had spoken to her mother.

Leyoca smiled wistfully. "Didn't expect me to miss my only child's wedding, did you?" She held out her arms, and Tamara ran into them. They embraced for a long time before Leyoca said, "I may not agree with your choice of a mate, but it's your choice, Tamara, and I respect your decision."

"Oh, Mommy, I'm sorry I said those horrible things to you," Tamara apologized, remembering the harsh exchange she had with her mother when Leyoca expressed her disapproval of Jared.

Leyoca waved away the apology. "Let's not get all mushy now and ruin that beautiful makeup." She held her hand and spun her daughter around. "You are beautiful, Tammy."

Tammy smiled. Having her mother at her side on her wedding day completed her happiness.

"Will you walk me down the aisle?" Tamara asked her mother.

"Of course I will. Just promise me one thing."

"What's that?"

"No babies yet. I'm too young to have a grandchild." Everyone laughed, and the light mood prevailed. "Or am I too late?"

"Don't worry, Mommy," Tamara said, rolling her eyes. Some things just never changed. "We decided to wait for marriage."

Leyoca smiled, relieved.

A few minutes later, the wedding planner came into the room, frantic. "Everybody's here except the groom," she announced to Tamara. "Maybe you should call him, find out what's the holdup."

Tamara called both his cell phone and hotel room, but there was no answer. "He's probably on his way over here right now." Tamara was worried. Brides were supposed to be late, not bridegrooms. "Do you think something happened to him? Maybe I should call the hospitals."

Yesterday, when she last saw him, he was excitedly looking forward to the wedding. Instead of going to a day spa as Ebony and Darlene had suggested, Tamara had spent the day with Jared, making last-minute financial transactions. They had opened a joint account and added each other's names to their personal accounts. At seven he dropped her back at her home in Rosedale, telling her she needed her beauty rest.

"Let me see the phone," Leyoca said. She called the hotel front desk and asked for his room. Slowly she turned around to face Tamara. "I'm sorry, Tammy. It looks like he checked out sometime around nine last night."

"Checked out?" Tamara asked dumbfounded. She closed her eyes. "There must be an explanation."

With trembling hands, Tamara dialed the car-rental agency. They informed her that the car was turned in at BWI airport some time after ten last night. Tamara felt a headache coming on. She looked up at her mother. "Did you have anything to do with this?"

Leyoca looked at her, hurt. "Tamara, we may not see eye to eye on everything, but you know I would never hurt you or embarrass you like this."

Tamara felt the tears, but refused to cry. There would be plenty of time to cry later.

She swallowed the lump in her throat and blinked back salty tears. She stood up, held her head high, her back ramrod straight. "Well, what are we waiting for?" she asked the silent room. "It's time for the reception."

"Are you sure you want to do this?" Darlene asked her softly.

"Whether or not that food gets eaten, I'm paying for it. We may as well make use of it."

Tamara forced a smile and led the way through the sunroom and onto the stone patio. As she walked up to the gazebo where the priest still sat, the guests trained their eyes on her. There were only about forty people, most of whom were her coworkers, family friends and distant relatives. Though she felt like hiding under her bed at this moment, she steeled herself.

"Well," she started, struggling to keep a smile on her face, "we know what most people come to weddings for: to see the bride, right? Here I am." There was a trickle of uncertain laughter. "As you can see, there'll be no vows exchanged today. Seems like the groom's got a case of cold feet." Another trickle of laughter. "Well, you know what they say: 'If you're not man enough to show up at your wedding, you're not a man at all.' I'd kinda prefer to marry a man." The guests erupted in laughter, stood and applauded. "Well, we've got lots of food, and we've got a band." Tamara fixed her eyes on Jordan and smiled fondly. "My best friend always says, 'Before good food waste let belly bust.' So, folks, let's get the party started."

The band struck up a hip-hop tune and Tamara danced her way down the aisle to the stone patio that would have been the dance floor. Jordan joined her, and then one by one the guests joined in. Finally the wedding planner remembered her duty and started co-ordinating what was turning out to be quite a party. Instead of a sit-down dinner, they served the food buffet style while the guests danced and partied into the night.

An hour later, Tamara slipped away and locked herself in her bedroom. She needed to be alone. She needed to think. Her head was throbbing and the pain in her heart was almost physical. There were people dancing and enjoying themselves at what should have been her wedding. How could Jared have not shown up?

Dammit! I deserve an explanation if nothing else. She stared at the phone, tears streaming down her face. *Why did he do this to me? Why?* She lay across the bed crying and hyperventilating. Just then she heard a knock on the door.

Slowly she got up, wiped her tears and opened the door. Leyoca entered and held her daughter in her arms.

"You were really brave to do what you did, Tamara. Believe it or not, I don't think I would have had such courage. I'm proud of you."

Tamara clung to her mother and sobbed. "You tried to warn me, Mommy, and I didn't listen."

"You see, Tamara, when people are in love they sometimes make bad decisions. They see and think with their hearts, and I understand. I know you loved him." They were silent for a while.

"Let's get you out of this uncomfortable dress," Leyoca said. She rifled through Tamara's still packed bags. Tamara had just moved her clothes and personal effects to their new home. She hadn't finished placing them in the closets and dresser. Tonight would be the first night she slept there, and she'd expected to share it with Jared. The thought brought fresh tears to her eyes.

When the tears subsided, Tamara asked, "What did you see in him that I didn't?"

"Intuition. He was just too smooth."

Tamara changed into a pair of jeans and a T-shirt. She walked over to the window and looked down at the revelers partying on her lawn. They were doing the Electric Slide, a mandatory dance at weddings. "You know, I have that honeymoon package. It's too late to cancel or postpone it now. Maybe you and Carl could take an impromptu vacation."

Her mother smiled apologetically. "I'm sorry, honey. My schedule is booked solid for the next two months. I canceled a series of meetings today to be here, and I still have to promote my book. Plus Carl is still in San Diego."

There was a soft rap on the door before Jordan entered. "You're in capable hands. I'll go check on the party." Leyoca hugged her daughter one last time and left.

"I wish there was something I could say to make it better," Jordan started.

"Companionable silence would be nice," Tamara responded, and they both laughed. Then she broke down in tears. After she regained her composure, she said, "You know, there's this part of me that hopes that he'll walk in here with some valid explanation—like he was unconscious at the emergency room or something—and we still get married. I've been such a fool."

"He had us all fooled," Jordan said comfortingly. "Time will heal the pain."

"I was supposed to be in marital bliss tonight. I was supposed to lose my virginity on this very bed tonight. Now I'll be sleeping in this mammoth bed all alone."

"Marriage and marital sex is overrated anyway. Three kids later and there isn't even a marital bed," Jordan confessed. "You're lucky if you can get one night without five people squashed in your bed."

"Yet you manage to keep Becky pregnant." Tamara laughed through her tears, thinking of Jordan's stay-at-home wife who was pregnant yet again. Tamara knew it was a difficult time for them since Jordan recently had been laid off.

Jordan sighed. "The last time we made love was probably when she got pregnant."

Tamara couldn't help smiling. She had never thought of marriage beyond the wedding night and the honeymoon. She moved to the window again and looked down at the partiers. The numbers were dwindling as guests slowly left.

"I know just what you guys need: a nice romantic vacation, just the two of you. How about an all-expenses-paid European cruise, complete with a honeymoon suite and every conceivable luxury?"

"Don't even think of it, Tammy..."

"Look, Jordan, it's too late to cancel, and I've already paid for it."

"What are we gonna do about the kids?" he asked, warming to the idea.

"Leave them with me. It beats being in this big house all alone. I can have Ebony's girls over, and it would be one giant party."

Jordan smiled. "Someday I'll repay you for this." He hugged her. "Let me talk to Becky about it."

A few hours later, the guests had all gone, and Tamara settled down for the night. She was not alone. Her relatives insisted on spending the night to keep her company. Since the master bedroom was the only furnished bedroom in this huge house, Darlene and Ebony shared the king-size bed with her, just like they had as kids when they lived in the tiny apartment in East Baltimore. Leyoca and Leticia slept in the sitting room on the sofa bed and Kayla and Katanya, Ebony's kids, slept on an airbed in one of the guest rooms.

Before drifting off to sleep, Tamara smiled ruefully. She expected marital bliss tonight, but instead out of the ashes of despair emerged the hope of familial unity, love and acceptance. Despite their diva ways, Ebony and Darlene truly cared for her. And her mother, amid her stoic self-controlled façade, loved her more than anything else. Maybe it wasn't a bad way to spend her wedding night, after all.

Chapter One

Eight months later

It was wet—soggy, soaking wet. Rain came down in torrents and ran off the glass walls of Tamara's sunroom in sheets. Thunder cracked loudly, sending Jordan's son Devon diving for cover. Eight-year-old Kayla, Ebony's oldest daughter, watched the sheets of rain flow down the glass.

"This sucks," she complained. "This really sucks."

"This sucks. This really sucks," echoed her five-year-old sister and emerging shadow, Katanya.

They were spending the week with Auntie Tammy, and Kayla was looking forward to wading in the stream and collecting strange-colored rocks. Ordinarily they would have been in summer camp, thanks to a generous Auntie Tammy, but this year the coffers were dry. Instead Ebony decided they would spend the time with Tamara, since, after all, she was unemployed.

Tamara looked at the bored girls as she rifled through her mail. Devon had finally left the safety of the throw on the sofa and found his way to the PC in the library. She could hear him playing some game. He was becoming so much like Jordan, a computer enthusiast. It didn't matter if it was raining, snowing, sleeting or bright and sunny, give him a computer and Devon was content.

She looked at her two disgruntled young cousins

staring forlornly at the window. Kayla was a little tomboy. She always wanted to be outdoors. Katanya, on the other hand, was more like Ebony, wanting to dress up and be pretty. If she could remain in princesslike attire forever, she would. Yet she followed her sister around and echoed whatever she said.

As Tamara turned her attention back to the envelopes in front of her, her heart skipped a beat. There was mail from New Image Tech, the firm she interviewed with a week ago.

She held her breath and crossed her fingers, saying a little prayer. She had been out of a job for eight months and had been on at least seventeen interviews. It was the same each time: you're overqualified, you're not qualified enough, you need a degree, you're not what we're looking for, we don't think you'll be a good fit for this company. Wherever she applied, it was the same. She was beginning to think that she was being discriminated against solely because of her weight. A few months of dallying with chocolate-chip cookies and Häagen-Dazs ice cream and she'd gained back all the weight she'd lost for the wedding and then some.

However, this last interview had gone really well, and she was optimistic. With trembling hands she opened the letter. Immediately hope turned to despair. They, like all the others, thought her experience was impressive, but didn't think she was a good fit for the company.

She held her head in her hands. Her unemployment checks had run out, and she now had zero income. She tried to budget her money carefully, but her credit card bills from the failed wedding and the new house were eating up everything she had. She had even hocked her engagement ring. She'd gotten six thousand for it, when it had originally cost over ten thousand. Two months ago, she'd borrowed money from her mother. She hated doing that because it always came with a lecture that ended with, "Sell your house and move back home." Last month, Jordan had thrown a consulting job her way. With four kids under five, including a young baby and numerous medical bills, Jordan needed every job he could get, yet he sacrificed and gave her that one. It brought in three thousand dollars, enough for her mortgage, utilities and car payment. Her credit cards just had to remain unpaid.

The phone rang. Tamara grabbed it on the first ring. "Hello?"

"This is Visa calling to remind you…" said the lady on the other end.

Tamara did not have the money to pay the credit card, so she did like any other American would do. "The check is in the mail," she lied, and said a silent prayer for forgiveness. She had no idea how she was going to find the money to pay her credit cards or her mortgage next month, for that matter.

Tamara looked out at the sheets of rain pouring on her windows. When it rains it pours—literally, she mused. Tamara closed her eyes. How did it get to this? Just last year she was so happy. She'd had lots of money in the bank and a dream job as an information technologist, making almost six figures despite not having a college degree. She'd gone to UCLA on a full scholarship but after two years had quit, completed a computer-networking course and had gotten a high-paying job in Silicon Valley. A year later, driven by nostalgia and loneliness, not to mention the offer of a lucrative job working closely with her best friend, she had moved back to Maryland.

Living rent free in one side of her mother's tiny duplex in Rosedale and collecting Section 8 subsidized rent from Aunt Leticia and Ebony who occupied the other, Tamara had been able to build a substantial savings. Her only indulgence had been the Lexus SUV she bought a year ago and the clothes and toys she often lavished on Kayla and Katanya and her godson, Devon. She had had no credit-card debt.

Then she met Jared. Tamara recalled her happiness after his proposal. Even Darlene and Ebony's lack of enthusiasm when she announced her engagement and Aunt Leticia's warning that three weeks was too soon for such a life-altering decision did not deflate her bubble. She chalked it up to jealousy. None of Aunt Leticia's boyfriends had ever proposed to her, Ebony had two kids and was still unmarried, and Darlene, despite her phenomenal beauty and her feminine wiles, rarely maintained a relationship longer than three months.

Instead she and Jared had excitedly gone in search of their dream home. They found it, this majestic sixty-five-hundred-square-foot house on a half acre of land in a new Burtonsville community in affluent Montgomery County. It was custom built, and Jared had insisted on every luxury that was offered. The mortgage was steep, but Tamara didn't mind. She was, after all, a very well-paid IT specialist, and Jared owned a lucrative financial-services company. Moreover, Jordan had bought a modest two-thousand-square-foot home a few blocks away in the same community a year ago.

She was living a dream.

All that changed after Jared abandoned her at the altar. Tamara felt tears of anger and frustration stinging the back of her eyes as she thought about Jared. Not only had he broken her heart, he'd wiped her out and left her in debt. She should have seen the signs when she paid for the engagement ring after his credit card got rejected. She should have realized something was amiss when he had insisted on taking control of her finances, setting up investment accounts with her savings, and adding his name to her bank accounts. She had trusted him as a professional financial advisor and as her fiancé. She should have listened to her mother when she compared him to a used car salesman. Instead, Tamara had been blinded by love and had cursed her mother.

Though her mother had forgiven her, Tamara cringed each time she recalled the harsh exchange between them the night she introduced Jared.

"You are making a big mistake. This guy has ulterior motives. I don't want you to marry him," Leyoca warned.

"That's not your decision to make. You cannot micromanage every aspect of my life."

"Don't be so conceited, Tammy. You shouldn't rush into marriage with this…this man. He reminds me of someone from my past."

"Who? My father?" Tamara asked sarcastically. *"Oh no, I forgot…I don't have a father. Mommy, Jared asked me to marry him, not sleep with him, not shack up with him. What more do you want from me?"*

Leyoca bit back tears. She straightened her back and stiffened her shoulders, holding her head high. *"Well,"* she said, *"for the record, I don't approve of this marriage, and I won't be attending your wedding."*

"That's fine," Tamara responded, *angry tears welling in her eyes. "You're not invited."*

Her mother had been right. Two weeks after he'd stood her up at the wedding, her mortgage check bounced. Tamara recalled the nauseating feeling she had when she discovered her bank accounts were all depleted, the investment accounts had never been created, and her credit cards were almost maxed out. Jared had stolen everything from her.

When she reported him to the police, she learned that Jared Turnbull was really Jeffery Walters, an elusive con man wanted for bigamy, embezzlement and fraud. She recalled the embarrassing moment when she'd mentally questioned his reason for postponing sex until marriage, not realizing she'd spoken aloud. When she saw the barely concealed mirth on the officer's face, she wished she could sink through the floor. That's when one officer explained, "Your guy likes men. Jared Turnbull was Jeffrey Walters's lover. When Turnbull died, Walters took his identity and used it to swindle unsuspecting investors out of thousands of dollars."

Tamara remembered leaving the precinct with a sense of futility. There was little she could do to recoup her losses since his name was on the accounts. Tamara was determined to rebuild her finances. However, three weeks later, she'd lost her job, a victim of corporate restructuring. That was the hardest blow. She knew the company was experiencing difficulty. She had seen Jordan, with his bachelor's degree in computer engineering and his master's in business administration, get laid off three months before her wedding. But Jordan, being the optimistic Jamaican immigrant he was, did not despair. He used the severance package offered by the company to open his own info-tech consulting business.

Tamara didn't have that option. Her severance pay was consumed by her huge mortgage and credit-card debt. With a good recommendation from her boss, she'd set out immediately to find another job. In fact, she had been so certain that she would have found one by now, that she'd taken some of the money from the sale of her engagement ring and purchased a bunk bed, dresser and swivel bookcase with a full-length mirror from Ikea for the girls. But here she was, eight months later, broke, and in debt with no income.

"Are you ok?" Tamara opened her eyes to see Kayla standing in front of her. "You look like you're about to faint."

"I'm ok," Tamara responded. "Just thinking."

"About what?" Kayla persisted.

"About what we're gonna do today. And you know what?" she asked, forcing enthusiasm into her voice. "How about we make some cookies?"

Katanya gave an excited, "Yay," while Kayla just shrugged and said, "Ok."

"Devon," Tamara called. "We're making cookies."

Devon strolled into the room. "Cooking is for girls," he said sullenly.

"And who told you that?"

"Daddy."

"Well, I'll have to have a talk with your daddy about that. Come on, it will be fun."

Half an hour later, they were elbow deep in flour. Just then the phone rang. "Kayla, you're in charge. Any of those little ones get out of hand, you just take care of them for me."

"Yes, Auntie," Kayla grinned. There was nothing she enjoyed more than being in charge.

Tamara answered the phone on the fifth ring, just before the answering machine kicked in.

"Please hold for an important call from…" a mechanical voice said over the phone. Tamara promptly hung up. She considered it insulting for a machine to call your home and ask you to hold for an important call.

As she headed for the kitchen, the phone rang again. It was the credit-card company again, but this time she spoke to a live person who warned her if she did not at least make the minimum payment in the next week, her account would be turned over to collectors.

Tamara took a deep breath and did what she had been doing for a while now. "The check is in the mail," she lied.

"Ma'am, our record shows that you claimed to have mailed it two weeks ago. We haven't received any payment as of yet."

"I'm sorry. It must be lost in the mail," Tamara said feebly.

"I suggest you contact your post office and track your mail, ma'am."

Tamara sighed and hung up. Twenty minutes later, the kids were putting the cookies in the preheated oven when the phone rang again. Quickly Tamara finished what she was doing, wiped her hands and ran to the phone, giving Kayla instructions to supervise the cleanup.

"Hello?" she answered breathlessly. It was the credit card company again threatening to take her to collections if a payment was not received within a week. "I just spoke to a rep a few minutes ago, and I told her that I already sent in the payment!" Tamara said, exasperated.

The lady apologized. Just as soon as Tamara hung up the phone, it rang. She picked it up angrily. "I said the check is in the damned mail!" she screamed in frustration.

"Whoa," Jordan responded on the other end of the line, laughing. "No wonder my palm is itching. I knew there must be some big money coming my way. I hope that check has lots of zeros behind it."

"Oh, it's you," Tamara said, smiling. "Thought it was those creditors again."

"Don't you check your caller ID?"

"Took it out. I have only basic telephone service now."

"That bad, huh?"

"That bad, but I'll survive."

"I know you will. So what's my little man up to?"

"He's in the kitchen baking cookies," Tamara responded, peering into the kitchen to ensure that the kids were still on task.

"Baking cookies? What are you doing to my son?" he joked.

"Making him a self-sufficient man!" Tamara responded indignantly.

Jordan laughed lightly. "What are you doing later?"

"Other than babysitting Kayla and Katanya, not much. Why? You have a hot date for me?"

Jordan laughed again. "Actually, I do. How about dinner and a movie?"

"Hey, buddy, I don't date married men," Tamara teased. "Don't you have a wife to take out?"

"This was Becky's idea."

"I'm flattered," Tamara said sarcastically. "When a man's wife begs him to take his best friend on a date, it screams charity case. Believe me, I'm not that desperate."

"Let's put it this way, I have two tickets for the premiere of a sci-fi B movie. I figured we'd catch a bite after."

Tamara couldn't help smiling as she remembered the one time early in their marriage that Jordan had taken Becky with them to see a sci-fi B movie. Becky had been silent throughout the movie, but the minute they walked out of the theater, she turned to Jordan and said, "Honey, you know I love you more than anything in this world, but if you ever take me to another crappy movie like this I will divorce you!" Since then Tamara accompanied him to sci-fi movies with Becky's most enthusiastic blessing.

"Ok," she agreed. "But what will I do with Kayla and Katanya?" Even if she could take them back up to Baltimore to their mother tonight, she knew Ebony worked the early shift and would not be able to bring them down in time before work.

"Becky will watch them."

"That's six kids, Jordan. That's a little much, even for Becky."

"Don't worry about that. Becky can handle them."

Chapter Two

Hours later Tamara found herself laughing hysterically at the sci-fi movie. The plot in itself wasn't funny. It was the poor acting that made it hilarious. After the movie they drove to a T.G.I. Friday's not far from home. The rain that had stopped midafternoon had returned in full force. Jordan and Tamara made a mad dash from Jordan's five-year-old Subaru Outback to the entrance of the restaurant.

As she sat across from Jordan, her best friend and greatest supporter throughout all life's changes and challenges, she was filled with nostalgia. They had been friends ever since sixth grade when Jordan was a scrawny kid with a nose and lips that took up his entire face, eyes as big as a frog's and a Jamaican accent so thick you swore he spoke a foreign language. She had saved him from a set of bullies who surrounded him calling him "bug eyes" and "tar face" and telling him to get back on the banana boat. Though Tamara was shy and often the object of their ridicule, she had been angry enough to stick up for him, telling the guys to pick on someone their own size. They immediately turned on her. She had hollered so loud that a teacher came to their rescue. Since then, she and Jordan had been inseparable.

Tamara and her mother had moved to San Diego a year later, and her mother had rented out their side of the duplex to Jordan's family. The next year Tamara begged her mother to let her go back to the duplex in Rosedale and live with Aunt Leticia and her cousins, who occupied the other section. She and Jordan became even closer then, often spending hours together playing computer games, talking and reading.

Jordan and Tamara remained close. Even after his summer trip back to Jamaica just before they entered ninth grade. He left Maryland a scrawny ugly kid and came back a hot sexy catch. His face filled out to meet his nose and eyes. His lips, considered thick and rubbery before, were now full and sensuous, according to her flirtatious cousins. The acne-prone skin was now a smooth coffee-cream complexion. He grew at least six inches and his body developed. He was suddenly popular. Even then he never excluded Tamara from anything in his life. He remained her best friend. A wife and four kids later, Tamara and Jordan were still like brother and sister.

Tamara looked around the restaurant pensively. It had been a while since she ate out, beyond the occasional Mickey D's. The last time she'd been to a restaurant was almost a year ago with Jared. Tamara smiled at Jordan. "It's been a long time."

"Yup," he responded. "We now know what reality feels like for the millions who made so much less than we did." Jordan's business was doing fairly well, but medical bills had been eating up quite a bit of his income. He failed to find an insurance that would cover Becky's hospital bills because she was pregnant before signing up, and the twins' asthma was a pre-existing condition not covered by most affordable insurances. Yes, Jordan was in a better place than Tamara because he had an income, but it was still a tough and unpredictable road.

They ordered the least expensive things on the menu and chatted and laughed.

"I have a proposal for you," Jordan said.

"A proposal?" Tamara asked.

Jordan looked at her carefully. "It's a marriage proposal."

Tamara laughed sarcastically. "I believe you're already married."

Jordan laughed in response. Then he said, "I have an associate who needs a green card desperately. He is willing to marry any American citizen, just to get it."

Jordan observed Tamara as her expression went from shock, to indignation and then anger.

"What the hell do you think I am, Jordan? *Desperate* for marriage? I thought you knew me and understood me better than that!" With that, she threw her napkin on the table, grabbed her purse and walked off.

A few minutes later, she returned to the table. "I don't have a ride home," she admitted.

"You done blowing off steam?" he asked as she settled again. He knew her well enough to give her time and space when she was angry. Her boiling point sometimes came quickly but never lasted more than a few minutes.

She smiled briefly, took her seat at the table and resumed eating her dinner.

"I guess I said it wrong. This is not a marriage as much as it's a business deal. He needs the green card, and you need the money."

She looked at Jordan from the corner of her eye.

"You didn't mention money before."

"You didn't let me finish."

"How much are we talking about here?" she asked, surprised at the desperation in her voice.

"Fifteen grand."

"Fifteen thousand dollars?" That was enough to pay her mortgage, car payments and credit cards for at least a few months. It could buy her some time until she got a job. But still, she wasn't going to marry a stranger for money. She had principles.

Jordan continued. "The deal is, you have a court marriage, file the papers and go your separate ways until the INS interview. A few months later when he gets his green card, you file for divorce and it's over. You get five grand when you file the papers, five grand when he receives the green card and the final five grand when you file for divorce."

Tamara was quiet while contemplating it. The money was tempting, and she desperately needed to pay her credit cards. She didn't even know how she would survive next month. But still, some things were just not right.

She looked at Jordan. "This is crazy and you are crazy to think that I would even consider that."

"Ok, it might not be right, but it worked for my grandmother. She came on vacation, married an American citizen, got her green card, then filed for divorce. It was strictly business, nothing more."

"The answer is still no."

"At least think about it."

The next morning, Tamara awoke to the sound of the phone ringing. This time, there were two collection agencies and the credit card companies. She definitely hated her life…but not enough to marry a stranger. However, the more she thought about it, the more she warmed to the idea. Yet she couldn't see herself marrying for money.

Over coffee she rifled through her mail from the previous day. This was her moment alone before Kayla and Katanya returned from their sleepover at Becky's. She was certain Devon would be with them; he had a crush on Katanya.

The mail was the usual: letters from creditors and potential employers turning her down. One letter was from her gynecologist reminding her to schedule her annual checkup. She didn't have insurance coverage anymore and she sure as hell couldn't pay out of pocket. She was down to her last packet of birth control pills, but who cared, wasn't like she needed them anyway. She must be the only celibate person on the pill.

Another letter was from IRS, saying she owed taxes from last year. *Maybe I should just go work at McDonald's, sell this house and move back home. But this is home.* The more she thought about it, the more attractive the marriage proposal looked.

Just then the phone rang. It was Jordan. He was on his way over with the kids and, "By the way, have you thought about it?"

Before Tamara could back out, she heard herself say, "Yes, I'll do it. When?"

"Next week."

"Next week!"

"There is a time factor involved. Otherwise he may face deportation."

Tamara took a deep breath. It was ridiculous, even bordering on insane, but she needed the money. "Ok."

Chapter Three

Tamara was driving on the rain-slicked road when her mother called. She did not have a hands-free device. Katanya had broken her earpiece a few weeks ago, and she never replaced it.

Cradling the receiver between her shoulder and her ear, she answered the phone. This was one time she didn't want to talk to her mother. Not today, when she was about to make the biggest mistake of her life. She was on her way to sell her soul for a meager fifteen thousand dollars.

"Where have you been? I haven't heard from you in two weeks," her mother accused. Tamara rolled her eyes. Though she hadn't lived with her mother since she was twelve, Leyoca still kept a stranglehold on her life. Tamara understood that her mother was overcompensating for not physically raising her and was trying to protect her from repeating her own mistakes. Leyoca, like her sister, Leticia, had been a teenage mother and high school dropout collecting welfare. But she went back to school, got her GED and attended college part time. Always an overachiever, she had worked her way up the corporate ladder, until her job took her to San Diego, California. Eventually, she'd left her firm to form her own advertising company. Since then, she'd written two books: *By the Bootstraps*, which detailed her struggles as a teenage mother on welfare, and *Out on a Limb*, which discussed the risk she took leaving a Fortune 500 company to form her own business.

"I don't have long distance on my phone," Tamara responded calmly.

"You do have a cell phone."

"I'm over the monthly limit. I have a very basic plan."

They talked while Tamara navigated the road, waiting for her mother to get to the point. She knew this was about her house. Finally Leyoca got around to the topic that Tamara knew was number one on the agenda.

"Maybe you should look into selling your house. You might make enough to pay off your debts and you can always move back home."

"Mommy, I already looked into it. I don't have enough equity in my house to break even on the mortgage if you consider the interest I'm paying. Besides, I like my house. It is the only thing of value that I own. I don't want to sell it."

"Tamara, you're not being practical!"

Tamara sucked in her breath and looked through her rearview and her side mirrors. She needed to get in the left lane.

"If things come to a point where my back is against the wall, I'll sell. Right now, I'll do whatever I have to do to keep my house. Even if it means working at McDonald's." *Or marrying a stranger.*

"If you'd stayed in college and gotten your degree, you wouldn't be in the predicament you're in now."

"Jordan has his degree and a master's, and he is in the same predicament...Oh no!"

Tamara heard the horn behind her as she swerved into the left lane. She tried swinging back into the middle, but by then another car was alongside her. It was too late. She heard screeching brakes and felt the impact as the car rear-ended her.

"Mommy, let me call you back I just got into an accident."

"Are you alright?"

"Yes. Some idiot just rear-ended me. I'll talk to you later."

Tamara hung up the phone and took a deep breath. She sat for another minute in her vehicle, trying to calm her frayed nerves. *Just what I need—a damaged car to fix!*

"Time to face the music," she whispered to herself and reached for the door handle. Before she could open the door, a very dark stocky man with thick bushy eyebrows pounded angrily on her window. She rolled her window down, suddenly fearful of leaving the safety of her SUV.

"Woman, are you crazy?" the man shouted in a thick African accent.

"Excuse me?" Tamara said softly, her voice shaky.

"You cut me off and now look what you've done to my car. You will pay for this," he yelled, waving his arms around melodramatically.

Tamara slowly got out of the vehicle. "Look, mister," she said, suddenly getting angry when she saw the beat-up old 1989 Chevy Celebrity he was driving. To fix a dent on her Lexus would cost a whole lot more than the value of that junk pile. "*You* were the one who rear-ended *me*."

The man put his hand on his head and huffing and puffing said something in a foreign language. In English he added, "Woman, you dense or what? You pulled into my lane without looking. If I didn't slam on my brakes, the damage would be worse. If you weren't talking on that damned cell phone, you would have seen me in the lane beside you."

"I'm not wrong here," Tamara argued. She walked around the car to assess the damage. There was just a little scratched paint on her rear bumper. If her vehicle wasn't as high as it was, the impact would have been worse.

"What do you mean, you're not wrong? You should have made sure it was clear before you changed lanes. Aye! You bought your license or something?"

Tamara looked at him and was totally disgusted. From his big rubbery nose flaring with anger to his bulbous red eyes and his thick sweaty neck. How dare he shout at her and accuse her of buying her license. "Well, why don't we just call the police and let them settle it?"

While they were talking, the passenger side of the old car rattled opened and out stepped the man's companion. He was tall and slim with a nice, chiseled physique. Tamara casually noticed his smooth coffee-cream complexion, his high cheekbones, his sensual lips and piercing, almond-shaped dark brown eyes. However, she was too preoccupied with the idiot arguing in front of her to pay much attention to the man with the confident swagger in his step.

Slowly the tall man walked around the vehicles, carefully examining them for damage, while Tamara and his friend stood arguing loudly about who was at fault. Calmly he said something to his friend in a foreign language Tamara assumed originated somewhere in Africa. His friend replied heatedly in English, "If she wasn't chatting on the cell phone, none of this would happen."

"Calm down, Edebe," he said in English. Then he turned to Tamara. "I'm sorry about all this. However, looking at both cars, I don't see enough damage to merit calling the cops or even getting insurances involved. Maybe we should just exchange numbers and if any further damage turns up, we'll take care of it."

Tamara looked at him through narrow eyes. "Aha! I see the trick. You think I don't know about these scams. You draw somebody into an accident, you don't get the insurances involved, and then milk them for money the rest of their lives."

"See, I told you the woman is a stupid American," the shorter, garrulous man exclaimed. "It makes no sense even talking to her."

"Why the hell don't you return to the rock you crawled from? We don't need you in America," Tamara responded heatedly. She took out her cell phone and began to dial for the police.

"Wait," the taller one said calmly. "Never mind Edebe. He has a short fuse. There's no scam here, but we are short on time. Yes, we can wait for the cops to get here, and we can go through the insurance company and pay the deductible for a scratch that a little ten-dollar paint job could take care of. And we can risk increasing our insurance rates for something as insignificant as this. But right now, ma'am, we're running late, and all I ask is your understanding."

Tamara looked at him. Her anger was slowly dissipating. Plus, he made sense. Why risk increasing her insurance premium when she was already so broke?

"Ok," she reluctantly agreed, and they exchanged information.

As she turned to enter her car, the taller one turned and fixed his gaze on her. Tamara couldn't help noticing his impressive height or how handsome he was. He said evenly with a relatively light accent, "For the record, you were wrong. It's your obligation to check that the lane is clear, before changing lanes." With that he strode calmly to the car and entered the passenger side.

"Hmmph!" Tamara huffed and walked to her vehicle. Some nerve!

Tammy entered city hall and sat in the waiting room. *Where in the world is Jordan?*

Her best friend was late as usual. He always claimed his tardiness was a Caribbean thing, but he'd been in this country long enough to get that out of his system.

To pass the time, Tamara looked around the room to see who might have been her potential husband. She knew he couldn't be too good looking. A handsome guy wouldn't have to pay for a green-card marriage.

A heavyset Hispanic man came into the room and sat down. He was nervously cracking his knuckles. He wriggled his tie in an effort to fix it, but his hands were shaking so much it made it more crooked. He gave up and just loosened the tie altogether. That must be him, Tamara thought.

A minute later, a petite Hispanic woman entered. His face lit up in a smile as they embraced and kissed each other on the lips. She fixed his tie affectionately, and he gave her the bouquet of flowers sitting on the bench next to him. Both made their way into the other room.

I stand corrected, Tamara thought and trained her eyes on the door. Just then Jordan walked in and made a beeline for Tamara. She was so glad to see a familiar face in this room full of strangers that she gave him a big bear hug.

"Save some of it for your new hubby, baby," he teased.

Tamara laughed nervously. "Where is he?"

"On his way. He had a little car trouble on the way here, so he's running a bit late. Are you nervous?"

"Oh no, I'm as cool as a cucumber," Tamara answered sarcastically. "Of course I'm nervous. I'm marrying somebody I've never even seen before. Suppose he's a serial killer."

Jordan laughed. "Keep your voice down before somebody hears you and has you committed. I know him personally, and he's a very nice guy. Plus, after you sign the papers today, you don't have to see him again until you prepare for the INS interview."

"You won't believe what happened on my way here," Tamara said, changing the topic since her nerves were getting the best of her. "I got rear-ended by some idiot who…"

Before she could finish the sentence, the two Africans who'd rear-ended her SUV stepped into the room. Tamara stared in shocked silence as the men crossed the room and each shook Jordan's hand. Jordan turned to Tamara, "Meet your fiancé…"

Tamara looked from Jordan to the two men and back. "The wedding is off," she said before anyone could speak. "I am not marrying this idiot. He is the one who rear-ended me."

"Calm down, Tammy. Let's go into another room and discuss this." With that, he shepherded the small group into a vacant conference room across the hall.

"I told you she was irrational. This whole thing is a bad idea. Let's go," Edebe said as soon as they got into the room.

"You're right," Tamara responded. "It is a bad idea and no amount of money in the world is enough to make me marry you. Jordan, I'm leaving." She stepped toward the door. The taller one followed her out of the room.

He extended a hand toward her. "I think we met under the wrong circumstances. Let me introduce myself. I'm Kwabena Opoku."

Tamara accepted his extended hand. His hand was big and slightly rough. "Tamara Fontaine. And I am not marrying that idiot in there you call your friend."

He smiled in response. "Good." Tamara looked at him, puzzled. "Because I believe you are to marry me."

Tamara looked up at him, surprised. He was more handsome than she remembered. He exuded an aura of effortless virility and sensuality. And in spite of this stressful situation, he seemed calm and rational. He looked like the type of man women would fight over. Why would a man like him have to pay for a wife to get a green card? Was this some kind of scam?

As if reading her mind he said, "It's a very long story, but this is the only way I can remain in this country legally at this time."

"Why do you want to stay here? I thought Americans were dumb?"

"Edebe said that, not me."

She looked up at him warily. He towered over her. She didn't trust him or his friend one bit. She hoped she was not getting in over her head—again.

"Your accent—" Tamara said hesitantly. "What is it?"

"Ghanaian." Kwabena's voice was melodic yet strong.

Shaking her head to rid soft thoughts, she said, "Let me see the money."

He removed a check from his pocket. Only the payee's name was missing.

"How do I know it won't bounce?" she asked. "I'd feel safer with a bank draft or cold hard cash."

He smiled calmly. "If it bounces, then you don't have to go to the INS interview, which means I don't get my permanent residence. So you have the power. Just to make sure we have it straight here's the deal: you get five thousand when you file the papers, another five thousand when I get the green card, and the last five thousand when you sign the divorce papers. Do we have an agreement?"

Tamara took a deep breath, and a minute passed before she answered. All kinds of things ran through her mind. Finally she exhaled and said, "Deal. And that's all it is: a business deal, a marriage of convenience."

They shook hands and rejoined Jordan and Edebe in the conference room. A few minutes later, Tamara was signing papers before the justice of the peace joining her and Kwabena Opoku in marriage.

Chapter Four

Tamara sat out at the poolside in her one-piece bathing suit soaking up the sun. Hidden speakers around the pool belted out Bob Marley's "Buffalo Soldier," played from the stereo in the den. Having lived most of her teenage years next door to Jordan's folks and spending so much time at his place, she had come to appreciate reggae music. Jordan's uncle, a vegetarian Rastafarian with clumpy dread locks extending below his waist and a penchant for calling any meat "deaders," visited their home on a daily basis to experience his mother's "Yardie" cooking. He would play loud reggae music, usually by Bob Marley, Peter Tosh or Burning Spear, which he dubbed "conscious" or "roots reggae." He frowned on the more contemporary dancehall-style reggae that Jordan played.

As the song ended, she heard her doorbell ring. She got up, wrapped a sarong around her and donned a T-shirt. Quickly she walked to the door. The postman was just getting into his van, leaving her house. I really should get that mailbox fixed, she thought. Strong winds in the spring had blown over her mailbox and she never replaced it.

She picked up several letters left on the semicircular front porch. Among them was a legal-size brown envelope. It was addressed to *Mr. and Mrs. Kwabena Opoku.*

As she headed toward the den, she turned over the

envelope and saw the Immigration and Naturalization Services return address. That's when it suddenly hit her. *She* was Mrs. Kwabena Opoku! At her insistence, she and Kwabena had used her address for filing the papers to ensure he didn't secretly receive the green card and stiff her the five thousand dollars. She had been scammed before, and she had no intention of being scammed again.

This must be about the interview, Tamara thought with some relief. It couldn't have come at a better time. The five thousand dollars had helped her through the last month and a half. A three-week job at a small library getting their database online helped her the rest of the way. It was a job that Jordan had passed her way and she was indeed grateful for that. But now she was broke again and not sure where next month's mortgage would come from.

She looked at the wall calendar and noticed the date. It was August 2, the anniversary of her wedding that never was. Quickly she shook her head to get rid of the thought and dialed Kwabena's number. She had all the information in her office.

Since filing the papers for his permanent resident card, Tamara had had no interaction with Kwabena. Admittedly, from the limited interaction of those few days, she found him to be a reasonable person, but his ever-present friend Edebe got on her last nerve. That was enough to squash any desire for more contact with her "husband."

The phone rang for a long while before a woman with a heavily accented, sexy, throaty voice answered. Tamara nervously asked for Kwabena.

Even though she expected his voice, the deepness of

it still startled her some. It took a few moments to gather her thoughts and get out the information she needed to communicate.

"What does the letter say?" he asked.

"I…I don't know. I didn't open it. It's got your name on it."

She heard him sigh. "It has both our names on it. Please, open it."

As she read the multipage mail, he gave out a shout of joy. "We've got a date!" Somehow reading aloud, she'd missed the gist of the letter. But the interview was in the next two weeks and a whole lot of paperwork had to be gathered for that time.

As Tamara hung up, she breathed a sigh of relief. She'd pulled it off. She took part in a green-card marriage and so far her folks were none the wiser. She couldn't wait for the next two weeks and the other five thousand dollars. Her bills waited.

"What the hell is a conditional green card anyway?" Tamara shouted the minute they left the INS office. Her face and neck were red with anger. She felt she had been tricked.

The interview was no interview. It involved Kwabena getting all kinds of medical tests, including HIV, tuberculin tests, chest X-rays and getting fingerprinted. On the day of the interview, the INS agent perused his immunization record as if he was going to bring a plague to the United States. They didn't ask any questions. They just wanted to know that they had the proper documentation. After going over the marriage certificate with a fine-tooth comb, the interviewer stamped his Ghanaian passport and said, "We're giving you a conditional alien registration number. We will schedule a follow-up interview within a year or two, where you will have to present proof that this marriage is legitimate. That can be in the form of joint tax returns, joint accounts, shared primary residence, et cetera." She stamped several papers mechanically, shook their hands and said, "Welcome to the United States of America." Then the interview was over.

Kwabena looked at Tamara and answered calmly, "It means we have to remain married for another year or two, and we have to share an address."

Tamara strained to look up at him. She felt angry and foolish and wanted to communicate that in no uncertain terms, but from her position so far below him she felt weak and ineffective. She wished he were seated at this moment. "Who said I wanted to live with you?"

"Too late for that," he responded calmly, trying hard to control his own rising anger. He was disappointed. With the laws enacted after 9/11, this delay would set him back a lot more than he'd anticipated. There was little he could do about it now, so he just had to adjust his expectations and his attitude. Kwabena looked down at his watch. It was already after one in the afternoon and he hadn't had lunch as yet. "Why don't you let me buy you lunch and we can discuss it then."

"I don't want to have lunch or anything else to do with you. And I am not moving in with you or adding your name to my bank accounts," she responded heatedly.

"Then I guess I'll have to move in with you," he responded, anger seething beneath the surface.

"This was not part of our agreement! I thought you understood the process." Tamara accused; even though she knew she should have investigated further before agreeing to the process.

Kwabena looked at her and tried hard to maintain his cool. "Miss Fontaine," he said slowly and carefully as if speaking to a child, "Immigration and Naturalization Services is not a department to argue with—in our circumstances. We just have to deal with it as it comes."

"I want my money," she demanded.

"When I get my green card, that's when you get your money," he stated firmly.

Tamara walked away in a huff, jumped into her Lexus and turned on the ignition.

"Where are you going?" Kwabena asked through the open window.

"Home!" she shouted bitterly and pulled out of the parking lot hastily.

Quickly Kwabena jumped into his six-year-old Honda Civic and pulled out after her. He had already invested five thousand dollars of his hard-earned money in this business deal, and they were going to have to see it through.

He should have questioned Jordan more about this woman. All he'd told him was that she was a bit down on her luck, had never been married and needed the money. He didn't tell him that Tamara Fontaine was a lunatic. He could barely keep up with her as she tore down streets and onto the highway like a madwoman. No wonder they'd gotten into that accident.

Kwabena was having a hard time keeping up with her. He barely noticed when she left the main road and turned into a gated community. For a minute he drove around the elegant complex, trying to figure out where she disappeared to. Then he saw it—her gold Lexus pulling onto a narrow road with new houses still under construction. The speed limit was twenty-five miles per hour. The maniac was doing fifty.

She turned left onto a narrow road with large, expensive-looking houses separated from one another and the street by large backyards and expansive front lawns. Suddenly she turned into a driveway.

Kwabena followed behind and hesitantly turned into the driveway. Maybe she was visiting friends. By the time he parked, she had already gone into the house, slamming the door behind her. He sat in his vehicle for a few minutes contemplating his next move.

He took a sip of day-old bottled water from the cup holder. The water was too warm to quench his thirst. Wiping sweat from his brow, he exited his vehicle and walked up the short path to the semicircular porch with its faux balcony. He stood before the burgundy door, flanked by multipaneled glass. He took a deep breath before using the brass knocker on the door to alert her of his presence.

Tamara paced the den. Her anger had dissipated but was replaced by worry. What had she gotten into? How would she keep this from her mother or the ever-prying eyes of her aunt or cousins? But even more importantly, how was she going to pay her next month's mortgage? She needed the five thousand dollars now, not a year or two from now.

She heard the rap on the door. She was expecting it and had left the door unlocked, yet the sound still startled her. She walked to the door and opened it without saying a word, then stepped back into the foyer, expecting him to follow her. When he didn't, she turned back to him and said, "Since you're gonna be living here, feel free to look around." With that she walked through the den and disappeared into the sunroom.

Kwabena looked around the two-story foyer with its large cathedral window and crystal chandelier. The place was beautiful. The décor was simple and elegant. The honey oak hardwood floor in the foyer was bare. The only furniture in this room was a marble-topped semicircular console and an antique mirror. Slowly he stepped up the single stair into the den. Again it was beautifully decorated, with a deep leather sectional with ottoman in cream and glass-topped coffee table. On one end of this large rectangular room was a wood-burning fireplace with slate hearth flanked by two un-adorned floor-length windows.

Kwabena looked around and wondered how this woman was paying for all of this. The house had to be worth a pretty penny. According to Jordan, she didn't work. The only answer that came to his mind was drug dealing or prostitution.

"Miss Fontaine," he called, not knowing where she had disappeared. When he didn't get an answer, he wandered into what looked like a formal living room. It was decorated with a light green floral Victorian sofa, loveseat and settee with cherrywood coffee and center tables. On one end was a double-sided fireplace with white marble hearth. Two archways surrounding the fireplace led to the formal dining room. The hearth on this side of the double-sided fireplace was gray stone, which gave the room a warm country feel. He looked at the elegant dark oak dining table surrounded by eight high-backed, cushioned chairs. Long-stemmed crystal glasses hung from the top of a wine cabinet. He walked over to it to look at her collection of wines, but was surprised to find only apple and grape ciders. Lots of expensive-looking china graced the china cabinet.

If this woman is dealing, she is big time, Kwabena thought. A butler's pantry gave way to a spacious gourmet kitchen that easily could have been profiled by *Home and Garden*. From the unscratched pots and pans hanging and the unscratched granite surface of the countertops and the large rectangular island, he could tell that not much cooking occurred here. A lone coffee cup sat in the sink yet to be washed, and a bag of half-eaten chocolate-chip cookies lay open on the countertop. Curiously he opened the honey oak door of the pantry, and a bag of potato chips fell onto the cream and tan ceramic floor. He bent to retrieve it, and the contents fell onto the floor.

"Shoot! Now she'll think I'm prying." He returned the bag of chips to the bare pantry and looked around for a broom or dustpan but came up empty.

"Miss Fontaine," Kwabena called again, wandering into the library with its floor-to-ceiling shelves of books and video games, large cherry desk and leather swivel chair. There were lots of computer books and romance novels. She appeared to be an avid reader. Not quite the profile of a drug dealer or a prostitute. Maybe a kept woman?

He stepped back into the foyer and opened a door on the right. It was a powder room with pedestal sink, antique framed mirror and expensive-looking bath rugs and accessories. Quickly he closed the door. He tried the door adjacent to it, but found himself staring into an empty two-car garage.

"Miss Fontaine," he called again a little louder. He

reentered the den, still wondering where she was. Kwabena took a short flight of four stairs off the den and found himself in the sunroom encased by tinted glass. As he looked out of the sunroom to the stone patio and swimming pool, he reevaluated the cost of the house. This place had to cost a small fortune.

Tamara sat on the arm of a white wicker sofa decorated with a bright floral cushion. She sipped slowly on a Coke while biting into Hostess Twinkies, staring out of the glass panels. He observed her from the doorway for a few seconds before announcing his presence. The fiery dragon was looking a lot less fierce from that position. She just looked worried, afraid and…vulnerable? Looking at her like that, he immediately ruled out drug dealing as a source of income.

"I think I made a bit of a mess in the kitchen. Where can I find a broom?" he asked.

Tamara jumped and immediately turned red. Quickly she regained her composure.

"Upstairs," she answered and led the way through the den and up the elegant staircase to the master suite.

Kwabena followed her silently. The air between them was tense. He looked at her expansive behind and round figure as she led him up the stairs. Ok, not a prostitute, he thought, as she did not try to seduce him or make a deal with her body. Plus, there was something about her that just did not look overtly sexual. Maybe it was the expression in her eyes when he saw her in the sunroom. There was a kind of innocence about her that made her seem sheltered and unexposed, characteristics that did not go well with that profession.

A kept woman. She has to be a kept woman, Kwabena concluded when he saw the master suite. The suite was built for romance. The sitting area, with its plush carpet, was decorated with a modern red sofa and white ottoman that sat in front of the gas fireplace. French doors from the sitting room opened to a small private balcony. The bedroom itself seemed to be built for two. A beautifully adorned king-size bed on a slightly raised platform was the anchor of the room. The brass and cherry head- and footboard, dresser and nightstands screamed romance.

She looked into a closet large enough to serve as a child's bedroom. Not finding the broom there, she entered the master bathroom with Kwabena in tow. If there was any doubt in his mind, now he was certain… Tamara Fontaine was a kept woman, and whoever her man was, he was rolling in dough, or at least had been at one time.

He looked around the spacious cream and gold bathroom. On one side was a marble shower stall. On the opposite end of the room was a sauna. Wow, he thought to himself, quite extravagant. The double vanity was marble topped with gold faucets. The crowning glory of the bath was the raised Jacuzzi amid a bank of bay windows. Three marble stairs on each side of the hot tub permitted entrance to it. It was a beautiful bathroom built for romance—the never ending honeymoon. He guessed the man supporting this effort was married. Maybe the relationship went bad, which was why she was broke now.

She found the broom leaning against a linen closet. She opened the honey oak doors of the vanity and removed a dustpan and brush and led the way out of the master suite.

"You're not sleeping in there with me," she announced coldly as they left the master suite. She opened another bedroom. In it was a bunk bed adorned with princess and BRATZ bedcovers.

She has kids?

As if reading his mind Tamara said, "My cousins."

She showed him three other guest rooms and a bathroom. "There's an airbed you can use if you like. You're welcome to sleep in any one of those rooms. The farther from mine the better."

There was no way he wanted to be that close to her. Not with that temper of hers. Plus, he needed his privacy. He had his own life.

"Do you have a basement?" he asked.

She nodded and led the way down two flights of stairs to the basement.

Perfect, he thought when he saw it. There was a bedroom and bathroom and an L-shaped recreation room that could serve as a sitting room. The laundry and utility rooms were separate. There was even an exercise room filled with empty boxes but no exercise equipment. The basement was unfurnished and had its own front and back exit. It could easily be turned into a two-bedroom apartment. That way he could move his furniture there. The only thing it lacked was a kitchen.

"I'll stay in the basement," he said after seeing the place.

"Whatever floats your boat," she responded noncommittally as he left through the basement entrance, got into his car and drove off.

Chapter Five

The sound of the doorbell ringing awoke her with a start. Tamara rolled over, looked at the blurred numbers on the bedside clock: 6:08. She moaned, rolled over and pulled the covers over her head. Maybe she'd been dreaming.

A few minutes later the doorbell rang again. This time the ringer was persistent. Tamara walked to the window and peered through the blinds. To her amazement a U-Haul truck was sitting in the driveway. Before she could question what was happening she saw Edebe's big ancient Chevy.

"Ugh," she groaned and proceeded to the bathroom. "The nerve of these people coming here this early in the morning, waking me up from my good sleep!"

She was going to make them wait. Slowly she dragged herself to the bathroom, brushed her teeth and her hair and put in her contacts. Then she took her dear time wiggling into jean capris and a bright yellow T-shirt. Before she was finished dressing, the old car was honking persistently.

"Oh boy," she sighed. This she didn't need—ill-mannered people waking her at six A.M. and making a big commotion for all the neighbors to see. She ran down the stairs two at a time and threw back the front door, intending to unleash her fury on the untrained coot. Instead she came face to face with a smiling Kwabena, his knuckles poised to rap on the door.

"Good morning," he said brightly in a thicker than usual Ghanaian accent.

Tamara hesitated a moment too long. She expected to see Edebe at the door with his dour demeanor. Instead it was Kwabena.

When she finally spoke she asked, "What are you doing at my house this early?"

He smiled. "I'm moving in with my wife. Thought you'd roll out the welcome mat."

She couldn't miss the sarcasm in his tone. Tamara did not answer. She rolled her eyes, then looked at the mid-size truck parked in the driveway.

"Aren't you gonna open the door to the basement?" he asked.

"When I said you could move in, I didn't expect a truck with all your junk."

"And I didn't expect to be offered an airbed for a year. Or will we be sharing that king-size bed? It's big enough for two."

The words she wanted to use right now were not fit for strangers to hear. How dare he come here so early in the morning and then be fresh with her? She ignored his comment.

"Why so early? I was sleeping."

"It's supposed to be really hot today," he said, walking past her and heading toward the basement. "We thought we'd beat the heat."

Too late for that, Tamara thought. At six it was already hot and humid. Today was destined to be a scorcher.

A few hours later, she watched in anger from the front porch as both men moved back and forth, sweat-soaked shirts sticking to their backs, lugging heavy furniture into her once unoccupied basement. The truck had been parked with one wheel on her grass, crushing the thriving azaleas lining her driveway. She had shouted at them about the truck, but they had chosen to ignore her. Now all she could do was stand and watch as they turned her life upside down.

A sweat-drenched Kwabena joined Edebe in the truck. Edebe did not even have the manners to acknowledge her presence. She detested that sour imbecile. Kwabena emerged from the truck shirtless. His lean, taut muscles rippled.

Wow! He may not be the nicest person, but he sure is fine. She admired his hard abs, his well-defined chest as he exited the truck, his ebony body glistening in the August sun. If she were to construct her perfect man, she would probably give him Kwabena's body—at least the butt, chest and abs—hell, she might just add the face too.

Suddenly he made a beeline for her. Tamara felt the heat rise in her face as she tried desperately not to stare. Despite her mistrust and anger toward him, she just couldn't help admiring him. But then, weren't the good-looking ones the most deceptive?

Kwabena looked directly at her as he asked for the house keys, and she immediately looked away. She tossed them to him rudely. *What is this woman's problem?* Since he'd met her, he had never seen her smile. She was always angry. He would make sure to keep his dis-

tance from her. All he really had to do was have his mail
come here and keep a few joint bills and a joint bank account. Beyond that, he would give her all the space she
needed. This was, after all, just a temporary setback.
These things happened all the time, and he just needed
to adjust to the change. But as soon as this was over, he
was moving his things out, and would probably find
himself a good wife. One who fit his tastes and not his
mother's. Arranged marriages were not uncommon
back home, even in big cities like Accra. That thought
put a smile on his lips as he returned to the still full
truck. All this effort and they hadn't made a dent in the
unloading. It was going to be one long day and an even
longer year.

As Tamara retreated to the air-conditioned comfort of
her den, she heard a vehicle pull up. She peered through
the curtains to see a minivan filled with several men and
two women stop in front of the house. Several people
got out and greeted Kwabena with friendly laughter
and hugs. They chatted casually in a mixture of deeply
accented English and what Tamara assumed was Ghanaian. One of the men removed a large cooler of drinks
from the minivan. All the men worked together and resumed moving the furniture into the basement. The
women could be heard arranging things downstairs.
They all seemed to be enjoying themselves, chatting
and laughing loudly.

In less than an hour, the truck was empty and Tamara
could hear furniture being moved around downstairs.
Two men removed a steaming silver pot from the minivan. As the men disappeared into the basement, a roar

of excitement and laughter erupted. It was like a giant party. The smell of the spicy stew wafted upstairs, reminding Tamara that it was time for lunch.

She scanned the refrigerator and pulled out some leftover macaroni and cheese. She heated it in the microwave and sat at the breakfast nook to eat. The laughter from downstairs reminded her just how lonely she was. Yes, she had Jordan and Becky, and her cousins and aunt, but it was not the same as having a group of friends.

She remembered the last time she had fun like that. It had been the day of her wedding, exactly one year and three weeks ago. And it did not end in laughter. Tamara brushed the thought from her mind, rinsed her plate and headed upstairs. There she shut the door hoping to keep out the sound of laughter.

Tamara was watching her favorite sitcom when she heard a light rap on the door. The noise downstairs had subsided, and one by one she'd heard the vehicles pull out of the driveway.

She got up and opened the door. Kwabena stood a full foot over her. He had recently showered and smelled of Irish Spring soap and aftershave. She could see his closely cropped hair was still damp. He now wore a pair of cotton shorts and a green tank top that showed his well-developed biceps.

Kwabena looked intently at her. "This is for you," he said, handing her an envelope.

She turned it over in her hands before opening it. In it was a personal check made out to her. "What's this for?" she asked, confused.

"Your payment for the green card."

She looked at the amount on the check. "It's short."

"You get half now and the rest when I receive the permanent card," he responded.

She looked at the check again and nodded.

At that moment Tamara wanted to wrap her arms around him and give him a big hug. If he only knew how much she needed that money right now. Thank goodness she now could meet her mortgage and her car payments. She could pay her bills again.

Tamara raised her eyes to see him still standing staring down at her.

"Is there something else you wanted?" she asked.

He smiled and shook his head. "That was all. Good night."

He turned and walked down the hallway.

"Kwabena," Tamara called to his retreating back.

He stopped and turned around.

"Thank you," she said softly, smiling.

Kwabena returned her smile. "You have a very pretty smile," he said. "Please call me Ben."

"Thank you, Ben," she responded before slipping back into the bedroom suite. *Maybe this isn't such a bad idea, after all.*

Chapter Six

In the two weeks since Kwabena had moved into her home Tamara had seen him only once. He was indeed a busy person. He left for work before she arose in the morning and returned at odd times. She was also learning he was a very social person. He had installed a phone line in the basement to prove his residency in her home. Since then his phone rang incessantly. At least six times in the last two weeks he'd had groups of friends over. There was always laughter and delicious smells of food wafting up from the basement.

Today Kwabena was the last thing on Tamara's mind. Today was her big interview. The job description fit her profile very well. The pay was not as high as she'd made with her old firm, but it was sufficient. There was only one problem: it was in Delaware, a two-hour commute.

She got up early and walked into the kitchen in her pajamas. Her uncombed hair stood out in every direction. Her eyes could barely make out the things in the kitchen as her contacts were still soaking in the bathroom and she'd left her glasses on the nightstand. It was the first time she'd been up this early since Kwabena had moved in, and she needed some strong coffee. By rote, she headed straight to the cupboard and removed the tin of coffee. She took it over to the machine and was surprised to see a fresh pot of coffee brewing.

Kwabena must have made it. She was certain he would not mind her taking a cup.

She got out her favorite coffee mug, with the UCLA insignia. Like the pajamas she wore, it was old and worn. The lip was chipped and there were brown stains on the inside, but she didn't mind. She poured the coffee and drenched it with cream and sugar. As she sipped the coffee she made a face. It was a very bold flavor, bordering on harsh, despite the cream and sugar.

"Ethiopian dark roast," Kwabena said, coming behind her and reaching over her for a coffee mug. "Good to see you decided to join me for coffee."

Tamara jumped, startled, spilling the coffee on her pajamas and scorching her lips. Slowly she turned around to face him, feeling guilty for taking his coffee without permission.

Kwabena stared intently at her. Under his gaze Tamara turned beet red, uncomfortable to say the least. The discomfort gave way to anger. "What are you staring at?" she demanded defensively. "Never seen a fat woman in pajamas before?"

"Not one revealing that much," he said without missing a beat.

Tamara looked down self-consciously at her well-worn pajamas. The threadbare material over her left breast was worn to transparency and her nipple was playing peek-a-boo behind it. Moreover, a few buttons had become undone, revealing a lot more skin than she'd intended.

Tamara immediately folded her hands over her wet pajamas in an effort to cover herself. She was embarrassed to the point of anger. "You…you…you lecher," she hissed and tried her best to hide her nakedness from his prying eyes.

"I don't think that word applies to married couples," he said with a twinkle in his eyes.

"Ugh," she groaned, gritting her teeth. "Is that how you get your kicks? Voyeurism?"

"Maybe you should try covering yourself. Or are you trying to seduce me?" he asked, taken aback at the vehemence in her voice.

With a thud, Tamara thumped the coffee mug on the counter, blew off and stormed upstairs. "I changed my mind about having coffee with you! I don't dine with Peeping Toms."

Kwabena shook his head and smiled. *That woman needs help.*

Sometime later as he ate breakfast, he saw her enter the den in a navy blue business suit. He was tempted to ask her where she was going, but thought better of it when he saw the expression on her face. She gave him a hard, cold scowl and disappeared through the garage door.

The company headquarters reminded her of a college campus. Redbrick buildings framed a large grassy courtyard with benches surrounding a fountain. People could be seen sipping coffee in the warm September sun, some tapping away at laptops. It was an environment where she would love to work.

As she entered the building she was greeted by a friendly secretary who ushered her into an overdecorated office.

"Hello, Miss Fontaine. I'm Fiona DesChamps. How was your commute?" the interviewer asked lightly.

"Oh, it was fine, thank you." Tamara shook Ms. Des-Champs's hand.

Tamara was relieved. Not only was the interviewer African-American, she was also overweight. That meant chances of discrimination because of her weight or her race were dramatically reduced.

They chatted for a few minutes. Then Ms. Des-Champs outlined the interview process. After interviewing with her, Tamara was required to take a computer proficiency test, after which she would be interviewed by Ms. DesChamps's boss. She would then be interviewed by a junior partner in the firm.

"Why the test?" Tamara asked before being escorted to the examination room.

"We get so many applicants claiming to be computer experts, and then when we hire them we discover that they are not even computer literate. A few months ago we decided to test each interviewee individually."

The test was like child's play for Tamara. She didn't even have to draw on her knowledge as an information technologist to do the silly test. She left the interview with Ms. DesChamps and the test feeling optimistic about this job prospect. As Ms DesChamps ushered her into her boss's office, Tamara was even more pleased to discover that her boss was a black man, a UCLA alumnus.

The interview was quite light and simple. They discussed the job, her work experience, why she wanted to work there, and then they reminisced about UCLA and the culture of that school.

Just before the interview ended, a secretary interrupted and gave him an envelope with her test scores. He raised his eyebrows as he read the paper. "Ms. Fontaine, congratulations. You've scored higher on this test than most of our prospective employees."

"Thanks," she responded, feeling confident that she would get the job.

As he ushered her across the grassy courtyard to the executive building for her third interview he said, "I'm very impressed with your experience, your eloquence, and I think you would fit in well with the rest of the information technologists in this firm. I will make sure I communicate this to Mr. Orson. Ultimately, he is the one who will make the final decision."

"Thank you, Mr. Carter," Tamara said, shaking his hand as she entered the door with the big *T. L. Orson III, Executive Office*r engraved in brass.

Tamara strode confidently into the office, shaking Mr. Orson's large hands. Unlike the other two interviewers, he was a middle-aged white man with thinning hair and a bad comb-over.

He smiled warmly and welcomed her to the firm. He asked her about her future plans, where she saw herself in ten years, the standard interview questions. Then he said to her, "You have very impressive experience, even without a degree. Your test scores were among the highest we've had in a long time, and you come highly recommended by Egbert Nurenburgh, who I must add is a good friend of mine. You had to be very good to gain such a glowing recommendation from him, both in a letter and when I spoke to him on the phone a few weeks ago."

Tamara smiled. "Thank you." She was relieved. Finally she was going to get a job offer. Finally.

He continued, "However, you've been out of work for almost a year now, so let me not waste your time.

The computer industry is very dynamic. Lots of changes occur within a year. This year especially we've seen new operating systems, new network interfacing mechanisms. A lot has been going on since you left this field of work. So even though your credentials are solid, I'm afraid it's outdated. I'm sorry, we can't hire you."

Tamara knew she was red all over. This was her last chance, her only hope. "Sir, the underlying programming languages haven't changed that much, and I have formal training in computer programming," She argued, "None of the changes were so drastic that without reading a few books, I cannot adjust. And I have been reading, doing some work and keeping up-to-date on the changes in this field. I am still very qualified for this position."

"I'm sorry, Ms. Fontaine."

Tamara felt angry, disappointed and defeated as she left the office. To make matters worse, the drive back home was long, and the traffic was bad. It was already after six when she reached home.

She removed her shoes and sat on the sofa in the den. This was so unfair. She had no other choice. She would sell the house and move back into the duplex. Right now there was enough equity for her to maybe break even on the mortgage—maybe. This was a bad time to sell. Even if she didn't make much on the house itself, she would make enough from the sale of her furniture to pay down her debt significantly. Without the mortgage, she could live on a small salary, maybe find work in the food-services industry. She would have to have a talk with Kwabena, make some arrangement for them to appear to share a domicile.

Tamara felt tears stinging her eyes. First she was downsized, and now she was obsolete.

"Dammit!" she cried out loud. She threw the cushions angrily across the room. "It's not fair!" she screamed. Tears streamed down her eyes as she sobbed. "Why, Lord, why me?"

These tears were long overdue, and now that the floodgates were open it was hard for her to stop. Her shoulders wracked with sobs as she cried for all the losses in her life. She cried for Jared's deception, she cried for her accumulated debt, she cried for her inability to meet her basic living needs, she cried for the frustration of finding a job, she cried for her loneliness. She just cried, shedding tears that should have been shed a year ago.

Tamara felt more than saw Kwabena's presence. She tried fruitlessly to pull herself together, but the sobbing would not subside.

He extended a hand, then drew her in his arms and let her cry on his chest.

"It will be alright," he comforted, caressing the back of her head. "It will be alright."

Kwabena had no idea what she was going through, but whatever it was, it was bad. He wished he could do more to make her feel better. He had been in the kitchen preparing dinner when she arrived. After this morning, he was reluctant to have any dealings with her, and therefore kept his distance. That was before he heard the things being tossed about and the sobs. He observed her crying for a while, uncertain what to do. But then his heart reached out to her. He wanted to shield her from whatever was causing her pain.

He liked the smell of her hair. It was like flowers and wild strawberries, and it filled him with the urge to kiss the top of her head. He liked the feel of her head against his chest and her ample body in his arms. Taking a deep breath, he tried to control himself. He definitely did not want to be accused of lechery or voyeurism again.

Slowly Tamara regained control of her sobbing and extricated herself from his embrace. He handed her a napkin to wipe her tears.

"I'm sorry," she whispered hoarsely. "You shouldn't have seen that. I…I…"

"It's ok," Kwabena assured her. "We all have our days. Would you like some dinner?"

She shook her head. "I don't feel like going anywhere right now."

"It's in the kitchen," he explained.

She looked up at him with soft eyes. Her expression one of defeat. Their eyes met and held. Kwabena had the strange urge to kiss away her tears and remove the hurt. He wanted once more to see that beautiful smile she flashed him the night after he'd moved in.

He got up from the couch and helped her up, leading her by the hand into the kitchen. The scent of the spicy food suddenly made her mouth water. She was hungry. She hadn't eaten all day.

Tamara watched as he silently placed two white balls of something on her plate and doused it with meat sauce. He proceeded to the dining room, a place she had never used except for Thanksgiving dinner last year. The food was absolutely delicious.

"This is delicious. Who prepared it?" she asked, biting into succulent meat.

"I did."

"I thought African men couldn't cook," Tamara replied.

"Where did you get that stereotype?"

She responded pensively, "I really don't know. It's just one of those things you hear somewhere along the road that becomes fact to you." She was suddenly ashamed she believed so readily.

"Well, I cook, and so do many of my friends."

"I thought you made your wives do all that for you."

He grinned. "You're my wife, and I don't see you cooking for me."

Her face lit up with a smile. "You know what I mean."

Kwabena returned her smile, satisfied to have elicited her rare smile. He noticed her eyes were dark brown, two shades darker than he recalled from that morning.

They ate in silence for a while. "What kind of food is this anyway?"

"This is plantain foo-foo," he said, pointing to the sticky balls. "And this is stewed goat in peanut sauce." He pointed to the meat.

"Goat!" Tamara exclaimed. She could feel the bile rising in her throat. "Like the kind in the petting zoo?"

"Yes, goat, like the kind people kill for meat."

She wanted to gag. The food was delicious, but this was goat. She stopped eating. "This is like eating a cat or a dog. We're eating Fluffy."

Kwabena laughed as if he had no care in the world. Tamara decided she liked his laugh. "There are some cultures that do eat cats and dogs. Many other countries, the Middle East, the Caribbean, Africa and some parts of Europe, eat goat as a staple meat. They are raised on farms just like your cows and chickens."

"Yeah, but goats are cute creatures you touch at the petting zoo."

"So are pigs, but I don't see you grimace at your ham."

Tamara laughed. He had a point. Maybe she was being too close minded. "I'll try some more goat meat, but I'll pretend it is lamb."

"Now that's my girl," he said as he spooned more of the goat stew over her foo-foo.

They were silent for a while before Tamara said, "I'm sorry you had to see me so upset. I don't usually lose control of my emotions like that."

"Do you want to talk about it?"

"No, but I have to, because it affects you." She twirled a bit of foo-foo on her fork and looked off at the fireplace. "I've been out of a job almost a year now, and things are really tight financially. I am in a lot of debt. I may have to sell this house and move back in my mother's house."

Kwabena was silent for a while. He hadn't realized she had been unemployed for so long. That explained why she agreed to marry a stranger for money.

"What kind of work did you do?" he asked. It was the first time they'd had an intimate conversation.

"I was an information technologist. Jordan and I worked at the same company. Last year we both got downsized. He was smart enough to start his own business. I've failed to find a job for this whole year. Now I'm apparently obsolete. My mother's duplex is much smaller than here. There won't be any separate apartment for you. We'll have to figure out how we'll establish shared primary residence. Maybe we can do the roommate thing."

"Would it help if I pay you rent for the downstairs apartment and the utilities?"

She smiled. *Why didn't I think of renting it out before?* That could have helped her with her mortgage. The rent from the Rosedale duplex could help supplement it.

"I'll only accept for half the utilities," she responded. "I don't want to be a kept woman."

Kwabena burst out laughing.

"What's so funny?"

"When I first saw your house, I thought you were a kept woman."

It was Tamara's turn to laugh. "Yeah, right! Why would you ever think so?"

"Your bedroom. It looks like a honeymoon suite. So I figured you were with a loaded man."

"When I bought the house, I was loaded. And as for that bedroom…it's a long story."

He reached across the table and patted her hand. "Everything will work out. God never gives us more than we can bear."

She smiled and got up from the table. "I'll do the dishes."

"No, I'll do them. I made the mess."

"Since you cooked, it's only fair that I do the dishes."

He didn't want her to see the kind of mess he'd made in her pristine kitchen. "You'll ruin your nice suit."

She removed the jacket, revealing a camisole that left little for the imagination. He didn't want to stare lest he be accused of lechery, but it was hard to keep his eyes off her ample bosom. Looking at her, he felt stirrings in places he could not reveal to her.

They argued back and forth until she saw the mess he made in the kitchen. "Ok, we'll clean the kitchen together," she conceded.

For the next few minutes, they cleaned the kitchen, chatting and getting to know each other. For the first time in a long time, Tamara felt like laughing.

"You know, you do have a nice smile. It's such a shame we don't see it very often," Kwabena observed as they finished the kitchen and walked out to the den where she'd cried in his arms an hour or two ago.

"I guess I didn't have very much to smile about this past year."

As he flipped on the LCD TV above the mantel, he said, "Happiness should be *in spite of* not *because of*."

"What are you, a philosopher?" she gently teased.

He shook his head.

"What work do you do?"

"Research." Kwabena did not elaborate.

They looked at a few sitcoms together. It felt so good to have another person to talk to and laugh with.

"Can I ask you a question?" Kwabena asked her.

"You already did, but you can ask me another," she teased.

"Do you wear contacts?"

"Yeah why?"

"This morning your eyes were a lot lighter than I had ever seen them."

Busted! She smiled. "I wear colored contacts. I cannot see a thing without them. Is that why you were staring at me this morning?"

"Yes."

Tamara smiled sheepishly. "I thought you were staring at other things. I'm sorry I accused you of lechery."

"That was a pretty egregious accusation. I can't accept your apology until you accept my invitation."

"What invitation?"

"To a gala ceremony at the Ghanaian Embassy in D.C."

"Why me? What about your friends or your girlfriend?"

"I'm a married man, or didn't you notice?" he teased.

She laughed. "I noticed. Why not? I accept the invitation. Just don't get any ideas about marital consummation."

He laughed as he got ready to head downstairs. It was almost eleven. "Don't worry. I don't want to be accused of overstepping my bounds again. By the way, it's a formal affair."

He said goodnight and headed downstairs. "Ben," Tamara called as he approached the stairs. "Thanks for dinner and for understanding. You can call me Tammy."

He smiled and nodded before disappearing into the basement. Tamara headed upstairs. It was the first time in a long while she'd enjoyed an evening in her house.

Chapter Seven

The gala came quicker than Tamara had anticipated. She didn't have any formal dresses that still fit, and she couldn't afford the brand name clothes in the mall. She and Becky went to a discount plus-size clothing outlet with four children in tow, and bought a black dress with thin-strapped corset bodice. It flared off the hips, then flowed into a handkerchief hem. The corset bodice restrained her loose flesh and accentuated her full figure. With it she wore a glittery shawl, silver earrings and black stilettos speckled with silver.

She applied her makeup and came downstairs to meet Kwabena in the den as they had agreed. Just then the doorbell rang, and Tamara rushed to answer it.

"Auntie Tammy." Katanya and Kayla rushed into her arms.

Ebony stood outside while a man in a black car waited impatiently. "Can you watch them for me tonight?"

As Ebony stepped into the foyer, her face registered surprise. "What's with the dress?"

"I'm sorry, Ebony, but I have plans," Tamara said.

"Come on, Tammy, how often do I ask this of you? The kids are all excited to sleep over tonight." Both girls had already run upstairs to their room, where Tamara kept an assortment of toys and books for them.

"I'm sorry Ebony, but I do have a life." Tamara shook

her head. "You chose a very bad weekend for this. You should have given me some advance warning."

"Did Jared come back?" Ebony asked, looking up the stairs and around the room.

Tamara frowned. "Don't even mention that name to me," she exclaimed angrily. "If he does, I will have a loaded gun waiting for him."

"Who's this mystery date? Don't tell me you're engaged again."

Tamara sighed. "Just take the kids and go. I…"

Kwabena came upstairs just then, wearing traditional Ghanaian attire. He wore kinte trousers with a flowing robe and what looked like a scarf diagonally across his chest. On his head he wore a matching kofia. His presence filled the room. From his head to his toes, he looked impressive, like African royalty.

Ebony and Tamara both stared at him, speechless. Tamara knew he was handsome, but she'd never seen him looking this fine.

"This is my cousin Ebony," Tamara introduced them when she found her tongue. "Ebony this is Kwabena."

"Hi," Ebony muttered breathlessly.

"Ebony was just leaving. Kayla and Katanya," Tamara called. The kids came running down the stairs.

Tamara introduced Kwabena to the kids. Kayla stepped forward bravely and stretched out her hand for him to shake while Katanya hid behind her mother.

"Nice to meet you, Kayla," Kwabena said, crouching to her level and shaking her hand. "You've got quite a handshake."

He put his hand out to Katanya for her to give him five. Katanya smiled and hesitantly stepped forward to slap his palms. Shyly she asked, "Why are you wearing a lady's dress?"

Kwabena smiled. Tamara tried hard not to laugh. Ebony outright giggled.

"That's not a lady's dress, silly," Kayla corrected impatiently. "Don't you see it's an African costume?"

"You're quite a smart young lady, Kayla. This"—he turned to Katanya and said in the soft voice of a kindergarten teacher—"is my traditional Ghanaian dress. People from Ghana wear it to special events that celebrate African culture, like the one we're attending right now."

"What's Ghana?" Katanya questioned.

"Ghana is a country in West Africa. It is the very beautiful country where I am from."

He stood back up to his full height and spoke directly to Ebony, "It was a pleasure meeting you and your two lovely daughters. Tamara and I really should get going soon. Maybe we'll meet again someday."

Tamara smiled as Ebony nodded and gathered the kids. Ebony was not too happy and Tamara couldn't care less. But when she saw the disappointment on Katanya's face she turned to her. "I promise you we'll have a sleepover sometime soon. I'll have Devon over too, deal?"

"Deal," Kayla and Katanya said in unison as they bounded through the door.

Tamara turned back into the den to see Kwabena staring intently at her. She blushed and turned away.

He took a few steps toward her. "You look wonderful tonight," he complimented. He had never seen her so well dressed, and she certainly looked ravishing. She was an attractive woman, despite her fiery anger and her sometimes unconfident disposition. The black dress contrasted well with her light complexion, giving her skin a healthy glow.

"Thank you," she whispered as they stepped out into the cool night.

The gala was held in an impressive suite at the Ghanaian embassy. An exhibition displaying the history, culture and art of Ghana was held in the anteroom. Paintings, carved stools, masks, jewelry, drums and photos of historic events were on display. Kwabena escorted Tamara from exhibit to exhibit, explaining the different crafts and some of the history. He stood before a lovely wooden mask with intricate details.

"This is a Dagomba mask," he explained. "It is a religious mask used ceremoniously by the Dagomba people, one of the larger ethnic groups in Ghana. Today it's mostly decorative."

"And this one?" Tamara questioned, running her fingers over another intricately carved, blackened wooden mask.

"This one's an Akan mask. It probably goes back to the time when the Asante united into one kingdom. And this right here is a replica of the golden stool," he explained, pointing to a wooden curve-topped bench. "This stool is pretty powerful. It is believed to contain the *sunsum*, which is the soul of the Asante people. In fact, legend has it that the original golden stool fell out of heaven right into the lap of the king and made the Asante people a powerful nation."

"And what tribe are you?" Tamara probed.

"I'm Asante, but the Akan is made up of both the Fante and the Asante people."

They moved over to a colorful picture of a woman with a basket of fruit on her head. To Tamara, it looked like an appliqué on canvas. She wondered what material it was made of. As if reading her mind, Kwabena asked, "Can you guess what this is made of?"

"It looks like some kind of fabric...or tissue paper. No, it must be leaves, I'm seeing veins," Tamara contemplated.

"Butterfly wings," Kwabena said and looked at the surprised expression on her face.

"Wow, I would never have guessed."

Kwabena greeted a few dignitaries, keeping short conversations in a rhythmic language.

"What language is that?" Tamara asked.

"Twi. Various dialects of it are spoken by the Akan people. It's probably the most widely spoken language in Ghana other than English," he responded.

Just then a tall man dressed in full Ghanaian regalia approached. From his entourage and the deference people gave him, Tamara could tell he was someone of great importance. He greeted Kwabena who bowed and shook his hand. They spoke for a few minutes before Kwabena introduced Tamara.

"I'd like you to meet the ambassador to the United States," he said.

Tamara bowed and shook his hands before being escorted to their seats.

Tamara leaned over to him. "How do you know all these important people?"

"The ambassador and my father worked together a long time ago," he explained.

The dinner was a formal affair. Many of the men wore traditional African attire. Others wore suits and ties. The women were decked out in their most elegant finery, some with majestic-looking headpieces. There were long speeches from people deemed great orators. Dancers in colorful costumes performing traditional dances to drums entertained them. Then there was an awards ceremony.

The master of ceremonies gave a long introduction about the work and contributions of each recipient, who then received the award with much fanfare and delivered a long-winded speech. Two hours into the ceremony, Tamara had tuned out most of the speeches. Though the ceremony was done in English, the heavy accents made it difficult to understand all that was being said. So it came as a surprise when she heard, "I now present this award to Dr. Kwabena Opoku for his contribution to the advancement of science and medicine."

Tamara stared in disbelief as Kwabena strode up to the podium amid loud applause. He ceremoniously accepted the award and gave a thankfully short, yet eloquent speech. After shaking the hands of a million and one dignitaries, Kwabena returned to his seat. He saw the shock on Tamara's face and smiled, indicating that he would explain to her later.

The minute they got into her Lexus, Tamara turned to Kwabena. "*Dr.* Kwabena Opoku. When I asked you what work you did, you said research. Why didn't you tell me you were a scientist—a doctor, no less?"

He smiled and calmly responded, "I did. I have a

PhD in biomedical engineering, and I do biomedical research. What difference does it make?"

"Ben, I don't know. At least I wouldn't be blindsided." She tried to explain, "I would have known you were being presented an award…that you are an accomplished scientist. What's the award for anyway?"

"It's really not a big deal. Every year the Ghanaian Association holds a gala and they honor a few ex-pats who they feel have done something to make the Ghanaian people proud. I'm a biomedical engineer. I published a few papers in respected scientific journals, which, quite frankly, most people do not read, so they decided to honor me. It's not the Nobel Prize."

"I don't understand why you are going through such great lengths to downplay your accomplishments," Tamara responded with annoyance. "If you're such a big shot why did you have to get married for a green card? Don't important researchers get national-interest waivers or something of that nature?"

Kwabena was quiet for a few seconds as he collected his thoughts. "You know, I had this really wonderful great-uncle. He was an old, frail, soft-spoken man. I'm named for him."

"But—" Tamara began.

"He always would say to me: 'Never boast of your accomplishments or your good works. If they've made an impact, they will speak for themselves.'" He paused. "I thought he was just an old wise man who never really left the village. But he was a well-educated and accomplished man. You know when I found that out? At his funeral. When they read the eulogy, I learned that he was a brave soldier in the fight against colonialism and an ardent advocate of Pan-African unity. He was also an accomplished author of several Ghanaian political and social commentaries and had traveled all over the continent promoting African unity. Bearing his name, I have a lot to live up to, but I emulate him because I admire his humility."

"Oh," Tamara responded. "But you haven't answered my question."

"Which one?"

"The reason behind the green-card marriage."

He thought for a minute about the circumstances leading up to the marriage. It was a simple story but hard to explain. He'd been forced to make a difficult decision to report his mentor's unethical behavior to the university. His mentor's reaction was extreme. He set out to undermine Kwabena's tenure and terminate his appointment. Failing to do so, he sought his deportation when his H-1B visa was about to expire. As Kwabena reflected on the difficulties of the last few months, he realized he was not yet ready to share that information with Tamara. "It's a long and involved story."

"I guess we all have our skeletons, don't we?"

Kwabena just smiled. "I guess."

They drove in silence for a short while. "I don't feel like going home now, do you?" Kwabena asked.

"What do you feel like doing?"

"Dancing. Let's go dancing."

They went to a West African night spot in Washington, D.C. As they entered the hall, a group of men greeted Kwabena with loud fanfare, congratulating him and patting him on the back. They were a few of his friends and associates from the West African Association.

One of the men looked over at Tamara. "Who is the little woman?" he asked curiously. "Quite a departure from your usual."

Kwabena just laughed. "This is my landlord, Tamara Fontaine."

"Quite a young landlord," the man said with admiration.

He laughed and waved his friend off lightly. Soon they were on the dance floor, moving to mostly quick tempo West African soukous and hip-hop. Tamara laughed with joy when she heard people rapping in a foreign language with heavy Nigerian accents.

For the first time in a long time she was having fun. Most of Kwabena's associates laughed, flirted with her and teased her, making her feel part of the group.

Sometime after two A.M., the music slowed down. Kwabena led her by the hand to the dance floor. Together they swayed to the music. She rested her head on his chest as they slow danced. She could smell his cologne through his shirt. For a moment she forgot about their arranged marriage, their business deal and just enjoyed the feel of his arms around her. She closed her eyes and lost herself in the dance. Soon she felt his head lower, and his cheek resting on the top of her head. Then his lips brushed her head ever so lightly. Or was she imagining things? Did he just kiss her head?

She stiffened momentarily, raised her head and looked up at him questioningly. He looked down at her and smiled sheepishly.

Suddenly she pulled away from him. The song hadn't

yet ended. "I'm tired. Maybe it's time we leave," she said quietly.

Kwabena nodded, embarrassed, and they left the night club. The ride home was quiet and tense. Tamara had suddenly turned cold. The camaraderie built in the last few weeks was gone.

When they entered the door, Tamara headed upstairs. "Tammy," he called quietly. She turned back and looked at him with eyes of steel. "I crossed the line. I'm sorry."

She nodded and ran upstairs to her room. As she lay in bed, she reflected on the night. This marriage was a business deal, and she did not want to lose sight of that at all. Yet she felt the attraction. It was not just that he was handsome or physically attractive. But he was the only person beside Jordan who made her feel special and secure. In their interactions of the past few weeks, he had listened to her as if she was the most important person in the world. He looked at her with respect and admiration. Most of all, Kwabena made her feel beautiful and feminine. But she knew in a year's time when he got his green card, they would be divorced and whatever pretend marriage they had would come to an end. She couldn't risk falling for him. She couldn't risk another heartbreak.

Chapter Eight

The delicious scent of stewed meat greeted Tamara as she entered her front door, reminding her of just how hungry she was. It had been a long week, and today an even longer day. She'd attended church with Becky and the kids, since Jordan was out working. Church was an all-day affair. Worst of all, she could not get what happened last weekend off her mind.

For the entire week, Tamara replayed the events at the gala and nightclub in her head. Though she hadn't seen much of Kwabena for the week, she could not stop thinking of the slow dance they shared and his light kiss on her head. She kept seeing the embarrassment on his face when she abruptly ended the dance. Even while at church, she could not clear her mind of the expression on his face as he apologized for crossing the line. But the more she thought of it, the more she realized that she had overreacted. His action was probably just a momentary lapse in judgment, stimulated by the slow music and the ambiance of the moment. Her reaction was not justifiable.

Yet Tamara recognized that her reaction was driven by fear. Not fear that Kwabena would intentionally try to take advantage of her. In the weeks between her failed job interview and the gala, she had grown to like and respect Kwabena as an honorable and charming person. They had shared a few dinners and conversations that left her feeling secure, as if she could trust him. He was easy to talk to, easy to be with. What she feared was herself...that growing attraction she felt for him. She didn't understand it. Yes, he was handsome. Yes, he had a body that could make a woman drool. But beyond that, she felt a growing closeness—a kind of emotional attraction she did not trust. Tamara had to keep reminding herself that their relationship was based on a business deal and nothing more. In a year's time it would be over and he would be out of her life. The most she could hope to get from this arrangement was a new friend.

Tamara drifted into the kitchen, lured by the aroma of delicious food. As was customary when Kwabena cooked, the kitchen was a mess. Pots, pans and ingredients occupied every bit of counter space. Something was sizzling in a large pot on the stove. Kwabena was nowhere in sight. Tamara draped her long ice blue jacket that complemented her straight sleeveless dress over her arms and headed straight to the pot. She lifted the cover, taking in the delicious aroma of stewed meat.

"Curiosity killed the cat," came Kwabena's deep voice behind her. She jumped and immediately turned red. She saw he was grinning from ear to ear.

Tamara returned the smile. "I hope that's not what you are cooking."

Kwabena laughed lightly, as if last weekend was all but forgotten. "Could be. Taste it and see."

"Goat I'm willing to try, but I draw the line at cats and dogs...and rabbits."

They both laughed. "It's just beef and chicken," he said, stirring the stew with a wooden spoon and lowering the fire beneath pot. "I'm preparing Jolof Rice. Want me to show you how to cook it?"

"I'd love to, but I've got to shop for groceries. As of this morning the cupboards resembled Old Mother Hubbard's." Tamara opened the refrigerator to see what she needed to purchase. To her surprise, the refrigerator was filled to capacity with many unfamiliar ethnic foods.

Kwabena glanced up at her. "That's been taken care of."

"Gee, thanks," Tamara responded. "How much do I owe you?"

Kwabena moved toward the island, where he began to peel vegetables. "Nothing. Just help cleaning up this kitchen when I'm done."

Tamara looked around at the messy kitchen and clucked her tongue. "I definitely need to change my clothes for this," she said and exited the kitchen.

Kwabena looked at Tamara's retreating back. He thought back to the dance they shared. His initial reason for inviting Tamara to the gala was twofold. First and foremost, he wanted to dispel a few myths she held about Ghanaian culture and lifestyle. The second reason was more important: he felt sorry for her. She appeared sad, lonely and vulnerable. He could not help noticing the paucity of friends or her nonexistent social life. That was in stark contrast to him, who constantly entertained friends. On several occasions, he had been tempted to invite her downstairs to join him and his friends for dinner, but was dissuaded by her hostility and hot temper. That night when he found her crying in frustration, his heart went out to hers, especially when she detailed the difficulty she'd faced in the past

year. He commiserated with her. It was not too long
ago that he faced similar tumults and uncertainty in his
life that led him to this desperate marital arrangement.

Since that night they had eaten together and watched
television on several occasions. They'd even played a
game of chess, and she'd whipped his butt—no small
feat. She was intelligent, witty, easy to talk to and did
not take herself too seriously. He enjoyed the time they
spent together. He genuinely liked her, but that was no
excuse for his actions last weekend. He had no idea
what had come over him or why he had felt such a
strong desire to kiss her. He was not usually that impul-
sive. Maybe it was just the night: the high of receiving
the award, the song or the dance. *Or maybe…*

"Maybe what?" Tamara returned, sweeping into the
kitchen in a pair of jeans, a green T-shirt and flip-flops.

He had spoken out loud. "Maybe…you can cut up
some veggies or chop some seasoning," he said, quickly
rebounding from his mishap. "Do you have a garlic
press?"

"No," Tamara answered, grabbing a full bottle of cider from the Lazy Susan and holding it up, "But I have
this."

Tamara began pounding the garlic with the bottle,
while Kwabena cut vegetables, only to be interrupted
by the phone ringing in the basement.

"Be back." Kwabena wiped his hands on a kitchen
towel and trotted down to the basement, but by the
time he got to the phone, the caller had hung up. He
looked at the caller ID, sighed and trotted back upstairs.

When he returned, Tamara was macerating the garlic, calmly humming a gospel song. Looking at her, he had to admit she was beautiful. Not the kind of obvious beauty that he usually found himself attracted to. He couldn't understand the attraction to her. He always went for the tall, slim, model type. Tamara was anything but that. But there was something about her that had him captivated. Her beauty came from within and radiated out.

Again his mind drifted to last Saturday night and the urge he had to kiss her. Tamara was several inches shorter, a whole lot heavier and definitely less polished than any woman he'd ever dated. Yet he found her attractive. Maybe it was her sheltered innocence or her smile, which lit up her face and made you feel like you were the most important person in the world. Or maybe it was her simple, sometimes self-deprecating, sense of humor…or her honesty. She was not coy. She did not flirt or throw herself at him like so many women did. Nor was she pretentious. Nothing like the women he dated or the beauty queen he almost married. Tamara was like a breath of fresh air.

"Ow!" she squealed, sticking her throbbing finger in her mouth. She'd missed the garlic and hit her index finger hard.

"You ok?" Kwabena crossed the room in two quick strides.

"No," she responded. "I think I just made mincemeat out of my fingers."

He laughed. Even in pain, Tamara had a sense of humor. "Let me see." He took her hand in his and looked at her red swollen finger, then reached in the freezer for a bag of frozen veggies.

"What's that for?"

"First aid," he responded wrapping the cold bag around her finger. "It will reduce the swelling."

Kwabena held the cold pack around Tamara's fingers, aware of the softness of her hands in his. They stood in the middle of the kitchen silently, her hand in his as he gently nursed her wounded finger. He wrestled the urge to draw her closer. His eyes searched her face. She raised her gaze to meet his and for a fleeting moment their eyes locked.

Staring into Kwabena's dark eyes, Tamara felt naked, as if he could see into her soul. Nervously, she lowered her head.

Kwabena placed one long finger beneath her chin. Gently he tilted her face upward. Tamara's heart throbbed as he lowered his head ever so slowly. Tamara closed her eyes, powerless to fight the invisible force that drew them together.

The scent of burning meat assailed their noses as the pot sizzled noisily on the stove.

"The meat!" they exclaimed in unison as realization hit them.

Kwabena rushed to the stove, hurriedly removing the pot from the fire. The spell was broken.

An hour later, Tamara and Kwabena sat at the table in the breakfast nook over steaming plates of Jolof Rice and fried plantains. Tamara savored the taste of the rice infused with stewed chicken, beef and various veggies.

"This is good," she said. "It's almost like a dish Jordan's grandmother used to make. I think she called it cook-up."

"It probably originated from West Africa and crossed the Atlantic during the slave trade. The more you travel, the more you realize the similarity among cuisines. The more diverse a culture, the more blended the cuisine."

"I guess you must be well traveled." She wanted to know more about him.

"I did a lot of traveling before living in the U.S.," Kwabena admitted. "Now most of my international traveling is restricted to conferences in Europe or Asia and trips back to Ghana to visit relatives."

Tamara looked out the bay window of the breakfast nook to the golf course in the distance. "I always wanted to travel outside the U.S."

"Any country in particular?"

Tamara smiled and took another bite of her food. "I always wanted to go to the Caribbean. When I had the money, I never had the time. Now I have the time, but not the money."

Kwabena chuckled, "One day you will." He spooned a generous helping of red pepper sauce over his food.

Tamara took the bottle from him.

"I don't recommend it," he warned before she poured it. "It's extremely hot."

"Hey, I've had Jamaican jerk. I can handle a little pepper sauce!" With that, she poured a generous amount over her rice. With the first forkful, Tamara felt her eyes water and her throat burn. "Water..." she croaked, her mouth on fire. After downing a pint of water Tamara asked, "What in the world is that?"

Kwabena tried his best to keep a straight face. "It's *shito*. My aunt Esi made it for me the last time I visited."

"They should call it fire sauce."

"My aunt uses it in everything, especially her Jolof Rice."

"Sounds like a recipe for perpetual heartburn," Tamara muttered, spooning more rice minus the *shito* into her plate.

"Believe me, Aunt Esi is a top notch cook. If you think my Jolof Rice is good, you should taste hers. When I was little, each time a man wanted to marry one of my aunts, his elder relatives, usually his uncles, would have these meetings with my uncle Kofi and several of the elder men of the family. After the meetings, there would be feasts and dancing. Aunt Esi would make her Jolof Rice. That thing was so good that my aunts used to say if the man seeking marriage had second thoughts, Aunt Esi's Jolof Rice would erase all doubts."

Tamara laughed, thinking of her own very small family. "You must have an incredibly large family. How many siblings do your parents have?"

Kwabena reached for some fried plantains. "They are not all my parents' siblings. Some are cousins, and some aren't even blood relatives. As long as they are within my parents' age group, they are aunts and uncles. Similar to the way your cousin's kids think of you as their aunt."

"I see," was Tamara's response.

They sat in a comfortable silence, savoring the sweet taste of the plantains. After a few minutes, Tamara asked, "How is it you've never been married?"

Kwabena raised one eyebrow.

"I mean before this…this arrangement," she clarified.

"Never found the right person." Kwabena looked far off as he reflected on his engagement several years earlier. It had been for all the wrong reasons with the wrong person. She had been more interested in his family status and his potential fame than in him as a person, and it had hurt him greatly. From her and some minor girlfriends, he'd learned not to trust women. For him it was too difficult to distinguish those who wanted him for who he was and those who associated with him for his status in life. It was also one of the reasons why he revealed so little of himself, his family history and his work to the people he recently met. As a result, he'd engaged in a series of noncommittal relationships and had not seriously considered marriage.

He turned back to Tamara. "Someday, when the right person comes along, I'd like to have a family. Someday…" His voice trailed off.

Tamara smiled. "Me too."

Chapter Nine

The October air was cool and crisp as Tamara stood out on the deck overlooking the pool. The trees in the woods behind the yard were already turning yellow and red, painting a picturesque scene of tranquility. Squirrels scampered in and out of the trees and scurried along the ground, enjoying the last bits of warmth before winter set in. Tamara smiled as she saw a rabbit hop by, and listened to frogs croaking around the creek. She inhaled the perfumed air, enjoying her home. She was thankful she didn't have to sell right away.

She heard the deck creak. She looked around and saw Kwabena enter the deck from the basement entrance.

"Hey," he said, leaning against the railing next to her.

She returned his greeting with a casual smile. In the past two weeks they had adopted the lifestyle of roommates. They split the grocery bill and the utilities. If he cooked, he left food for her. If she cooked, she left food for him. And if they were both home at the same time, they ate together. Other times they cooked together. They respected each other's space. It was a feeling of camaraderie and belonging that Tamara had been missing most of her adult life. Yet, he never went upstairs, and she never went downstairs. At times, she heard him with friends. Other times, she suspected he entertained women. Tamara had to constantly remind herself that what he did was his own business, despite her curiosity—and jealousy.

Kwabena looked at the sun slowly going down behind the trees across the yard. It left the sky with brush strokes of orange and pink. "This is my favorite time of year," he said, looking far off. "It's not too hot, and it's not too cold."

Tamara smiled. "Enjoy it while you can. Our first arctic blast moves in next week, or so the weatherman says."

They stood in silence for a while, enjoying each other's company. "I love this place," he said. "I'm glad you don't have to sell."

"Who says I don't? Unless I get a J-O-B I will have to sell sooner or later. I hope it's later than sooner."

"Maybe a job is on the horizon," Kwabena said, his eyes twinkling mischievously.

"Are you offering me one?"

"Actually, I spoke to this friend of mine who is looking for an IT specialist to set up and maintain a data communication system. I ran your name by him, and he would like to interview you."

"Are you serious?" she asked hopefully. "I hope you're not teasing me."

"I'm not," he assured her. He fished in his pocket and retrieved a business card from his billfold. "You need to give him a call to arrange an interview. I took the liberty of directing him to your resume online, so he's already familiar with your qualifications."

She read the card. The location was about ten to fifteen minutes from her home. "Thank you." She smiled gratefully, closing her eyes. Suddenly a mixture of inexplicable emotion overwhelmed her. She looked up at

Kwabena with awe. Not only was he an extremely modest accomplished scientist, he was also a very sensitive and generous person. Kwabena was fast becoming her personal hero.

"It's an academic institution, so don't expect a six-figure salary."

"Any salary is better than none," she said. Overcome with emotion, she threw herself in his arms and gave him a big hug. "Oh, thank you, Ben. Thank you so much."

Her happiness was infectious. Kwabena found himself lifting her effortlessly off the ground and spinning her around. When her feet returned to terra firma, they were both laughing.

She looked up at him with soft brown eyes, sparkling with happiness, relief and gratitude. Her heart swelled with a strange feeling so strong she could hardly speak. "Thank you," she whispered her voice thick with emotion.

He looked down at her. Their eyes met and held. Kwabena sighed deeply, his eyes searching her face. Surely she must be feeling the same thing he was feeling. He wanted to feel her soft moist lips on his. With his back against the banister, he bent to bring himself closer to her height and tenderly drew her to him. Slowly he lowered his head, his eyes asking permission to ravish her lips.

Tamara looked up at him with wide eyes. His eyes were filled with desire that she knew reflected her own. Her heart was racing, her knees weak and shaky. She looked at his generous lips and breathed deeply. She wanted to feel his lips on hers, to taste the sweetness of his kiss. Her lips parted as his face drew close to hers.

Gently his soft, moist lips touched her forehead, then brushed her closed eyes, the tip of her nose and her lips. Tenderly his lips possessed hers in a soft, sensuous kiss.

Slowly he moved his lips against hers, enjoying the sweet sensations that showered him. He closed his eyes savoring her sweetness. Gently he released her. His eyes searched her face seeking permission to ravish her. His heart thumped erratically in his chest.

Tamara looked up at Kwabena, her cheeks flushed, her heart racing wildly. She held her breath as he lowered his face to hers once more. His lips covered hers again in a gentle yet passionate kiss. Ever so tenderly his tongue probed her mouth as his kiss deepened in passion and intensity. Tamara responded passionately, opening her mouth and welcoming his teasing tongue. Slowly they explored the deep recesses of each other's mouth, filling each other with desire. Tamara closed her eyes and submitted to the sweetness of his kiss. Bolts of desire coursed through her body, igniting her passions. She felt her breathing deepen as he ravished her with his lips and tongue.

Their kiss intensified as Kwabena felt arousal course through his body. He didn't want to let go. He drew her closer to him, letting his hands caress her back, feeling her soft flesh beneath his fingers.

Reluctantly he drew back, trying desperately to control himself. She opened her eyes, her expression one of fear and desire. He kissed her again hard, pulling her into him. He could not get enough of her lips. She returned his kiss with fiery passion. Her body was tingling all over with desire as she caressed his lean hard body. She could feel his arousal pressing into her belly. Her heart was like a drum in her ears.

Slowly he released her lips and pulled her in a tighter embrace nestling her head on his chest. She heard him sigh deeply as he struggled to gain control. She felt him shower her temples and forehead with tiny kisses. They remained locked in a tight embrace, her head on his chest, his cheeks on her head.

He raised his head, took a deep breath and in a hoarse scratchy voice whispered, "I'm sorry, Tammy."

"Sorry for what?"

"Taking advantage of your vulnerability."

She looked up at his still wet lips glistening in the dim twilight and whispered, "You have my permission to take advantage of me."

He smiled and kissed her again passionately. He wanted to do so much more with her than just kiss. He wanted to ravish her body. He wanted to make her moan with pleasure. He wanted to make love to her from the setting of the sun to the first rays of dawn. His hand found her bare flesh at the waist beneath her blouse. He felt like he would explode with desire as they kissed each other hungrily. Then the doorbell rang.

Tamara heard the surreal ringing from a distance. Reluctantly she released his lips.

"I should get that shouldn't I," she breathed, her passions still ablaze.

"You should," he responded thickly. He didn't release her right away. His lips possessed hers, and they kissed passionately.

The doorbell rang again. "I should get that," Tamara repeated.

He nodded and kissed her again. Neither of them wanted the moment to end. Finally he released her. She remained rooted in her spot, waiting for him to kiss her again.

"Aren't you gonna get the door?" he asked with a sly smile on his face.

She giggled and stepped in the wrong direction, toward the basement.

"I think it's that way," he said, physically turning her to face the door.

"Yeah, I knew that," she said, giggling girlishly. She was happy, she was elated, she was giddy and her body was on fire.

He couldn't help laughing. She glanced at him before entering the doorway and flashed a smile. Her expression spoke volumes.

Oh gosh! One kiss and I'm acting like an idiot. He probably thinks I've never been kissed before. One kiss! Well three kisses or is it four? But who's counting? Tamara wrestled with herself as she walked to the front door. What they did felt so right. He was a good kisser. No, he was an extraordinary kisser. She just hoped her face was not all red right now. It was probably Jordan anyway—or Becky. They were the only people likely to visit midweek.

Tamara opened the door without looking. "Darlene!" she exclaimed in surprise. "What are you doing here?"

"Visiting my cousin," Darlene answered, stepping into the foyer.

"You're the last person I expected to see at this time of day." When she'd first bought the house, Darlene visited often, mostly to use the swimming pool. It was also her pickup and dropoff point for dates she wanted to impress and a place to host pool parties. But as the winter set in, her visits became less frequent. A steady boyfriend over this last summer kept her occupied, but that relationship ended a month or so ago.

"I was on my way home from work and decided to drop in to see you."

"You work in downtown Baltimore, and I live south of the city. You could hardly call that on your way home."

"Ok," she said, getting to the point. "Who's the man?"

Tamara knew that was the purpose of the visit. Ebony must have told her about Kwabena, and she was curious.

Tamara blushed. "What man?"

"The one Ebony saw you with."

"That was weeks ago! Why you all up in my business like that?" Tamara responded annoyed.

"Ebony said the guy looked like he was living here. I want to know who he is. Inquiring minds want to know." Darlene pushed her way past Tamara and entered the den, looking around curiously.

"Then read *The Enquirer.*"

"Come on, Tammy, you can talk to me." Darlene turned to face Tamara, staring her down, daring her to tell the truth. "Who is he? I heard he was hot."

Under Darlene's probing gaze, Tamara blushed and leaned against the back of the couch. "Ebony made a big deal out of nothing," she said with a shrug. "It's just a guy who needed an escort to an awards ceremony, and I agreed to accompany him."

* * *

Kwabena stood outside, watching the exchange. Through the closed sliding doors he could not hear the conversation, but he had a feeling it was about him. The air outside was getting chilly. Without Tamara's warm body next to him, he was feeling the cold through his thin polo shirt. He ran down the stairs toward the basement entrance. It was locked. He must have locked it behind him when he came up earlier.

He looked down at his pants. He needed to go inside but didn't want to risk it—not with the telltale bulge. A shiver ran through his spine. The temperature was dropping rapidly. He had no choice but to enter through the kitchen. He untucked his shirt, letting it hang casually over his pants in an effort to hide his protrusion. Then he opened the sliding door and stepped inside.

As he entered the den, he heard Tamara say, "It's just a guy I rented the basement to in order to pay my mortgage, that's all."

He tried to sneak quietly past them, but Darlene looked up and saw him. She smiled slyly and looked at Tamara expectantly, silently demanding an introduction. *Busted!* He strolled over to the girls.

"I kind of locked myself out of the basement," he explained. He looked at the woman standing next to Tamara. She was the type he easily went for—tall and slim with shapely curves and long legs. Relaxed hair with drop curls framed her oval face. Large eyes with unending lashes, high cheekbones and full red lips made her a drop dead beauty.

"Kwabena, my cousin Darlene; Darlene, my tenant Kwabena," Tamara introduced them.

"Well, hello," Darlene said in a throaty, seductive voice. "It is certainly good to see you again."

Kwabena observed her. He could tell that this was a woman who'd seen the world. He shook her long-fingered, well-manicured hand. "Have we met before?"

"Not really, but I've…well, I work for Kulper, Cleveland and Rollins, so I've seen you before, but we've never officially met. It is a pleasure to finally meet you."

"The pleasure is mine," he responded, still holding on to her hand.

Tamara looked at the exchange and wanted to gag. Darlene was pulling out all the stops flirting with him—and he was falling right into her feminine trap.

Just then the phone in the basement rang. "I'd love to stay and chat some more, but I'm expecting a call, so good night ladies." With that he disappeared into the basement.

Darlene looked at Tamara excitedly. "Do you know who that is? That is Dr. Opoku, *the* Dr. Opoku."

"And?"

Darlene stared at her as if she was from outer space. "He invented some kind of smart prosthetic or something, and our law office is handling the patent. When his invention goes to market, and the military gets a hold of it, he is going to be rolling in dough. Your tenant is *famous*. He was on CNN Health and they profiled his work on the Discovery Channel. Don't you watch the news?"

"I don't have cable." Tamara was going to have a talk with Kwabena. Why was he so secretive about his accomplishments? Shouldn't he be proud of them? His behavior surpassed modesty and humility.

Darlene kept talking. "He is just your tenant right? Nothing between you, no secret engagement, no little hanky panky right?"

"He's my tenant," Tamara asserted.

"Good, then he's fair game. You'll be seeing a lot of me."

Tamara heard the garage door open and Kwabena's car drive off. *So much for my evening.*

"Since I'm already here, what's for dinner?"

Tamara dished out the food that she expected to share with Kwabena. She was distracted. She couldn't get the look on his face or the feel of his kiss out of her mind. Maybe this is the beginning of something, she thought with a smile as she placed both plates on the table.

Chapter Ten

Tamara called Dr. Botanga the next morning. She was surprised that he answered the phone himself. Then he asked her what time was good for her. Less than two hours later she was dressed in her navy blue interview suit on her way to Independent Laboratories.

When she arrived, there was no secretary to greet her and escort her to the interviewer's office. Instead she found herself wandering through a maze of corridors until she found the room number listed on the card. She found Dr. Botanga in a laboratory placing red liquid into a tissue culture dish. He was dressed in jeans and a sweater, over which he wore a white lab coat with the name *Michael A. Botanga, MD, PhD* embroidered over the left pocket. He was a five-foot-ten-inch medium-built, dark-skinned man in his forties.

"You must be Tamara Fontaine," he said in a light African accent different from Kwabena's. He didn't stop what he was doing. "I'm Mike."

He placed the tissue culture dish on a rocker and set a digital timer. He discarded his purple nitrile gloves, washed his hands in the heavily stained sink, and then shook her hand.

"Welcome to Independent Laboratories," he said.

He introduced her to some of the other members of the lab, who gave her a brief summary of their projects.

Then they walked into his office, which was little more than a large walk-in closet near the front entrance of the lab. Shelves on the wall held an untidy array of bound scientific journals, laboratory and supply manuals, reference books and oversized binders. His desk was littered with journal articles. Somewhere amid the clutter were a laptop computer and a framed photograph of his wife and three children.

He cleared a microfiber chair of books and offered her a seat.

"Independent Laboratories is a loose conglomeration of research labs scattered throughout Maryland," Dr. Botanga began. "Some of our labs are with academic institutions. Others, like the four in this building, which you can tell was once an old strip mall, are private labs. When we started, our focus was on drug development; in particular, two rheumatoid arthritis drugs—one of which is on the market, and the other now in phase-three clinical trials. Since then we've branched off into drug discovery and the development of smart prosthetics. Recently we've added two bioinformatics labs. So you see, our labs are scattered all over. We have one at Johns Hopkins Medical Institute, several at University of Maryland College Park, two at UMBC and one at the National Institutes of Health. Then there is the biomedical engineering lab that Ben heads over in Bethesda. For the longest while, we've shared data by e-mail, FTP or physically transporting data on zip disks or CDs. That's where you come in. We need to get our computers to communicate with each other so that we can transfer large amounts of data from any computer in the network securely, and we can freely access a central database. And we need someone to maintain the system once it's in place. Do you think you can handle that?"

Tamara spoke for the first time. "Much of what you describe is what I did for the last five years. I am certain I can handle it. If there is anything that I'm unfamiliar with, I am confident that I can learn it within a short time."

"Good. When can you start?"

Tamara was shocked. "Don't you need to see my qualifications and references?" she asked.

Dr. Botanga smiled. "I saw your resume, and your experience is impressive. I've already checked your references. Moreover, Ben recommended you highly. I trust his judgment. As part owner of this company, I know he would not do anything that would affect it negatively."

Tamara felt another piece of Kwabena's identity puzzle fall in place. Not only was he a hotshot biomedical engineer, he was also part owner of Independent Laboratories. She had a lot of questions to ask her husband.

As if reading her mind, Dr. Botanga continued, "I know you are Ben's wife and I am aware of the circumstances surrounding your marriage. Not only are Ben and I business associates, we're very good friends. We go back a long way."

"In that case, I can start tomorrow."

"I'll see you tomorrow."

"By the way," Tamara asked, wondering exactly how to phrase her question. "Your lovely accent…Where are you from?"

"Cameroons," Dr. Botanga responded. "Yu Ming will accompany you to the conference room. We have a really interesting seminar today." He donned a tweed jacket and headed out the door.

It was after five when Tamara returned home. She couldn't wait to tell Kwabena and was relieved to see his car parked in the driveway. She'd accompanied the postdoctoral fellow, Yu Ming, to the seminar. Then the lab members took her and the seminar speaker out to lunch. The rest of the afternoon she spent with an administrative assistant filling out paperwork. The pay wasn't much. It was a little more than half of what she made at her former job, and she was salaried, which meant no paid overtime. But there were no set hours as long as she put in a forty-hour week. Moreover, they would pay for college courses at any of the affiliated universities.

Brimming with excitement, Tamara rushed downstairs to tell Kwabena the good news. This was the first time she'd been down there since he'd moved in almost two months ago. He had done a wonderful job transforming the place. Two large potted palms greeted her at the foot of the stairs. He'd divided the L-shaped recreation room into a living room and dining/recreation area. In the smaller part of the L, he'd placed a small glass-topped dinette set close to the built-in minibar. On the wall over the table was an oversized painting of an African woman in traditional dress, walking through tall grass with an earthen jug on her head and an infant tied to her back. On either side of the painting were two Akan masks. Her pool table occupied this part of the recreation room.

The wall in the living room was lined with Akan and Dagomba masks and framed crafts made of butterfly wings. The only furniture in the long rectangular room was a brown and beige microfiber futon and a beige sofa bed with leopard-print throw pillows. A leopard throw rug sat on the ceramic floor between the chairs. Two cedar-accent round tables—with a wood-carved kneeling, bejeweled girl in Ghanaian dress as the pedestal—served as end tables. His center table was a black Asante throne ottoman, the pedestal for which was a carving of a naked woman kneeling prostrate beneath it. Creeping pothos ivy in two Akokyem ceramic vases sat on the cedar tables.

Tamara ran in search of Kwabena. As she passed her once empty exercise room, she was surprised to see a treadmill, weight bench, free weights and an elliptical machine occupying the room. She spotted him on the sofa and approached, barely able to contain herself.

"Guess what?" she asked excitedly. "I…" Her voice trailed off as the couch came into full view. Kwabena was sitting on the couch. In his arms was a sobbing brown-skinned lady, her head on his chest. His large hands caressed her back comfortingly. They both looked up to see Tamara standing there. Despite the red, tearstained eyes, Tamara could see the woman was a beauty.

Tamara stood frozen for a minute. When she found her voice she stammered, "I…I…It can wait. I'll come back some other time."

Before Kwabena or the woman could respond, Tamara fled. She left the house and walked around the neighborhood, looking at the new houses going up and the newly constructed golf course. She walked around the darkened lake, which was merely a water runoff area.

How could I be so stupid? How could he kiss me like that one day and be in the arms of another the next? Tamara closed her eyes. She felt disappointed, but she knew sharing a kiss with a man didn't amount to a commitment. She continued walking until she found herself at Jordan's house.

When she entered, the family was seated at the kitchen table having dinner. Immediately the kids got excited.

"Auntie Tammy," shouted Devon and the twins, Kaia and Michele, rushing from the table to embrace her. Kadeem, the baby, started bouncing in his high chair, kicking his little feet as fast as a hummingbird's wings. He banged his spoon against the tray of his high chair, splashing green mush all around.

"I'm disrupting everything," Tamara said. "I'll come back later."

"Where you think you're going?" Jordan asked. "You ain't disrupting anything. Now sit down with us." He turned to his wife. "Becky, can you get Tamara a plate of food please?"

"I'm not hungry," Tamara said.

"You're never not hungry," Jordan responded as Becky disappeared into the kitchen.

Tamara sat at the table, and the kids finally settled. Jordan took over spooning green mush into Kadeem's mouth. Soon Becky returned with a plate stacked with ackee and saltfish over large white dumplings.

It was delicious. "I see you've learned to cook island style," Tamara said slyly to Becky.

Becky responded, "When the madam was here a few months ago, she insisted that I learn to feed Jordan like a real Jamaican man. So she taught me to prepare ackee and saltfish, callaloo, fungi, cow foot soup, curried goat, oxtail and Manish water. She doesn't realize how expensive those things are at the Caribbean Market. For the six years we've been married, Jordan was quite content with my soul food, but now he keeps hinting that he wants Jamaican food."

Tamara laughed. Becky always referred to Jordan's mother as "the madam." In the first few years of their marriage, Jordan had a hard time balancing Becky's needs with his mother's demands. It made for a strained relationship between Becky and Jordan's mother. Things changed for the better when his mother returned to Jamaica to take care of his grandmother, who had a stroke.

"What brings you here tonight all dressed up?" Jordan asked. "Since your husband moved in, I haven't seen you much at all."

"No fault of mine," Tamara responded. "Becky and the kids see me often. If you didn't work so much, you would too."

"True," Becky concurred.

"Mon, I tell you, you work harder when you own your own business than when you working for someone else," he said, his Jamaican accent showing through.

"Talking about work, I got a job!"

"Congratulations!" they both said in unison and high-fived her. The kids each came around to give Tamara high-fives too. They had no idea what was going on, but they had to be part of the fun.

"Where?" asked Becky.

"It's at Independent Laboratories."

Jordan asked, "Isn't that Kwabena's company?"

"So I've heard. I guess it really isn't what you know but *who* you know," Tamara responded with a smile.

They finished eating and cleared the table. "I'll clean up," Tamara volunteered.

"You're a guest here," said Becky. "Let Jordan take care of it."

"Oh please, I'm here so often I practically live here."

"Jordan's not getting off the hook that easy. Cleaning the kitchen is the only work he does around here. His mother wants him fed like a 'big man,' so he's got to prove he is a big man and clean the kitchen like one." Becky shot Jordan a glance.

He walked over and whispered in her ear. She giggled like a schoolgirl, and he slapped her butt.

"Kids," she called. "Who wants a bubble bath?"

The three older ones came running, screaming, "Me!" Becky shooed them upstairs and walked up behind them with a food-covered Kadeem on her hip.

Tamara and Jordan set about cleaning the kitchen together. They worked in companionable silence. That was what she loved about being with Jordan. They could be silent together or they could be chatting up a storm, it was still comfortable. He was as close as she got to a brother and she was as close as he got to a sister. Not that he lacked siblings. His father, who never left Jamaica, had a wife and five younger children, all of them boys.

"Ok, what's on your mind?" Jordan's question caught her off guard.

"Nothing except work tomorrow."

"You're not fooling me, Tammy. You just got a job

after a year out of work and a million and one interviews. You should be excited, jumping through the roof. Instead you look sad, even a little hurt."

"You're imagining things," Tamara denied.

"I'm not. Something happened between you and Kwabena?"

Jordan always read her like a nursery rhyme. Tamara was silent.

"You're falling for him aren't you?"

Tamara wiped her brow with a soapy hand. "I don't know," she surrendered with a sigh. "I'm such an idiot. I allowed myself to get carried away, and now I feel like such a fool."

Jordan stopped drying the dishes and looked at her expectantly, waiting for the details.

"We kissed…and I'm not talking about a casual peck on the cheek." Tamara looked up at Jordan as he resumed drying the dishes. "You don't seem surprised."

"I'm not. I knew there was that risk when he moved in with you. Kwabena is honorable, but he is an attractive man and his reputation with the ladies is not much of a secret. The prettier the better."

"I wouldn't quite describe myself as pretty."

"That's because you've got self-esteem issues," Jordan dismissed. "I've told you before, you are a beautiful woman, no matter what you think."

Tamara sighed. "How could I be so stupid? Yesterday we shared this wonderful intimate moment and I thought it means as much to him as it did to me. I allowed myself to feel things that I haven't felt since Jared. Today I walk in on him in the arms of another woman in my house. I'm an idiot. I'm a magnet for dishonest creeps."

Jordan gave her a bear hug. "I'm sorry I got you into this. The last thing I want is to see you hurt again. Besides his reputation with women, which may or may not be exaggerated, Kwabena is a nice and relatively honest guy. Just promise me you'll be careful. Else, he'll answer to me."

When Tamara returned, she heard Kwabena in the kitchen. She tried sneaking past him and up to her room when she heard him ask, "What was it you were trying to tell me earlier?"

She sighed and walked into the kitchen. "I got the job."

"Good. This calls for a celebration," he said exuberantly. "Let's break out the champagne."

"I don't drink," she said cooly.

"How about those chilled bottles of apple cider in the wine cabinet?"

"I'm tired. I don't feel like celebrating right now."

"What's the matter?" He was standing so close to her, Tamara felt she could not breathe. He reached out and embraced her, drawing her to him. It took all her willpower not to submit to the warmth of his body next to hers, or to place her head on his chest and let herself go. But Tamara knew better. She'd suffered enough at the hands of one man. She wasn't going to risk making the same mistake.

Tamara placed her hands between them, gently shoving him away. "Let's be clear. What happened between us last night was a temporary lapse in judgment. I'm sorry I led you on like that. I promise it won't happen again." Before he had a chance to respond, she quickly turned and ran upstairs.

Kwabena realized she'd seen him with Afie and jumped to the wrong conclusion. "Tammy, you don't understand," he called after her. He heard the door to her bedroom suite slammed. He knew nothing he said to her now would make a difference. He was quickly learning that like Edebe, she was quick to anger.

He sighed. So they shared a few kisses. He'd shared more than that with women who never interpreted it as monogamous commitment. It was only a kiss.

Then why the hell do I feel like I've lost my best friend?

Chapter Eleven

True to her word, Darlene became a regular visitor to Tamara's house. Once there, with the pretense of visiting her favorite (and only) first cousin, she flirted with Kwabena, who enjoyed the admiration of a beautiful woman. After the second week, Darlene no longer needed Tamara as an excuse to visit. She visited Kwabena in his basement apartment.

For Tamara it was hell. She avoided Kwabena as much as she could. She did not want to have any part with that philanderer. Each time she ate alone in her sitting room before the TV, she longed for the shared dinners and casual conversations. She missed hearing him talk about his Ghanaian heritage or the many places he traveled. She missed the camaraderie that they shared as they prepared meals. She had to admit— she was lonely.

Kwabena, however, was anything but lonely. He had no shortage of friends. She often heard him with guests downstairs laughing and talking. One Saturday night at about eleven she heard familiar laughter. When she looked out the window, Kwabena was escorting Darlene into his apartment. Tamara steeled herself and went back to watching television.

Only her job kept her from despair. She enjoyed the fast pace of the work. She liked Mike and the camaraderie of the postdoctoral fellows and technicians in the lab. According to Mike, there were three kinds of work-ers: the nine-to-fivers go-home-to-your-wifers, the twenty-four-seven all-around-the-clockers, and the ten-to-whenever happy-hour winers.

For the first time since she began work a month ago, Tamara accepted the happy-hour winers' invitation to go to the Friday five o'clock happy hour at a local wa-tering hole. She, of course, was the designated driver as she never touched alcohol, due to her extreme sensitiv-ity. It took only a small amount for her to get drunk and make a total fool of herself. Consequently, she was con-tent to sip on virgin daiquiris and diet colas while the others got wasted. It was not something she enjoyed, especially having to chauffeur so many people home.

It was after nine when she arrived home. She'd stopped by the grocery on her way and done her weekly shopping. As she entered, she heard Darlene's deep, throaty, seductive laugh coming from the kitchen. Ta-mara took a deep breath and entered the kitchen. Dar-lene was standing, her hands deep in a bowl kneading flour. Kwabena stood behind her, hands around her waist reaching into the same bowl. They were both laughing. The sight of them together like that disgusted Tamara.

"Tammy, dear," Darlene sang in her sweetest voice as she glanced up at her. "Kwabena is showing me how to make puff-puffs, but we're low on cooking oil. Can you be a darling and run to the grocery store?"

Tamara ignored her question and headed to the freezer where she placed the frozen goods.

"We'll make do with what we have," Kwabena said.

Darlene pressed the issue. "I'm sure Tammy won't mind. Would you, Tammy?"

"Yes, I mind," Tamara said sharply. She continued putting away the groceries, then removed a large bottle of olive oil from the bag and placed it on the counter. "Anything else, your highness?"

Just then the phone in the basement rang. "I'll be right back," Kwabena said as he trotted downstairs.

Darlene came over to Tamara. "Look, I'm trying my best to get something going here. How about you give Jordan a visit?"

Tamara looked at Darlene irritated. "If you want privacy, go to your own home! And since when do you cook?" She resumed packing away the groceries, angrily slamming them into the pantry.

Darlene strolled over to the sink, rinsing the flour from her hands. She smiled coyly. "Ever since I learned that that sexy hunk living in your basement loves to cook."

Tamara stopped putting the groceries away and turned to face Darlene, hands on her hips. "And what happens when he finds out you actually hate the kitchen?" she demanded.

Darlene dried her hands on a dish towel and glided over to Tamara, smiling slyly. "I won't tell him and neither would you," she purred with a wink.

"No wonder none of your relationships last," Tamara said with derision. "They're all built on dishonesty. Sooner or later he's going to find out you're a pretentious fake and he'll dump you like all the others have."

"What's with you, Tammy? Why so bitchy tonight?" Darlene asked, surprised at Tamara's anger. "Are you jealous? You told me that there was nothing between the two of you."

"As if that ever mattered to you!" Tamara argued

raising her voice. This was not the first time that Darlene had hit on someone Tamara was interested in. She had tried to pick up Jared at a bar just moments before Tamara introduced him to the family. And even after learning he was engaged to her cousin, she still flirted openly with him.

In high school both Darlene and Ebony had dated guys after Tamara confided she was attracted to them. It was easy for them to steal guys from her. They were slim, curvy and pretty extroverts. Tamara had always been overweight and shy. How could she forget what happened to her first date when she was sixteen? It was with La'Mont, an athlete she'd harbored a crush on for some time. Her mother had flown in from San Diego unannounced just in time to grill La'Mont exhaustively, and then forbade her to date him. Darlene and Ebony had saved the date by volunteering to chaperone the couple, then spent the entire time flirting with him. Needless to say, he never asked her out again. A few months later, Ebony tearfully announced that she was pregnant by La'Mont.

"Oh, I see what's going on. You have a crush on him. You want him for yourself, don't you? Well let the competition begin."

"Just how much do you know about him?"

"I know he's intelligent, I know he's accomplished, and I know he's sexy as hell. That's all I need to know."

"Do you also know that he's married?" Tamara pulled the trump card.

"What? I don't believe you. He's not married," Darlene challenged, standing a few feet away from Tamara, arms folded. "Who is he married to?"

Tamara didn't answer. She hadn't expected to reveal so much to Darlene. She just felt so angry.

Darlene asked again, "Who is he married to?"

"Why don't you tell her who I'm married to, Tamara?" Both women looked up in surprise at the sound of Kwabena's voice as he reentered the kitchen. Tamara felt her heart thumping in her ears. She never expected him to challenge her like that. She remained silent, feeling her face heat. Kwabena kept his eyes trained on Tamara. "You're the honest one. Go ahead, tell her who my wife is."

Tamara remained silent.

"I'm married to your cousin," he said to Darlene never taking his eyes off Tamara's face. "Tammy is my wife."

"Is that true, Tamara?" Darlene whispered, disbelief registering on her face.

"Yes," Tammy said quietly looking down at the floor.

"How could you do that? How could you marry someone and keep it from us like that? How could you lie to us like that?" Darlene said, hurt lining her voice.

Tamara swallowed the lump in her throat. She took a deep breath. Since the cat was already out of the bag, she may as well tell the whole truth. "I married him so he can stay in the country and I could pay my mortgage. It is a business deal, nothing more."

"Are you sure it's nothing more?" Kwabena asked taking a step toward her.

Tamara forced herself to look up at Kwabena. She could not answer his question truthfully. The sexual tension between them was almost visible.

Darlene looked from Kwabena to Tamara. From the

expression on both their faces, she could tell there were deep emotions involved. Whether they knew it or not, they were in love with each other.

"I think, I'll leave you two alone," Darlene said. Neither Kwabena nor Tamara acknowledged her. Their eyes remained locked. "I…I'll see myself out." Darlene left quickly.

"It's nothing more than business," Tamara forced herself to lie. Deep down she knew she felt something for him. But he was a womanizer, and Tamara didn't want to be used and discarded by any man.

"Then why do you care if I date Darlene, or any other woman for that matter?" He strode over to her, his long legs easily closing the distance between them. His nearness was constricting her, making her unable to breathe or think.

"Because…because…"

"Because this is more than a business deal. Because you have feelings for me."

He reached down and kissed her. Tamara tried to resist, but found herself submitting to his kiss. She felt weak in the knees and leaned on him for support. Despite what her mind was telling her, she kissed him back with passionate fury.

When he finally released her, she whispered breathlessly, "We can't keep doing this."

"Why?"

"Because we're gonna do something we will both regret."

"Is that why you've been avoiding me?"

"I haven't been avoiding you." Tamara walked away from him and sat at the breakfast table. She needed space to collect her thoughts.

He followed her. "Yes, you have."

She looked away. "No, I haven't."

He sat across from her. "I thought we had an unspoken agreement to be honest with each other."

"Honest?" she asked with a sarcastic laugh. "What do you know about being honest? First you come here pretending to be a nobody, and it turns out you're some big shot scientist. You send me for a job with a friend's company, but you never told me you're part owner of the company. You kiss me as if I'm the only woman in your world and the next day another is in your arms, and now you're drooling all over my cousin. Do you call that honest?"

Kwabena ran his hand over his short-cropped hair and sighed. Placing his elbows on the table, he clasped his hands under his chin and whispered, "You don't understand, Tammy."

"Enlighten me."

He sighed. "Why do I get the feeling that you won't believe any explanation I give right now?"

Tamara turned to him and stared directly into his dark brown eyes. Quietly she said, "Because trust when violated is hard to regain."

Kwabena remained silent for a long while, contemplating Tamara's words. He looked up at her, his eyes staring directly into hers. A smile tugged at the sides of his mouth. "I have a wedding to attend tomorrow," he said. "Come with me."

"Why should I go out with you?"

"You said to enlighten you. If you come to the wedding with me you'll understand."

Chapter Twelve

"What's taking you so long?" Kwabena called upstairs from the den, their meeting room whenever they went out.

"I need your help," Tamara squeaked, barely loud enough for him to hear. The short notice didn't allow her time to shop for a new dress, so she tried putting on the red form fitting dress she'd worn over a year ago. It was a little tight around the waist and she had trouble zipping it. Finally she bent her head back sucked in her breath and pulled. The curly pony tail extension she'd added to her hair got stuck in the zipper. Now she could neither get it up nor down. With her head bent back at that awkward angle, she could barely whisper.

Kwabena entered the room and burst out laughing at the sight of her.

"What are you laughing at? I need help." Tamara could not help noticing how stunning he looked in his black tuxedo and silver fish scale vest.

"Is that thing sewn in or does it come off?" he asked, referring to her hairpiece.

"I paid a lot of money for this, so don't refer to it as 'That thing.' And, yes, it comes off."

"Fake hair, fake eyes, what else is fake?" he teased.

"My boobs are real," she responded sarcastically and immediately regretted it.

He smiled playfully and whispered in her ear, "How do I know for sure?"

"You won't."

He stood behind her and removed the ponytail from her hair trying not to mess up her natural hair beneath it. Her naturally wavy brown hair was soft and silky beneath his touch. Kwabena couldn't resist running his hand through it. He then tried yanking the zipper downward. "You have a pair of scissors?"

She pointed to the dresser. He cut the hair and tried yanking the zipper up. It wouldn't budge. "I have to unzip it," he said.

Tamara sighed. The thought of him peering at her naked back was unnerving. Slowly he eased the zipper down to the waist until the last strands of hair fell out. He observed her light brown soft skin beneath the dress and had to fight the urge to caress her. He pulled up the zipper.

"You're not wearing a bra," he observed.

Tamara blushed. "T…the dress has cups," she stammered. "But that's not your concern."

"Really? We're married, remember. Most married men see, feel and taste their wife's breasts."

Tamara looked up at him. From the twinkle in his eyes she could see he was teasing, but she had no intention of falling unguarded into his trap.

"Our relationship is not like that."

"Not yet," he whispered, letting his lips brush her ear lightly. Just that small gesture made her heart beat frantically and turned her face and neck red. Her hands shook as she replaced the hairpiece. "By the way, do you realize that in Ghana, red is a color of mourning?"

"Well it just happens to be my favorite color," Tamara replied defiantly. She had no intentions of changing the dress.

"You look very beautiful in that color," he said as she donned a bolero jacket over her dress. "And for the record, I prefer your natural eyes and your natural hair."

She smiled at him. "I can't see without my contacts."

"I still prefer to see your own beautiful eyes."

Tamara was in for a few surprises at the wedding. First off, Kwabena never told her he was a part of the wedding party. At the church Tamara found a seat in the second pew. A few minutes later, a tall, stately looking woman in pink and gold traditional African dress with a large scarf around her waist and hips, and a matching head dress sat next to her.

The woman looked at her and smiled and immediately began talking in a deep Ghanaian accent. Though she spoke very fluent English and it was obvious that she was well traveled, Tamara had difficulty understanding her. In time, it was obvious that this woman was the mother of the bride and she was brimming with pride. Tamara learned that the marriage was arranged, and though her daughter was resistant at first, she'd finally come around. She learned that this woman, who introduced herself as Akwape, had tried unsuccessfully to arrange a marriage for her very picky thirty-one-year-old son. No woman was good enough. She'd almost given up hope of grandchildren from him and so had focused on getting her twenty-three-year-old daughter married. From the initial contact by the groom's important maternal uncle to the wedding took over a year and multiple feasts and ceremonies.

To be polite Tamara asked, "Are they your only kids?"

"Unfortunately, yes. I wanted more children, but my husband traveled so much and we lived in all kinds of countries, it was not feasible. You see, my husband was the ambassador to the United Nations. If I have to count the countries where we lived, I'd run out of fingers and toes."

Just then the bride arrived on the arm of a six-foot-two elderly gentleman dressed in full traditional African regalia. The mother stood, beaming with pride. "That's my Afie. Isn't she the most beautiful person you've ever seen? I know that man will make her happy. He's studying to be a medical doctor. Comes from a good family, and I know he will take good care of her."

The second surprise was the bride. She was the woman Tamara had seen crying in Kwabena's arms that night. Tamara breathed a sigh of relief as the ceremony got underway.

She leaned over to the mother of the bride and asked, "Why a Christian wedding and not a traditional African wedding?"

The woman looked at her as if she was dense. "Because we're Christian, obviously."

Tamara remained quiet for the rest of the ceremony.

The biggest surprise came at the reception hall. While appetizers were being served, Kwabena came to her table. "Enjoying yourself?"

She nodded in reply.

"There are some very special people that I want you to meet," he said with a twinkle in his eyes. He escorted her to a table where Akwape sat with her husband. The couple stood and hugged him.

"This is my wife, Tamara. Tammy, meet my parents, Dr. Kwame and Akwape Opoku."

Tamara stared speechless. These were his parents? *How do you behave when you meet the parents-in-law in Ghanaian culture? Do you bow? Do you shake their hands? Do you embrace them?*

They stared back, equally stunned. Finally, ever the diplomat, Dr. Opoku came around and embraced Tamara. With an awkward grin, Akwape did likewise. Tamara did not understand why he introduced her to his parents as his wife when they had agreed to keep their marriage a secret.

Tamara looked up at Kwabena and smiled, suddenly making the connection. "Then Afie is your sister."

He looked at her and smiled, seeing the comprehension on her face.

"Can you excuse us for a second?" Akwape asked Tamara. She turned to Kwabena and spoke to him in Akan. From the tone of her voice, Tamara could tell she was giving him a scolding. Kwabena answered her with the respect of a child to an adult.

When they returned to their table, Dr. and Mrs. Opoku requested she sit with them. Then the grilling began. Mrs. Opoku wanted to know Tamara's background, her family history, her level of education, her job, how they met and if they planned on having children. Tamara realized her own mother's interrogation of Jared was tame in comparison. She wished for an escape.

Escape came twenty minutes later when Kwabena whisked her off to the dance floor. "We need to talk," she whispered to him.

He took her by the hand and led her to a darkened

balcony just outside the reception hall. The November air was chilly, but she didn't mind. It was the only quiet semiprivate place where they could talk.

"Why did you do that?" she demanded as soon as they stepped onto the balcony.

"Do what?"

"Introduce me to your mother as your wife. I thought we agreed to keep this marriage private. How was I supposed to act?"

He pointed to a woman in her midfifties standing close to the glass doors separating the balcony from the reception hall. "You see that lady? I'm trying to stop my mother from arranging a marriage."

"With her? Isn't she a little old?"

"Not with her; with her eighteen-year-old daughter. I figured if I tell her about our marriage, she would quit trying to find me a wife that suits her taste. And," he said, drawing her into his arms, "I want to do this to you without questions." With that, his lips covered hers in a slow, tender kiss.

Tamara closed her eyes and enjoyed the feel of his full lips on hers. Everything disappeared around them as they lost themselves in each other's kisses.

Akwape cleared her throat loudly.

Kwabena released Tamara and looked up at his mother sheepishly.

"We're ready for family photos," she said tersely.

Tamara stayed behind while Kwabena followed his mother. Akwape turned around at the door. "Come. You're family too."

As they gathered for photographs, Tamara was surprised at the few family members present. Besides Kwabena and his parents, only Afie's husband's parents and a few siblings were present. She whispered to Kwabena, "I thought your family was large."

He whispered back, "This is the American wedding. They are going to have a traditional wedding in Ghana when he finishes medical school. That's when the family will be out in full force."

Suddenly Akwape took Tamara by the hand and announced to the small family gathering, "This is our new daughter, Ben's wife." She glanced sternly at Kwabena clearly indicating her displeasure in the way he'd sprung his wife on them.

All eyes turned to Tamara as the small group greeted her graciously. Tamara turned beet red, uncomfortable with the sudden attention. Kwabena put his hand around her waist possessively and smiled reassuringly.

Afie hugged her closely and whispered apologetically, "I'm sorry our first meeting was under such unfortunate circumstances." She looked around furtively at her new husband and then lowered her voice even more. "When you saw me a few weeks ago, I was having second thoughts about this marriage. I guess I was really scared because I don't know him that well. Ben assured me it would be ok. After all, you have an arranged marriage and it's ok."

Flattered, Tamara smiled.

As soon as the photos were taken, Kwabena placed his arm around Tamara and led her to the dance floor.

Hours later, as they prepared to leave the reception, Akwape said something to Tamara that she did not quite understand but interpreted as a request for a visit.

"I'd love to host you before you return to Ghana,"

Tamara responded. From the horrified look on Kwabena's face she knew she said something wrong.

As they entered the car, Kwabena said, "Do you realize that you've just invited my parents to stay with us?"

"I did?"

"Fortunately, they're going to visit some friends in New York this week. It means they're spending Thanksgiving with us. We have to make this marriage look real."

Chapter Thirteen

Tamara was quiet the entire ride home. Their marriage just got complicated. Darlene knew about the marriage, and his parents were spending Thanksgiving with them. That was less than two weeks away. Between now and then they had to develop what appeared to be a real marital relationship. Moreover, she expected her mother to call anytime to berate her about her foolish decision. She glanced over at Kwabena as he concentrated on the road. If he was worried, he did not show it.

Kwabena looked over at Tamara as he drove the car. "You worried?" he guessed, seeing the expression on her face.

"Of course I'm worried. First you tell Darlene that we're married, and then you tell your mother. My mother is going to call anytime now and chew me out for it. If you think that scolding your mother gave you was bad, just multiply it by three and you'll know what I'll get from mine."

Kwabena smiled. He could not imagine anyone as domineering as his mother. She had indeed scolded him. She told him she could have arranged a marriage for him with any amount of good Akan or Asante women from distinguished family lines. She didn't see why he needed to marry a fat American woman who did not understand his background or culture. Even when his father calmly reminded her that Kwabena spent most of his life outside of Ghana and had been in the U.S. for more than twelve years, she did not stop. It was only after he pointed out to her that most of the people around understood the language that she had quieted down. Smiling sheepishly, she kissed Kwabena's cheek and told him he always was an independent thinker anyway and promised to accept his choice of a wife, but only if she didn't disgrace their family.

He reached over and grasped Tamara's hand in his, steering the car into the driveway with his left hand. "It'll be ok."

They walked to the door still holding hands. "I know just what would make you feel better. Some hot tea," he offered as they entered.

Tamara kicked off her shoes and sat barefoot on the sectional in the den while Kwabena headed to the kitchen. A few minutes later, he returned with a steaming pot of aromatic herbal tea and two teacups. He removed his jacket and vest, slinging them carelessly over the chair arm and sat next to her.

Slowly they sipped their tea in silence. Tamara's mind raced as the warm drink soothed her. Kwabena was like a layered mystery flower unfolding one petal at a time to reveal something new and intriguing. She wished he would tell her things up front rather than revealing little tidbits on a need-to-know basis.

"Tell me something," she said quietly, holding her teacup in both hands. "Why did you marry for your green card? Looking at your accomplishments and contributions it seems logical that your employer would have sponsored you or you could have obtained it by a national-interest waiver. It's time you answered my question. Why marriage?"

He was silent for a few seconds, gathering his thoughts. "I came to this country when I was nineteen years old on an F-1 visa to attend college. After I completed my doctorate, I did a postdoctoral fellowship with Dr. Thomas Cronin. Through him, I got an H-1 visa, which permitted me to work in this country. It was in his lab that I began work on the smart prosthesis. It was a very successful three years. After I completed the fellowship, the university offered me a tenure-track faculty position and start-up funding for my own lab. I hadn't thought about getting permanent residence then because I fully intended to return to Ghana. Thomas continued to mentor me throughout. We collaborated on multiple projects, held joint lab meetings and shared many resources. Then last year, he showed me a paper he had to review for publication. It was from a Japanese group. The work was excellent, though it was written poorly and they needed a few more controls. But Thomas told me he intended to give the paper a negative review, recommending several tedious experiments that would take months if not years to complete. He planned to set several postdocs immediately to work on the same project and publish before that other lab. It's something we call scooping, which is not illegal but highly unethical. I told him so and that I wanted no part in it. I tried to convince him to reconsider his actions, and he promised me he would. A month later, I found out he had indeed set six postdocs to work on the stolen project. If such information was made public, it would tarnish the credibility of our work and the university.

Since he wouldn't listen to reason, I took the matter to the department chair. Needless to say, Thomas was furious.

"Unfortunately my appointment was up for review this year. Thomas, being my mentor and closest collaborator was required to evaluate my tenure. I heard through the grapevine that he was going to give me a bad review. Rather than lose my position, I tendered my resignation and moved my lab to Bethesda. However, my H-1 visa was about to expire. I found out that Thomas was waiting for it to expire so he could call INS and have me deported. At this point, I have invested too much in this country to leave just yet. The only way I could have gotten a work permit to reside legally in the U.S. before my H-1 visa expired was to marry a U.S. citizen."

"Seems like your year was as bad as mine," Tamara observed, finally understanding Kwabena. "Do you have any regrets?"

"Other than receiving the sharp end of your fiery temper, no," he responded teasingly, slipping his arm around her shoulder.

Tenderly, he traced her lips with his fingers. Tamara's breath caught in her throat. He kissed her nose, her cheeks, her eyelids and her double chin. Slowly and gently his lips captured hers, his tongue gently teasing hers, exploring the sweet pleasures of her mouth. Tamara closed her eyes and submitted to the flood of emotion she felt, letting her tongue discover the sweetness of his mouth. She drew close to him, her chest against his. She could feel his heart beating loudly beneath his muscular chest.

His fingers traced a line down the center of her back,

sending shivers through her spine. Their kiss deepened in intensity and passion, sucking the very breath from her lungs. He sent a trail of light feathery kisses down her neck and chest. Tamara gasped. Her body was a fiery furnace, her passions ablaze.

She unbuttoned his shirt, running her hands over the muscles of his smooth, hairless chest. The feel of her hand on his bare chest sent him wild with desire. Kwabena trailed moist kisses down her chest to her exposed cleavage. His hands fondled her breast through the thin fabric. A moan escaped her throat. He unzipped her dress, caressing her exposed skin, driving her crazy with lust.

"I want to make love to you," he whispered between kisses as he lowered her onto the sofa. The feel of her soft smooth skin beneath his fingers made him moan with desire. He wanted her more than anything else right now. He took her hand and guided it to his groin, letting her feel his desire.

Then the phone rang.

"Don't answer it," he whispered breathlessly, but Tamara pushed him off her, still breathing deeply and rolled away from him.

"Hello," she answered hoarsely, trying to catch her breath and control her racing heart. She took a deep breath and closed her eyes as she tried to keep her unzipped dress from falling.

It was her mother. The call she was dreading. "What the hell were you thinking? You married a man so you can pay your mortgage? Tamara, all you had to do was ask me for the money. How could you?"

"This is not a good time, Mommy."

"When is a good time? After he strips you of everything you own? You didn't learn from Jared?"

Tamara put her head back and sighed. She wished she could say it was just a business deal. But after what happened tonight she could not even convince herself that it was just a business deal.

"Apples and oranges, Mommy."

"What in the world is wrong with you?" Leyoca continued with a long tirade and a full-length lecture before concluding, "I'm coming up there next week and we're having Thanksgiving at your house. I want to see what this new leech is like!"

"You can't come for Thanksgiving. His parents will be here."

"Better yet, I get to see which rock he crawled from."

When Tamara hung up the phone, she looked at Kwabena and shrugged. "My mother is coming for Thanksgiving."

"Speaking of marriage, how about we consummate this thing?" he whispered huskily, kissing her exposed shoulders.

Tamara shook her head. "I...I don't think I'm ready for that yet."

Kwabena struggled to control himself. Ever since that first kiss, he wanted her more than he'd ever wanted anyone. She was warm, passionate, loving...and he could not get her out of his mind. But he was willing to wait. She was worth the wait.

He held her to him. "It's ok. Whenever you're ready," he said, kissing her forehead.

Kwabena closed his eyes and sighed. He didn't know

who surprised him more, Tamara or himself. He couldn't recall a time when his sexual advances had been rejected. Yet he was surprised by his willingness to wait for her. If this was another time or another woman, he would have been a little more forceful. Not that he would have taken her against her will. He had too much integrity for that. But when he was finished kissing and touching her, she would be begging him to make love to her. However, this was Tamara and for some reason what she thought about him was important.

What is it about Tamara that makes me want to do whatever she asks? He wanted to make love to her more than anything else, but beyond that, he wanted her to want him. He wanted her to need him. He wanted her to love him. *You're in love with her.* Kwabena quickly dismissed that thought. He had never truly been in love with anyone in his life, not even his ex-fiancée. He held Tamara close to him. He didn't ever want to let her go.

Chapter Fourteen

It was the Saturday before Thanksgiving, and they were on their way to a party at Kwabena's friend's house, or as Kwabena dubbed it, their last fling before judgment day. His parents were due to arrive the next night and her mother was due on Wednesday of that week. Tonight they were going to forget about the impending stress and enjoy themselves. They were going to party the night away.

Tamara dressed in a pair of fitted black boot-leg jeans and a loose bell-sleeve blouse with molded bra cups and pointed hem that ended below the hips. Her outfit flattered her full figure. A pair of gold hoops and knee boots completed her attire.

She brushed her naturally wavy hair up and added a curly synthetic ponytail. The curls cascaded over her head, framing her face and hiding most of her own hair. Tamara observed herself in the mirror. It didn't look right. She adjusted the ponytail. She sighed as she recalled Kwabena's words: *I prefer your natural hair and eyes.*

She looked at herself in the mirror again. Tentatively, she reached for the hair extension. *Should I?* Tamara took a deep breath, debating with herself. It had been so long since she wore her hair natural. As a kid, she hated her hair because it didn't stay braided and beaded as long as Ebony's and Darlene's had. It would unravel and fray within a few hours, so that it always looked unkempt. She recalled when she'd become attached to fake hair. She was in high school and she'd overheard a conversation between Ebony and a boy she'd had a crush on.

"Her weight doesn't bother me. I like girls with a little junk in the trunk," Tamara heard him say to Ebony. *"But she thinks she's white because she has 'good' hair. I don't do coconuts."* Later she learned that was the general sentiment of her classmates. They thought she acted white because she had light skin, wavy hair and light brown eyes and took school seriously. The next week she'd gotten her hair braided with extensions. Since then, she'd kept using hair extensions, covering as much of her natural hair as possible.

Tamara reached up and yanked the ponytail from her hair, placing it on the dressing table. Rigorously, she brushed her hair to a shine, highlighting her natural waves. She clipped her hair back in a ponytail and placed a colorful scarf on the end.

"There!" she breathed. To her amazement, it looked beautiful. She felt beautiful.

Removing the colored contacts was a tougher decision. Her mind was in turmoil as she debated aloud whether to use the clear contacts she kept for emergencies. Finally she said to herself, "This is me, take it or leave it!"

With that, she traded her colored contacts for clear ones, revealing her naturally light brown eyes. She decided on no makeup, except lip gloss. As she looked in the mirror, she couldn't help noticing the woman staring back at her was striking, with lovely wavy hair and gorgeous brown eyes. She smiled. Leaving the room, she grabbed the hair extension from the dresser and dropped it into the garbage. That part of her life was over.

As she stepped into the foyer, Kwabena whistled. He couldn't resist running a hand through her soft hair. She was indeed beautiful. The simple hairstyle revealed her full face, giving her an air of elegant sophistication, something he'd never before seen in her.

"You are beautiful just like that," he said, kissing her cheek. "I have no idea why you hide such lovely eyes."

Tamara smiled, gaining confidence in her new look. For a fleeting moment she feared he would dislike it. Now she felt beautiful, thanks to him.

As they walked to the car, she explained, "All my life I've been using my cousins and aunt as the measuring stick for beauty. I wanted to be dark like them, tall like them, have thick hair that I could relax like them, have wide dark brown eyes and long lashes like them. I guess I tried so hard to prove my blackness that I never appreciated my skin tone or eye color. I loved summers because tanning made me a shade darker." Winking up at him, she added, "But someone recently taught me to appreciate God's natural gifts to me. So here I am, all natural, nothing artificial."

He put his arm around her before opening her door for her. "Just how I like you. You are best when you are you."

When they arrived at the party, a big roar went up. The guys, most of whom were Kwabena's friends from various African countries greeted him with loud laughter and teasing. Most of the people were Nigerians, but there were a handful of Ghanaians, Kenyans, Cameroonians and Tanzanians and one from the Republic of Benin. Tamara was the only American in the room.

"*Muti, Muti,*" several greeted patting him on the back and laughing. "This your new girl?"

Kwabena just laughed. It was quite clear that he was used to being the center of attention.

He introduced her to the guys simply as Tamara, with no explanation. Like those at the nightclub they attended a few months back, these fellows accepted her at face value, laughing, teasing and even flirting with her. It was a group of close friends. Most of them were highly educated, some with advanced degrees, who had met in college or graduate school. Most came for college but for one reason or another decided to remain in the U.S.

The air was relaxed and Tamara felt comfortable and confident around them. The women were just as loud as the men. Edebe was there, and much to Tamara's surprise, he greeted her with a hug, saying that any friend of Kwabena was a friend of his. It was then she learned why he only went by his last name. His first name, Zikorachukwudi, was unpronounceable to most Americans. She also learned why he was such a loyal friend to Kwabena, when he told her that Kwabena had literally saved his life. He'd come to this country fleeing political conflict with little money. He needed an operation that he could not afford. Kwabena, in college at that time, used his tuition money to pay for Edebe's surgery, knowing full well Edebe, a cab driver, could not repay him. For Tamara, that was another piece of the puzzle and attested to Kwabena's generosity. Pride filled her heart.

The party swung into full gear. They laughed, talked and danced. At one point, the host of the party, a Tanzanian named Christopher Ngala, challenged Tamara to a *Soul Train*–style dance off. It was the most fun she'd had in a long time and she had Kwabena to thank.

The only people who seemed aloof and uninvolved were four women sitting on stools at the periphery of the room. With the light atmosphere, Tamara felt comfortable enough to approach them. She sat on a stool next to the girls and asked where they were from. Two of them, who appeared rather shy, smiled and said they were from Ethiopia. Another introduced herself and said she and her friend were from Nigeria. Tamara didn't even dare attempt pronouncing her name. Her friend, whom she referred to as Adeola, a brown-skinned graceful beauty, quietly ignored Tamara's attempt at a conversation.

Christopher joined the group. "Beer?" he offered Tamara, handing her a bottle.

"No, thanks," she responded. "I don't drink."

"Against your religion?" Christopher pressed.

"Against good judgment. Alcohol turns me into a nutcase."

Adeola silently observed the conversation, then got up and left in a huff. Her friend followed.

Tamara looked at Christopher. "What's her problem?"

Christopher laughed and said, "It's a case of the fox and the sour grapes."

"What do you mean?"

Edebe joined them, beer in hand. "You don't want to know."

A group of guys came in, and they greeted Kwabena laughing, "*Muti* man."

Tamara turned to Christopher. "What is *Muti*?"

Christopher and Edebe both laughed out loud, "Believe me, you really don't want to know," Christopher said. "Come on, it's party time. Let's get a dance off going again."

Tamara had the distinct impression that that term had sexual connotations.

Tamara was sweating when she flopped down on a chair against the wall. She and a whole group of people had been dancing to upbeat, high-tempo music. She took a sip of some soda and fanned herself. That's when she realized she hadn't seen Kwabena for a while.

"Where's Ben?" she asked Edebe.

"I don't know, maybe the bathroom or something," he answered vaguely.

"Have you tried the fruit punch yet?" The Nigerian girl with the unpronounceable name approached Tamara.

Tamara shook her head no.

"Well, you've got to try it," she said. "Come on."

Kwabena stood out on the dark cold deck off the kitchen facing a glaring Adeola. "What's your problem?" he asked, frustrated.

"Why did you bring *that girl* here?" she asked.

"That girl," he said, "is my wife."

"You said it was a green-card marriage," Adeola complained.

"It is," he confirmed.

She took a step closer to him and placed her arms around his neck. "Well, then nothing has to change between us." She kissed him seductively, running a hand down his belly and toward his groin while rubbing her breasts against him.

He pushed her away, glancing furtively over his

shoulders as if they were being watched. "We cannot do this!"

She looked hurt. "Why the hell not?"

"I'm married!"

"You didn't say that when you were screaming my name a few weeks ago," she challenged.

"Stop it, Ade. Just stop it now." He regretted ever doing that now. He'd needed a woman, and she was available. A temporary lapse in judgment. "Things are different now."

She looked up at him through long thick lashes. Her full lips pouted petulantly. "Don't tell me you're sleeping with her? I didn't realize you were into cows."

Anger burned deep within him. He grabbed both her wrists in his large fists, pushing her roughly against the wall. Through clenched teeth he said, "Don't you ever disrespect my wife like that!"

He released her and walked to the far end of the deck in effort to control his anger. Right now he was angry at himself for losing his cool like that. Adeola knew how to get to him; she always did.

She came up behind him, rubbing her body against his. "I'm sorry, Ben," she whispered. She placed one hand on his chest, caressing his nipples. The other she lowered to his groin, feeling him grow hard beneath her caresses. "I know you still want me," she whispered, nibbling on his neck. "No one will have to know."

Kwabena closed his eyes and moved away from her. She definitely knew how to get to him. His body reacted to her the way it always did. She was, after all, a physically attractive woman with a sexy body that she knew how to use. But at this moment, her actions disgusted him.

"No," he said decisively. "Whatever we had is in the past. It's over. It's been over a long time."

He still could not believe he almost married this woman. They'd met in college and had been together while he was in graduate school. A few years ago he had asked her to marry him, more because it was the expected thing than because he was in love with her. He'd even started the official marriage process back home. But then she'd gone off and had an affair with a high-ranking Nigerian ambassador. Kwabena's status hadn't been high enough for her then. Yes, he'd had his indiscretions in the past. So had she. But this time it was different. She'd flaunted the affair openly. It was only when the ambassador refused to leave his wife for her that she came crawling back. He refused to take her. What happened between them recently was indeed a lapse in judgment.

"I still love you."

He looked at her. This woman had no idea what love was. She knew sex, she knew opportunity, she knew status, but love was foreign to her. If she loved him, she would never have treated him so carelessly.

"You don't love me, Ade. You love Dr. Opoku: the name, accomplishments and the status associated with it. That's why you want me now. No more, Ade. It's over."

He headed for the door.

She had to have the last word. "It won't last. We always return to each other."

He hesitated at the door, looked at her and left.

Chapter Fifteen

Tamara opened her eyes. Light was filtering through the bedroom. Her head pounded like a jackhammer drilling into concrete. She rubbed her temples and crawled out of bed. Nausea forced her to run to the bathroom, where she dry heaved over the open toilet. Her headache grew worse. She searched her medicine cabinet for aspirin, but it was devoid of pain killers.

After another round of dry heaves, she dragged her sluggish body to the sink, splashed water on her face and gargled Listerine. She couldn't remember how she got home last night. The last thing she remembered was drinking fruit punch with the Nigerian girl. After that, it was all a blur.

She looked at her reflection in the mirror. Her eyes were bloodshot, and she still had her contacts in. She never slept with her contacts. The scarf was missing from her head, and her hair was a tangled mess. Then she saw the nightgown. It was a baby blue satin shortie with black lace that ended just below her hips and fit tight across her breasts. She'd never worn it before. It was one of those in her nightstand that she'd purchased in preparation for her marriage to Jared. Since then she'd gained a lot of weight.

Then it suddenly hit her. *Oh my God! Ben must have put this on me. Did we make love?* The thought was frightening.

Her head pounded even more as she put on an old tattered robe and went in search of Ben. She needed to borrow some aspirin from him and find out what happened.

She found him in the exercise room, lying on his back on a bench doing bench presses. He wore only a pair of maroon gym shorts. With every lift he made a guttural sound. Tamara watched his sweat-shined muscles tighten with each lift of the weights. If her head wasn't pounding so much, she might have been turned on.

"Hey," she said shyly as he dropped the weights and sat up. He took a swig of bottled water and observed her unkempt hair and red eyes.

"You look like a ray of sunshine," he teased. "How are you feeling?"

"Like a nuclear bomb went off in my head. Do you have aspirin?"

He walked past her to the bathroom and came back with a bottle of painkillers. She was sitting on his discarded bench when he returned. She downed several and chased it with the bottled water he was drinking. He resumed his workout, lying on the floor doing crunches. Tamara looked at his six-pack abs and wondered why he needed to work out so hard. He already looked like a Nubian god.

"What happened last night?" she asked. "I can't remember a thing."

"You got drunk."

"I didn't have any alcohol," she protested.

"The fruit punch was spiked."

That explained the nausea, the headache and the lack of memory, which was why she never touched alcohol. The first time she drank had been at Auntie Leticia's birthday party when she was in her late teens. She only drank half a beer on a dare from Ebony. Within minutes she had passed out. She'd never been able to live down the stories of her wild actions, which became grander each passing year. She had tried alcohol again on her twenty-first birthday while in college. A half glass of margarita was all it took for more embarrassing stories to generate. Since then she never touched alcohol. Tamara took a deep breath and asked, "How bad was I?"

Kwabena finished his crunches and used the bench she sat on to stretch. He looked at her and saw fear and uncertainty in her eyes. He smiled. "Let's put it this way, everybody now knows that we're married and you're the only twenty-six-year-old married woman who's still a virgin."

Tamara cringed. "I said that?"

"You weren't too bad. Other than that sexy table-top dancing, you were a decent drunk," he teased.

He could now look back at it and laugh, but last night he was not as amused. When he came inside, he was surprised to see a group of his friends in a circle listening and laughing to Tamara's self-deprecating humor and loose-tongued chatter. After a few minutes, it was obvious she was drunk. Christopher assured him that she only had fruit punch.

Kwabena tasted the fruit punch. "Who spiked the punch?" he demanded. Christopher and Edebe looked at each other and gave vague answers. Kwabena got angry. "Who spiked the damn punch?"

"Come on, Ben, you know it's not uncommon for someone to spike the punch at a party. Let's not make a big deal of it."

"Just answer me."

"Adeola," Edebe finally answered.

"And I guess her best friend offered Tamara the punch, right?" he asked. They nodded.

He heard a loud roar of laughter and looked around. Tamara was on the table dancing seductively. He got angry at the leering men watching his wife. He stopped the music and got Tamara off the table.

"Dance with me, baby," she purred, gyrating her hips suggestively. He took her from the party. The minute she stepped out of the car, she'd thrown up on herself. He lifted her upstairs and held her head over the toilet as she puked her guts out. By the time he'd removed her clothes and wiped her with a washcloth, she had passed out.

Tamara's headache was pounding but she needed to know. "Did we…did we do…you know…it?"

Kwabena almost laughed at her discomfort discussing something as natural as sex. "No," he answered. "I don't take advantage of drunken women. When we make love, I want you to be wide awake and actively participating." He paused, then added with a slow, sexy smile, "And believe me, when we make love, you will remember every detail."

He saw her face flush bright red. He liked her innocence.

"One last question," she asked. "When you changed my clothes, did you look at me naked?"

"No, I closed my eyes," Kwabena answered sarcastically. "Of course I looked at you. And I like what I saw."

"You're not supposed to see me naked! That's inappropriate."

"We're married. I'm probably the only man who has to wait until his wife is drunk to see her naked!" he teased. "And by the way, what is a virgin doing with all that sexy lingerie and paraphernalia?"

She smiled to cover her embarrassment. "They were for my bridal shower. I was engaged to be married."

"Really? What happened to him, and how come you guys never made love?"

"It's a long story."

"Mama and Papa won't be here before tonight. I have all day."

With a heavy sigh, Tamara confessed, "He never showed up to the wedding. Turned out he was a con artist. Took every cent I owned, including what my mother had put aside for my education, and disappeared. As for the experimentation thing, turns out he was also gay."

"I'm sorry," Kwabena said sympathetically "Your year was definitely worse than mine."

The doorbell rang. He looked at her in her lopsided robe, her bloodshot eyes and unkempt hair and said, "I'll get it."

Kwabena trotted upstairs and opened the door to face a well-dressed couple. The woman, a tall, slim, good-looking lady who appeared to be in her early- to midthirties wore a dark brown skirt and leather boots and a long wool coat. She looked vaguely familiar. The accompanying man was one or two inches shorter than Kwabena with slightly graying hair at his temples.

"Hello. May I help you?" Kwabena asked politely.

The lady spoke in a businesslike tone, "Hi I'm Leyoca Novak. Is Tamara in?"

Tamara, who had come up the stairs behind Kwabena,

exclaimed in surprise, "Mommy, Carl, what are you doing here?"

Leyoca stepped into the foyer past Kwabena and hugged her daughter. Carl followed. Leyoca assessed Tamara's rumpled hair and lopsided robe and Kwabena's shirtless body with a skeptical look on her face. "I decided to come a little early, meet my son-in-law and see how you were doing. It's a little late for you to be in your bedclothes, isn't it?"

Tamara looked at Kwabena's shirtless sweaty body and her own state of dress and dreaded what her mother must be thinking. Then she remembered her manners.

"Mommy, Carl, this is my husband, Kwabena. Kwabena, this is my mother, Leyoca, and her husband, Carl."

Kwabena shook their hands, realizing only then that Tamara had never talked about her father. "I'm pleased to meet you. Is there anything I can do for you? Can I get your bags, or get you something to drink?" Kwabena asked.

"You can get some clothes on," Leyoca said to him coldly.

"I'm sorry," Kwabena apologized. "I was working out when the doorbell rang. I'll go change." He trotted downstairs.

She turned to Carl. "Honey, can you get the bags please?" As soon as Carl stepped out the door, she turned to Tamara and ordered, "Go make yourself presentable. Have you looked in the mirror?"

"I was at a party last night, and I just woke up," Tamara explained, escorting her mother up the stairs to the kids' room. "I have to apologize for the lack of accommodations. I haven't furnished the other rooms, so I'm afraid you and Carl will have to share the bunk bed."

She looked at the bunk bed with the full mattress on the bottom and the twin mattress on top. "It's fine. We've slept in smaller spaces. Now please go make yourself decent."

Chapter Sixteen

A freshly showered Kwabena dressed in jeans and a polo shirt met Leyoca and Carl in the den. Tamara was still upstairs. "Have you eaten yet? I'm about to prepare breakfast."

"I'll help you," Leyoca volunteered.

As they went into the kitchen, the grilling began. While Kwabena chopped onions and peppers to make omelets, Leyoca inundated him with questions.

"Let me be frank with you," Leyoca finally said. "Tamara is very impressionable and, unfortunately, easily fooled by good-looking men. I am not going to stand back and let you screw her out of everything she owns. I let it happen once. I won't allow it again."

Kwabena decided to be honest. "Mrs. Novak, I like and respect your daughter very much, but what we have is a business deal. I get my permanent U.S. residence, and she gets paid. Everything was discussed and arranged upfront. I have no intention of defrauding her in any way."

"And you get to live in her fine house and a few other fringe benefits, right?"

He knew exactly what fringe benefits she was talking about. If only he was getting that. "I rent the basement, ma'am. We have a mutual agreement. And we've also developed a very close friendship."

"So what work do you do? Or do you work at all?"

"Research."

"What kind?"

"Biomedical research."

"Really. What do you work on?"

Kwabena tried his best to explain his line of work in layman's terms. It was always difficult, even when speaking to scientists from different fields of work.

"Don't dumb it down for me, Kwabena. I work closely with many people in the medical profession and it insults my intelligence when they assume I won't understand."

Without going into too much detail, he outlined his specific area of research, which included smart prosthesis and rheumatoid arthritis drug development.

Leyoca's face slowly brightened. "That means you must be familiar with Dr. Michael Botanga's work."

Kwabena was pleasantly surprised. "You know Mike? He was my mentor in grad school. Now we're friends, collaborators and business partners."

Leyoca looked at him quizzically. "Wait. Are you Dr. Benjamin Opoku?"

He smiled broadly. "Yes."

"Then we've met before. Five years ago when I had just started my marketing firm, Mike hired me to do a marketing campaign for a new rheumatoid arthritis drug. He introduced me to you as his business partner." She remembered thinking he looked young for a business partner. Back then he was slight, bordering on scrawny.

Kwabena vaguely remembered. "You're Ley Fontaine?"

Leyoca laughed. "Yes, I am. That was before I married Carl. In my experience, having a name like Leyoca that readily identifies your race and gender makes it harder to gain clients. So when I started my business, I used Ley to be race and gender neutral."

They started discussing science and business, comfortably chatting and laughing until Leyoca was finally satisfied that he wasn't there to rob her daughter blind. The more they talked, the more she respected and liked him. He was well mannered and appeared decent and honest.

When Tamara came downstairs, she was shocked to see her mother and Kwabena chatting and laughing like old friends. She whispered to Kwabena, "What miracle did you work?"

He replied with a smile. "Just my good old charm."

Her mother, who had been setting the breakfast table, came over to her. "You didn't tell me that Kwabena was Dr. Benjamin Opoku. We actually met before. I've done work for Independent Labs."

Tamara looked at Kwabena. "Benjamin? Ben isn't short for Kwa*bena*?"

He smiled. "Benjamin is my middle name. My parents gave us both traditional names and Christian names. When I came to this country, I used my Christian name because it was easier for Westerners to pronounce."

This was going better than she anticipated.

Just then the doorbell rang. Kwabena was at the stove, expertly flipping omelets. "I'll get it," she said and went to the door.

"Dr. Opoku, Mrs. Opoku!" Tamara exclaimed in surprise. They weren't supposed to be coming until late that evening. She and Kwabena intended to move most of his clothes out of the basement and into her room before they arrived to make his parents believe their marriage was real.

Tamara stood at the open door, staring idiotically.

"Are you going to invite us in?" asked Akwape irritably. "It's rather cold out here."

"Oh, where are my manners? Come on in, make yourselves at home." She ushered them into the foyer. Carl jumped off the couch and went to help Dr. Opoku remove the bags from the waiting taxicab.

Akwape embraced Tamara perfunctorily. "Where is my son?" she asked.

Tamara led the way to the kitchen where Kwabena was still at the stove, now making flapjacks. Akwape hugged her son, then asked in highly accented English, "Why are you cooking and not her?"

"Because I enjoy cooking," Kwabena answered, kissing his mother on the cheek.

"That's why you have a wife."

"Never mind her," Dr. Opoku said, entering the kitchen and embracing his son. "She left her brain-mouth filter at the airport."

Tamara led them to the breakfast nook, where Leyoca had resumed setting the table, and introduced her mother and stepfather.

"Where is your real father?" Akwape asked Tamara.

Tamara hesitated. Leyoca stepped in and said vaguely, "He's not with us."

"Oh, I'm so sorry he passed," Akwape said.

Leyoca quickly changed the subject. "I hope you guys are hungry because we've got a big brunch here."

"This table is too small for all of us. Maybe we should try the dining room," Tamara suggested, and they began moving the settings into the dining room.

It was a brunch to remember. It started out a bit awkward as both sets of parents observed each other, indirectly interrogating each other.

"You look quite young to be the mother of a twenty-six-year-old," Akwape said.

"I take that as a compliment," Leyoca responded. "I'm forty-three years old."

Akwape did a mental calculation. "You married rather young."

"I was not married to Tamara's father."

A shocked expression came over Akwape's face. She turned to Kwabena and said in Twi, "You are going to bring disgrace to our family."

Leyoca did not understand the words, but she couldn't miss the tone. Smiling pleasantly, she went for the shock factor. "Yes, Mrs. Opoku, I was a statistic."

"Statistic?"

"Yes, an unmarried teen mother on welfare. And as for Tamara's father, he's not dead. She doesn't know who he is."

Akwape's face turned red, and her jaw dropped. Indignation was written all over her face.

Kwame looked at his wife and frowned. "Get off your high horse, Akwape," he said in English. "The Opokus have always been a humble family, regardless of their accomplishments or status in life. We have been around the world enough to know about challenges and successes. Your family is an example of great success. Apologize, Akwape."

Akwape was embarrassed but not deterred. "I just want to know about these strangers Ben chose to…"

Kwame responded deliberately, "Akwape, they are no longer strangers. They are our family now." He turned to Tamara. "I don't know how familiar you are with our culture and customs, but for us, marriage is not between a man and a woman—it is between families. Now that you are Ben's wife, our families have become one." He looked at Kwabena. "That is why the marriage process is so long and complicated back home. I assume you will initiate the process belatedly."

"Akwape," Leyoca chimed in. "If you want to know more about me, you can read my book, *By the Boot Straps*. It's all written and out in the open for all to see. That way I don't pretend to be what I'm not."

"You wrote *By the Boot Straps*?"

At the mention of the book, the discussion took a different direction. Both Akwape and Kwame had read the book and found it inspiring. It described Leyoca's journey from a teenage single mother and high-school dropout on welfare, to a high-achieving advertising executive. Detailed in it were her struggles to complete her GED, take college courses and work full time at several menial jobs while taking care of her daughter, without the support of a father. They had also read her second book, *Out on a Limb*, where she described her struggles as a single mother trying to climb the corporate ladder and the risk she took in leaving a Fortune 500 company to open her own advertising and marketing firm. Akwape and Kwame had found both books quite enthralling. However, it was written by Ley Fontaine, not Leyoca Novak.

Akwape looked at Leyoca with a new sense of respect. Then she surprised Leyoca by announcing that she herself was an author. She had written several books on the Ghanaian culture and the role of the midwife in the local villages. She had been a midwife for many years before her husband's work forced her to travel. The books were published and circulated only in Ghana, and she was interested in expanding the readership to America.

The initial tension out of the way, both families were talking and laughing like lifelong friends. Kwabena looked at Tamara across the table and smiled. Tamara smiled back triumphantly. They had done the impossible. They had tamed the most dominant women in their lives and made them friends with each other.

As Tamara looked around the table at everyone getting along amicably, she sighed. *If only this were a real marriage, it would be perfect.*

Chapter Seventeen

Thanksgiving Day rolled around quickly. It was one of those upside down days, mild and pleasant in the morning but cold and harsh in the evening. A clipper system was moving through the Northeast, with blizzardlike conditions in Pennsylvania, New York and points north. To the south, where Tamara lived, rain was expected.

Everyone gathered for Thanksgiving dinner at Tamara's home. In addition to Tamara's folks and Kwabena's parents, Kwabena had invited Mike Botanga and his family, Christopher Ngala, and Edebe, his wife and teenage daughters. Afie and her husband, recently back from their honeymoon, were spending the day with them. Jordan and his brood along with Tamara's cousins and aunt were also joining them this year.

The first to arrive was Ebony, and she brought a guest. It was the same guy who had been sitting in the car the night of the gala when she asked Tamara to babysit. She introduced him as her boyfriend, Rashid, then announced to Tamara with a wink, "The kids are sleeping over tonight."

"But Mommy and Carl are in their room," Tamara protested.

"No sweat. They can't wait to try out their new Dora and BRATZ sleeping bags." Kayla and Katanya entered just then, lugging what looked like duffel bags.

Darlene and Leticia arrived not too long after. Darlene brought a bottle of wine and whispered in Tamara's ear while handing it to her, "That little incident with your husband last month—water under the bridge." Tamara nodded in agreement. She was too happy to hold grudges.

Leticia brought her famed garlic mashed potatoes. According to Leyoca, there was enough garlic in it to kill a vampire.

A little after two, Tamara removed the turkey and basted it. Darlene came into the kitchen just as the doorbell rang.

"Can you put this back in for me? I need to fulfill my role as hostess," Tamara said and rushed to get the door.

Tamara opened the door to Christopher Ngala, holding a large pitcher of red punch covered with Saran wrap. He greeted her with a one-armed hug, the other carefully holding the pitcher. "Don't forget, you owe me a dance off at the next party we have," he teased.

"I'll remember that," Tamara laughed. She looked up and saw Mike Botanga and his family walking up the driveway. She said to Christopher, "The kitchen is to your left. Just place the drink in there."

Kwabena guided Christopher to the kitchen. Darlene had just closed the oven door and stepped away when she collided into him. The drink spilled, soaking Darlene's sweater.

"Oh no!" Darlene squealed, looking down at the deep red stain in her sweater.

"Oh, I'm so sorry," he apologized, grabbing a napkin and trying to wipe the stain from her sweater.

"I'll get towels," Kwabena offered as Darlene slipped

on the wet floor. She fell right into Christopher's waiting arms. "Damn!" she exclaimed.

They were both standing in a slippery puddle of bloodred drink, hugging each other, soaked to their skin. They looked at each other and laughed.

Kwabena reentered the kitchen with towels as Darlene went in search of a mop. Without taking his eyes off Darlene's retreating back, Christopher said to Kwabena, "Do you believe in love at first sight?"

Kwabena took one look at him and said, "Man, you've got it bad."

Christopher smiled and responded dreamily, "I think I've just met the most wonderful woman to walk this earth."

Kwabena just smiled. "You can borrow one of my shirts."

By three o'clock, everyone except Jordan had arrived. It was snowing lightly. The weather pattern had changed and instead of rain, they were getting snow; a light dusting to an inch, according to the weatherman.

While the kids played and the men watched television, Akwape, Aunt Leticia, Mrs. Edebe and Mrs. Botanga had taken over the kitchen. Every now and then, Kwabena entered the kitchen, trying to help with something, but he was promptly shooed out by his mother, who stood to her policy that the kitchen was no place for a man.

Around five-thirty, Jordan and his family finally arrived, late as usual. When Tamara opened the door, she was surprised to see the amount of snow that had already accumulated outside. The wind swirled the flakes violently, howling loudly. She couldn't see as far as the neighbor's house across the street. Jordan shooed the kids inside behind Becky, then ran back into the swirling white snow to the car. He returned with a bundle of blankets and comforters. Dusting off the snow he announced, "I brought two airbeds, some extra blankets and a few snow shovels. Nobody's going anywhere tonight. The blizzard that was supposed to hit Pennsylvania just decided to pay us a visit."

Jordan's kids promptly joined the five other children, and Becky joined the ladies in the kitchen, leaving Jordan to watch the game with the men. With the exception of the turkey and stuffing prepared by Tamara and Aunt Leticia's mashed potatoes, there was nothing traditional about this meal. Akwape, Mrs. Edebe and Mrs. Botanga prepared a variety of African dishes. Becky brought jerk pork and fried plantains.

Just before they announced dinner, Akwape went downstairs to shower and change. Leyoca was in the dining room setting the table. Tamara stayed in the kitchen, putting the final garnishes on the turkey. Just then Kwabena entered and tried to grab the turkey neck. Tamara promptly slapped his hand. He whispered in her ear, and she laughed. He hugged her from behind and stole a quick kiss, certain no one was looking.

Leyoca watched the exchange from the dining room. She smiled to Carl. "They are fooling themselves if they think they can come out of this marriage at the end of a year or two unscathed. I can tell they're in love with each other, whether or not they realize it. I just hope they realize it before they end the marriage."

Thanksgiving dinner was lovely. Tamara had to increase the size of the table and add a few chairs from the storage room. They moved the breakfast table into the dining room and the kids sat around it. After a long prayer by Kwame, they all sat down and dug into the delicious food. Multiple conversations went on around the table in four languages. Yet the air was casual and enjoyable.

Tamara looked around with a satisfied sigh and thought it was a fitting climax to an unusual week. After the snubbing on Sunday, Akwape had humbled herself, and she and Leyoca got along fine. In fact, they were getting along so well that Leyoca and Carl had taken them sightseeing on different occasions.

The only difficulty for Tamara was balancing the perceptions of both their parents. Kwabena's parents thought their marriage was real while Leyoca knew it was a marriage of convenience. So they made a compromise. Kwabena moved into the master suite with Tamara, but slept on the red love seat with the pull-out sofa bed in the sitting room.

Tamara looked across the table at Christopher and Darlene sneaking glances at each other. She smiled at Kwabena. They could not help noticing the growing closeness between Christopher and Darlene. It seemed the beginning of something—something much deeper than Darlene's usual superficial flirting.

After dinner, the kids went off to play Nintendo on Kwabena's television in the basement, while the females cleaned up the kitchen. Some of the men and teenagers went into the basement to play pool. The others took perches on the sectional in the den to watch the Baltimore Ravens play their archrivals, the Indianapolis Colts on Tamara's giant flat screen. With the surround-sound speaker system at full blast and the men drinking beer and bellowing loudly every few minutes, it was almost as much fun as being at the game. And it was a close game. By the time the women finished in the kitchen and joined the men, there was less than a minute to go in the game. The Ravens were three points behind, but a fumble by the Colts had put the ball back into the hands of the Ravens, who were now knocking at their door.

Everyone was holding their breath, waiting to see if Baltimore would score the touchdown for the win, when suddenly the house was plunged into darkness. A collective "ahhhh" could be heard around the room and from the children downstairs, followed by silence. Looking through the windows, Tamara could see the entire neighborhood was in darkness. Power was out.

Ebony's boyfriend, Rashid, an avid Ravens fan who had donned a purple Ravens jersey over his clothes for the game, was the first to speak. "Anybody got a portable stereo or something that works with batteries. I need to hear the game."

That put everyone in motion and they all scampered around to find candles, flashlight, batteries and a portable radio. They dug up Tamara's old portable stereo from college. Wood from the garage was brought inside and the fireplaces lit. In the hustle, the game was promptly forgotten until Rashid shouted out a few minutes later, "We won!" Then the cheering and celebration began.

Even without electricity, there was no shortage of entertainment. Everyone gathered around the fireplace in the light of candles and listened to Akwape and Kwame tell stories about Juju and Anansi the clever spider. The only people absent from this storytime entertainment were Darlene and Christopher, who had disappeared somewhere in the darkened house.

Kwabena sat on the floor, his arm around Tamara as they listened and laughed to the stories. Tamara leaned her head on him. As he looked down at her beneath the flicker of candlelight, he smiled. This felt right. The way a marriage should be. This was what he was missing in life.

Chapter Eighteen

It was almost one A.M. when Tamara got everyone settled and retired to her room. The sleeping arrangements took a little imagination, but it all worked out. The kids camped out in Kayla and Katanya's room, using the bunk beds and their sleeping bags. The red love seat with pull-out sofa bed was dragged from the master suite to the room across the hall for Carl and Leyoca. Air beds were inflated and placed in the other bedrooms for the many guests to use. Edebe and his family slept on the futon and sofa bed in the basement. Others occupied the sofa bed in the sectional.

At the end of the night everyone was accounted for except Christopher and Darlene, who had all but disappeared. Tamara finally located them in the sunroom, cozily warming themselves by the fire of the patio furnace. From their startled expressions, Tamara could tell that she'd interrupted something intimate.

When Tamara returned to the darkened bedroom, she heard the water running. Kwabena was taking a bath in the dark. The only light was the soft, ethereal glow of the night sky reflecting off the snow outside the bedroom windows and the flicker of the fireplace from the sitting room. Tamara searched around for candles and found only a few votive candles left. As she lit them, they gave off a delicate jasmine scent, their dim flicker giving the room a romantic glow.

Tamara began her nightly ritual of moisturizing, brushing, and braiding her hair into two cornrows. After that she would have a shower.

As she stood in front of the mirror brushing her hair, Kwabena stepped out of the bathroom naked, the candlelight casting long shadows on the wall. Tamara took in his long, lean muscular frame, his ripped abs and his slim hips. Her eyes rested on the triangle of hair around his groin and his huge protruding manhood. Immediately she turned her head away in embarrassment, her face and neck flaming red. It was the first time she'd seen a grown man naked other than on television.

Kwabena smiled at her reaction. He thought she was still running around organizing everybody. He hadn't expected to see her there with candles lit, illuminating the room or his nakedness. The thought of her looking at him naked sent a warm rush of blood through him, giving him an erection the size of Texas. He yearned to hold her in his arms and bury himself deep inside her.

"You could at least wear a robe or something," Tamara said, nervously trying to hide her embarrassment. She resumed brushing her hair.

He pulled on a pair of boxers and strode over to her. "You're my wife, Tammy. I don't have a problem with you seeing me naked," he whispered.

He took the brush from her hands and began running it through her hair. He liked the texture. He liked its smell. Then he began braiding her hair.

"Where did you learn to braid?" Tamara asked, not expecting a man, even one from Africa, to know how to braid.

"During my teen years we lived in different European countries. In some of the communities there were no other Africans and locals knew nothing about hair braiding. Mother had a very busy social schedule as the wife of the ambassador, so I found myself having to braid Afie's hair quite often. During my freshman and sophomore year at college, I braided the fellows' hair and moonlighted at a barber shop to supplement my living expenses."

Tamara closed her eyes and enjoyed the feel of his hands in her hair, the fresh scent of soap, the feel of his body standing close behind her, and evidence of his arousal poking into her lower back. The romantic aura of the flickering candles, the tenderness in his touch as he combed her hair made her feel all warm and tingly inside. She'd never felt closer to him. She sighed, "Tonight was so perfect. We get along so well. Our parents get along well. You're the only guy I've ever brought home that Mommy approved of. Sometimes I wish this were a real marriage."

He whispered in her ear sultrily, "For tonight, let's pretend it's real. When you get out of the shower, I want to touch you. I want to taste you. I want to lick you from the crown of your head to the tip of your toes and hear you scream my name. I want to make love to you in the candlelight until the break of dawn."

Tamara felt her body throb at his seductive words. She looked up at him and nodded yes. She wanted to make love to him. Her body, mind and soul were telling her this was the right thing to do.

His lips covered hers in a slow, sensual kiss. Tamara felt her knees grow weak and her heartbeat quicken as she closed her eyes and submitted to his sweet kisses. Her body came alive as his tongue dove deep into her mouth, setting every nerve on fire. The heat spread from her lips to the warm moist place between her legs, leaving a dull ache. She wanted him more than she wanted anything in her life. Reluctantly he released her lips, running his tongue along their smooth softness. "Don't take too long," he said. "I'll be waiting."

Tamara stepped into the shower, relishing the warm spray of the massaging shower head. Her heart was racing, her body throbbing. This was the first time she was sharing her bed with a man. She was going to lose her virginity tonight. She would finally feel what it was like to be ravished by a man. She would make love to Kwabena. She would feel his hard, muscular body against her and inside her. She had to make it perfect.

She splashed Victoria Secret body splash on her skin and chose a long, sexy nightgown to wear to bed. It was red satin trimmed with black lace with a deep plunging bust line that barely covered the nipples of her ample bosom, and two slits that went up to her hips. With it she wore matching crotchless thong panties. Satisfied that she looked her sexiest, Tamara climbed into bed next to Kwabena.

"I'm ready," she announced huskily.

There was no answer.

"Ben," she whispered in his ears. "I'm all yours."

Still no answer. Tamara shook him. "Ben?"

He mumbled something unintelligible and turned over. Kwabena was fast asleep.

Sunlight flooded the room, rousing her from sleep. Tamara opened her eyes slowly. The digital clock on the nightstand flashed twelve o'clock. Power had been restored. She looked over at Kwabena whose arms were slung loosely around her shoulder. His legs hung over her thighs. She felt his erection poking into her back. Gently she tried to extricate herself from his embrace.

He held her tightly, not letting her go. He gently nibbled at her shoulders and neck, caressing her exposed upper arm. Annoyed, Tamara jabbed him beneath the ribs with her elbow.

"Ow," he exclaimed hoarsely. "What's that for?"

"I got all dressed, up freezing my ass off in this sexy nightie, and you fell asleep."

He smiled sheepishly. "I'm sorry, Tammy. I was tired. You took so long in the bathroom."

"I wanted to be nice and ready for you," she said.

" 'Nice and ready' is you walking out of that bathroom naked, dripping wet, letting me lick every drop of water from your body."

Tamara was not going to fall for his graphic description again. "Yeah, right."

"It's not too late, you know," he whispered, nibbling on her neck. "We can still make love right now."

Tamara heard the patter of footsteps outside the door. She heard the bustle of activity and laughter of her guests downstairs, and the scraping of snow shovels outside. "Of course it is. Everyone else is already up and about."

"I'll make it up to you," Kwabena promised. "Tomorrow night when they're all gone we'll go out to a romantic candlelight dinner. I'll wine you and dine you like you've never been before, and when we get back, we'll make love until we're exhausted. Then we'll make love again."

Tamara smiled. "I guess we have a date." She got up from the bed and sashayed to the window. Kwabena looked at the way the tissue-thin nightgown clung to her round backside. It definitely was a turn on. "What are you wearing under that?" he asked.

Tamara turned around and cooed seductively, "That's for me to know and for you to find out. Oops, too late. You forfeited your chance."

He laughed. "I'll just have to settle for a cold shower, like I've done these past few times."

Tamara looked out of the window. The kids were out building snowmen and having a snowball fight. Kayla and Devon were using her laundry basket as a make-shift sled, coasting down the incline from the edge of the woods to the middle of the backyard. She could hear the men shoveling the driveway.

"Let's go lend a hand. We can't stay in bed while our guests slave away."

Chapter Nineteen

Leyoca gave her daughter and son-in-law a big hug. She and Carl were leaving for the airport. The storm had forced quite a few cancellations. The dusting to an inch expected in Montgomery County turned out to be ten inches—a lot less than the eighteen inches Baltimore and points north of the city got. But BWI was fully operational by that Saturday. Not only was Leyoca and Carl's flight not canceled, it was actually on time.

"It was the best Thanksgiving I've ever had," Leyoca said, smiling at them both. "It was the first time I've seen Tamara truly happy in a long time."

As Kwabena retreated to the basement to help his parents pack, Leyoca spoke directly to her daughter, "Tammy, you are fooling yourself. What I see between you and Ben is not a marriage of convenience, but one of love. And don't bother trying to convince me that all that smooching and closeness was an act for his parents. Whether you realize it or not, you are in love with each other."

Tammy smiled. "It is what it is, Mommy."

Leyoca shook her head. "I hope you realize it before it's too late. Whether you chose this marriage or this marriage chose you, it's the best choice you've made in a long time. Take care of yourself. I love you."

"I love you too, Mommy. Safe flight."

Tamara stood by the door, watching until the rental

Carl and Leyoca drove was out of sight. She then went downstairs to join Kwabena and his parents. Their flight was in a few hours' time.

As soon as Tamara entered the basement, Akwape said to her, "Sit. We have to talk."

Tamara joined Kwabena on the futon, where he was already sitting, looking uncomfortable. Kwame and Akwape sat on the sofa across from them and looked at each other. They then looked at Kwabena and Tamara before speaking.

Akwape took the lead. "You know since your father retired we've been doing a bit of marriage counseling back in Accra."

Kwame took over. "I can see the two of you care deeply for each other. And we would love for you to have a good marriage and have children. We're getting old. We need grandchildren. But your marriage is in trouble."

"Why do you say that, Papa?" Kwabena asked.

Akwape and Kwame looked at each other. Akwape replied, "This little lovey-dovey act you put on isn't fooling us. You guys don't even sleep together. Ben, the closet here is full of your clothes. It is quite clear that you live separate lives. If things aren't working out for you, you can come to us. We counsel married people all the time."

"Ben," Kwame said. "We like Tamara. We think she is a good wife for you. We would hate to see you end up in divorce court like so many others."

Tamara and Kwabena looked at each other, not certain what to do. They thought they had succeeded in convincing his parents that things were real. Apparently they'd done that and more. Finally Kwabena realized the only thing to do was tell the truth about their relationship.

Kwabena took a deep breath and spoke, "Mama, Papa, I'm afraid Tamara and I weren't very forthright with you."

"What, are you pregnant?" Akwape asked hopefully. "That would explain it all: the rushed marriage without our knowledge, the separate living quarters. I know when I was pregnant I had a hard time having Kwame anywhere near me."

Tamara spoke for the first time. She threw her hands up in the air in exasperation. "Pregnant? I've never had sex a day in my life!"

Everyone, Kwabena included, looked at Tamara as if she'd lost it. Complete silence followed.

Kwabena spoke slowly and calmly. "What Tamara and I have is an arranged marriage of convenience. I had a little trouble with immigration, and Tamara agreed to marry me so I can stay in the country. It is a business deal. Part of the agreement involves divorcing when I get my green card. As for this basement, I'm renting it from her. That's why my clothes and furniture are here. I'm sorry I wasn't more open with you both."

Kwabena waited for the melodramatic wailing from his mother. He'd grown accustomed to her reactions when things weren't as expected. Instead he got silence.

"Say something please," Kwabena begged.

Akwape said softly, "Why didn't you tell us this from the beginning?"

"Because I didn't want you arranging a marriage for

me with Mrs. Anan's daughter. I knew if you thought this marriage was real, you would give up on that one."

"You know I wouldn't force you to marry anyone. Maybe a little subtle urging, but if you told me you weren't interested, I would desist."

"I believe he did," Kwame informed her. "We just never listened carefully enough." He looked at Kwabena and Tamara sitting next to each other, Tamara as red as a vine-ripe tomato. He smiled. "However, I can tell you care for each other deeply."

Chapter Twenty

"Wow! This is absolutely gorgeous!" Tamara breathed, twirling around in the mirror. The red satin dress swirled seductively around her calves. It was as sexy as she could imagine, and she felt sensuous and desirable in it. The backless, spaghetti-strapped bodice clung seductively to her upper body, the low-cut front accentuating her full bust and cleavage. The skirt clung to her large hips, enhancing her round bottom before flaring out and ending somewhere midcalf with a handkerchief hem. She loved it.

She'd walked out of the shower still wrapped in her favorite bath sheet when she saw the dress lying across the bed. A handwritten note on it simply read, *Wear something sexy tonight.* And sexy it was. Because it was backless, she could not wear a bra with it. It clung so close to her hips, only a thong could be worn without panty lines being seen through the light material.

Tamara looked at herself in the mirror, satisfied with what she saw. Her hair was corn-rowed away from her face, the ends pinned up in a French roll. Her makeup—light silver eye shadow, a little blush and bright red lip gloss—matched the dress perfectly and highlighted her light brown eyes. She was beautiful.

Kwabena stepped into the room and whistled. The dress on Tamara had his head reeling, and other parts of him doing flips. His heart thumped in excitement.

He wanted to ravish her then and there. She looked up at him, her brown eyes filled with gratitude and awe.

Tamara's heart pounded as she looked at his tall, lean frame resting casually in the doorway, his smoky gray silk shirt and pleated, loose-fitting black trousers giving him debonair elegance. He was sexy. "Thank you," she said, breathless. "It's beautiful."

"You're beautiful," he said huskily, striding over to her. "But the dress is missing something."

She looked at him questioningly as he positioned himself behind her. He placed a silver half-inch-thick choker around her neck, leaving several links hanging down her bare back. His hand gently caressed her as he did, sending shivers down her spine. He next removed her gold studs and placed matching chandelier earrings in her ears. He stepped back to admire his handiwork. "Now it's complete," he said with a slow, sexy smile.

Tamara looked at the beautiful stranger in the mirror smiling back at her. She was so happy words failed her. Kwabena was indeed a man of impeccable taste.

He helped her into her full-length wool coat, then proffered his arm. "Shall we go m'lady?" With a gracious bow he escorted her down the stairs and out the door to a waiting limousine.

Tamara looked at him, her eyes sparkling with excited surprise. "A limousine!" The uniformed driver removed his hat and bowed. Tamara smiled as she recognized Edebe. He opened the door, settling them into the back of the limo. She looked up at Kwabena, eyebrows raised. He shrugged.

"Edebe runs a wedding and limo service," he explained as they sank into the plush leather seats. "This particular one is usually reserved for weddings and other special occasions." With that, he popped the cork on a bottle of cider and poured two glasses for them. "To us," he toasted, looking deep into Tamara's eyes, his deep voice sending chills down her spine.

"To us," she repeated, her hands trembling slightly. Her mother was right. There was no way they could come out of this marriage unscathed. In the past few months, he'd grown to mean so much to her. He was warm, loving and sensitive. He made her feel beautiful and alive; he made her feel like the most important person in the world. She liked the way he talked—how her name rolled melodically off his lips. She liked the way he looked at her, as if he could see into her very soul. She liked his calm rational thinking, his sense of humor, his humility, even his mystique. She loved the times they spent cooking, talking, laughing. She loved how her heart pounded every time he came near. He made her feel things she had never felt before, not even for Jared. She loved how his kisses lit her body on fire and how his presence made her feel complete. He had filled the void in her life, taking away the loneliness and emptiness and filling it with joy and excitement. Tamara couldn't fathom going back to her lonely existence. She was in love with Kwabena and wanted to spend the rest of her life with him.

Dinner was wonderful and romantic. They had the upper floor of the exclusive restaurant all to themselves. They dined by candlelight on succulent lamb with a Mediterranean flavor. They enjoyed light conversation filled with an underlying sexual tension that they both recognized was growing between them. Tamara gazed at Kwabena across the table, admiring how his dark eyes sparkled in the candlelight. She yearned to feel his full lips on her own. With every look, with every touch, she knew she wanted to share more than just a kiss with him. She wanted him, his heart, his body his soul—especially his heart.

After dinner they strolled hand in hand around the indoor garden. They looked at beautiful tropical flowers, blooming in the glass-encased greenhouse, while outside snow from the storm the day before piled high on the ground. It was a dreamlike escape from the reality of the harsh winter outside the walls of this faux paradise.

"This has been a very lovely evening," Tamara said as they sauntered through the large ferns and ginger lilies. The sound of soft jazz wafted through the air.

"It's not over yet." He smiled.

Returning to the dining room, the soft voice of a DJ came over the speakers. "This song is dedicated to Tamara, from her husband, Kwabena."

"Lady in Red" began to play. "May I have this dance, my special lady in red?" Kwabena asked, gently leading her to the dance floor.

They danced slowly to the beautiful song, their hearts beating in unison as their bodies moved to the slow rhythm. Tamara looked up at Kwabena, her eyes filled with emotion. She knew what she felt was real. She just hoped he felt the same way.

The sexual tension building between Tamara and Kwabena was almost palpable. They sat next to each other in the limo on the ride home in silence, their legs lightly touching. She glanced furtively at him, and he smiled. He touched her face lightly, his fingers tracing her lips. Her breath caught in her throat, her mouth went dry, her heart raced in anticipation of what she knew was going to happen tonight. He never said a word, yet his eyes spoke volumes. Tamara could see the desire in them.

He reached for her, his lips covering hers possessively in a long, deep, passionate kiss. Tamara closed her eyes, lost in his kiss, her tongue reaching out, entangling with his as bolts of electricity shot through her veins. She surrendered herself into his arms, feeling his hard body against her own, their labored breathing communicating their passionate need for each other. Neither of them noticed that the car had stopped until the door opened and Edebe cleared his throat loudly.

They thanked Edebe and ran inside, barely able to contain themselves. Kwabena wanted to take it slow, take her upstairs and be gentle. It was, after all, her first time. But he couldn't control himself, and neither could she. They were barely inside the door when they attacked each other in heated passion. He devoured her lips, his hands caressing her exposed back, reaching below her waistline to cup her round bottom. The feel of her naked creamy skin beneath his hands drove him wild.

She quickly unbuttoned his shirt, needing to feel his bare flesh beneath her hands, and discarded it somewhere on the floor of the foyer. She kissed his chest, her mouth hot and wet as she sucked at his nipples, her hands caressing the rippled muscles of his back and arms. He gasped, breathing deeply, needing her more than he needed air to breathe.

They fell onto the couch. In one swift motion, he lowered the dress straps to expose her breasts. His mouth covered her breast, his tongue licking, sucking, tasting. Tamara moaned, arching her back invitingly. His left hand reached beneath her dress, caressing her thighs, creeping up to her bottom.

She unbuttoned his pants, desperate to touch him, to feel him, to connect to him. She held him in her hands. He was large and throbbing. Her face grew hot with passion.

"Oh God, Tammy," he breathed, his deep voice hoarse and scratchy. "I want you."

Her body arched invitingly. She was hot with desire. She was on fire, a fire only Kwabena could quench. Yet fear hit her like a bolt of lightning. She froze beneath him. She felt tears come unbidden to her eyes. She could hardly breathe.

"Stop, Ben," she gasped, barely a whisper. "I can't...I can't do this."

Kwabena froze. He looked at her, confused. Her eyes glistened with unshed tears, wild with fear.

"I won't hurt you," he assured her, his voice hoarse.

"I'm sorry," she whispered, getting up from the couch, holding the remnants of her clothes together.

"Why?" he demanded.

"You won't understand," she replied and fled up the stairs.

Kwabena closed his eyes in frustration. *Why?* He couldn't understand why she ran whenever they got close. He loved her. He wanted her. But she always pushed him away. He ran his hands over his face and through his hair and sighed. He heard the door to her suite slam shut. He wanted to scream. He wanted to follow her upstairs and ravish her. He sucked in his breath and tried desperately to control himself.

It seemed a lifetime ago since he'd been with a

woman. Ever since he and Tamara had become intimate, he couldn't think of another woman. He was obsessed. He wanted her and nobody else. Yet she denied
him every time they got close. *Dammit!*

He walked down to the basement, shirtless, his pants
still open at the waist. He was so hard it hurt physically.
He flopped down on the couch and flipped on the television. He had to find a way.

Tamara leaned against the door, hyperventilating, trying not to cry. *Why did I stop?* The answer came to her in
a flash of reality. She was in love with Kwabena. Pretending to have a marriage was not enough. She wanted
a real marriage. She wanted all of him, not just his body.
She wanted him to love her like she loved him.

*Why is life so complicated? Maybe I should just tell him
how I feel. What am I afraid of?* But she already knew the
answer. She was afraid to give herself and be hurt. She
was afraid that she was just another conquest, a notch in
his belt, and nothing would really change about their
relationship. She was afraid in a few months, he would
leave and all she would have was memories of the scent
of a man. She wanted more. She wanted forever.

Chapter Twenty-one

Kwabena was sitting in front of the TV still mulling over the events of the evening when the basement plunged into sudden darkness. He groaned. He knew exactly what had happened. Tamara had turned on the sauna and it had tripped the fuse. For some inexplicable reason, the fuse tripped every time the sauna and the television were on simultaneously. He got up slowly, walking shirtless to the freezing garage in search of the fuse box. He found it, but it was locked. Shivering he returned inside and went upstairs to the foyer where Tamara kept a bunch of keys in a small cherry cabinet. The cabinet was bare. He looked in the junk drawer in the kitchen where tools and sometimes spare keys were kept. He found nothing resembling a key that would fit the fuse box.

He sighed and proceeded upstairs to the master suite. He was not sure he could face Tamara tonight, but he couldn't well sit downstairs in darkness and he was too wired to sleep. Taking a deep breath, he knocked hesitantly on the bedroom door. There was no answer, but he heard the jets of the Jacuzzi running and Kenny G's saxophone softly playing. He knew she would never hear him over the sounds. Images of her lying naked in the tub waiting to be touched flooded his mind. He quickly put those thoughts out of his head and entered the room. He came there for one thing. He was going to get it and leave.

He opened the bathroom door cautiously. She lay peaceful, her eyes closed, her naked body enveloped in a sea of sudsy bubbles. She looked like a juju queen, working her evil magic, transcending this body into the spiritual realm. Yet she looked calm and at peace. She was beautiful. He stood watching her for a few minutes before announcing his presence.

"Where are the keys to the fuse box?" he asked softly.

"On my key ring on the dresser," she answered without opening her eyes. She was expecting him. Once the sauna tripped the fuse, it was only a matter of time before he came looking for the keys.

He started retreating. She opened her eyes slowly, observing the rise and fall of his muscular chest. He still wore the black pleated trousers from earlier.

"Join me," she invited boldly, her brown eyes looked up holding him in her gaze.

He froze in his tracks. What was she, a tease? "Only so many cold showers I can take."

Her voice was soft, smooth and seductive. "I promise no more cold showers." She smiled encouragingly. He hesitated. "Please," she pleaded.

Kwabena held her gaze and dropped his pants and underpants to the floor. Tamara didn't wince. She didn't look away. She didn't blush. She admired his body. She looked at his manhood—big, hard and erect—and felt her body throb wildly. She had made up her mind. Whatever the consequences, she would submit to her desire. She would give herself to him. He was her husband, after all, temporary or not.

Kwabena stepped into the warm bath and sank beneath the suds. He looked at her sitting opposite him. He wished he understood her. "Why do you run every time I get close to you?"

Tamara closed her eyes and sighed. "You won't understand."

"Try me."

She spoke softly, her voice heavy with emotion. "Before you came along, I was in control of my emotions. I knew what I wanted. I understood myself. But somewhere between you moving in and us ending up here, I fell in love with you. Now I don't know who I am or what I want." She swallowed and continued, "It's not enough for us to pretend that our marriage is real, Kwabena. I want it to be real. I want you in my life. I love you."

"Come here, babe," he said, sliding her close to him so she sat in front of him between his outstretched legs, her back against his chest. "Our marriage is as real as we want it to be. What we feel for each other is real, and I want you in my life."

"What happens when you get your permanent green card?"

"We'll deal with it when the time comes. Right now, Tamara, the way I feel about you I've never felt that way about another. I love you."

Tears of joy came to her eyes. He loved her!

He took her pouf and tenderly washed her body, lingering around her breasts. She raised her arms round his neck while he washed her, touching her in the most intimate places. He discarded the pouf and gently stroked the soft flesh between her legs.

"Mmmmm," she moaned, feeling the pleasure of

arousal course through her body. She'd never been touched there before.

He stepped out of the tub and helped her out, then dried her soft, smooth skin. He looked at her body, luscious and supple in the glow of the candlelight. She was beautiful. Big and beautiful. He hoisted her in his arms and laid her gently on the bed.

He kissed her mouth, sweet and tenderly. He kissed her throat, his tongue licking, tasting, sampling the delicious softness of her skin. His long fingers caressed her legs and bottom, setting Tamara ablaze. She closed her eyes, arching toward him invitingly. She wanted him as much as he wanted her.

He moved his mouth over her body. He took one breast in his mouth, licking, tasting, suckling. Tamara moaned deeply, submitting to the flood of sensations that filled her soul. Their breathing deepened, coming in short rasps. He cupped her bottom, kissing her belly, letting his tongue linger around her belly button. She felt herself grow moist and hot. His fingers caressed the inside of her thighs and crept up to her warm, wet center. He touched her there, gently caressing its soft sweetness, driving Tamara into a frenzy of ecstasy.

"Take me, Ben," Tamara whispered passionately. She needed him within her, to be one with him. She wanted him to fill her and bring her to that place of ecstasy. She needed him to extinguish the fire burning in her, to fulfill her longing. But it was not yet time. Kwabena wanted her ready. It was her first time and he didn't want to hurt her.

Slowly he kissed her belly, her legs, his long arms reaching up and caressing her naked breasts. Then his mouth found the center of her being.

She moaned, writhing in pleasure, holding his head in her hands as his tongue sampled her sweetness, driving her wild. It was the most beautiful of sensations. Panting, she felt herself climbing to heights of passion, a feeling she had never before experienced.

"Oh, Ben," she gasped as she climaxed explosively, her body convulsing violently.

Slowly she laid him on his back, exploring his hard lean body with her hands, her lips and tongue. She wanted to know every intimate detail of this nubian god sharing her bed and her body. She licked his tiny nipples until they stood hard and erect. Kwabena moaned, a deep guttural sound escaping his lips. She caressed his long legs and butt, enjoying the feel of his steely muscles beneath her fingers. She kissed his belly, lingering around his navel, then took his length in her hands. It was the first time she'd felt anything this beautiful.

Kwabena moaned loudly, his breathing ragged. He gasped, "Tammy, I need you now," as he strained to hold himself back.

He straddled her. She opened her legs invitingly, willingly, wanting nothing more than to feel him inside her, to be joined as one with her husband. She heard the soft sound of plastic crackling as he removed a condom from its wrapper.

"Let me," she said, putting it on for him.

Slowly, gently he entered her. She was tight, but he had prepared her body well. Tamara felt a sharp jolt of pain, but it was soon replaced with pleasure as they moved against each other. Then panting, moaning and sweating, they moved in a fast rhythm, dancing to music only they could make. The moaning and groaning and panting grew louder. Just when Kwabena thought he could hold back no longer, Tamara suddenly came, her body shuddering, convulsing against his. Only then did he allow himself to let go, a climax so great it felt like an explosion.

"Tamara!" he screamed her name as his body shuddered and he lay against her—spent, satisfied, satiated but exhausted.

Lying in her arms, Kwabena whispered, "I love you Tamara. I love you."

Tamara stretched languorously. Her body tingled deliciously. Sunlight filtered through the blinds, alerting her that morning had arrived. A new day; a new Tamara. No longer a married virgin, but a wife, loved by a sexy hunk of a husband, having enjoyed the most wonderfully satisfying expression of love. She smiled, remembering their beautiful lovemaking. Remembering how he reached for her again in the middle of the night and before the first rays of dawn. Remembering the feel of him inside her, loving her like a real woman should be loved by her husband. He was absolutely right: when they made love, she would never forget it…and yes, she was begging for more.

Tamara stretched and reached for Kwabena, her body still naked beneath the satin sheets. But he was not there. She sat up and sighed, putting on her glasses. 7:49. Then she smelled the heavenly scents from the kitchen—bacon and eggs; or was it ham and eggs intermingled with fresh coffee? She got up pulling a satin robe from the brass coat tree near the bed. She looked at the jumbo pack of condoms still on the nightstand. Kwabena had placed them there Thanksgiving night when their plan to make love had been thwarted by his need for sleep. The rate at which she and Kwabena were going, they would finish the box by the end of the day. With that thought, she walked into the bathroom to freshen up. She would join Kwabena for breakfast in a moment.

When she emerged from the bathroom, Kwabena was sitting on the edge of the bed, wearing only boxer shorts. The sight of his chiseled upper body sent ripples of arousal through Tamara's core. On the nightstand was a tray of bacon, eggs, toast and coffee and a few peeled tangerines.

"I made you breakfast in bed," he said in his deep, melodic voice.

"Mmmmm…smells delicious."

He drew her toward him so she stood between his outstretched legs. "You look delicious," he said, untying her robe.

The sight of her naked body beneath the robe made him rock hard.

"I'm hungry," she whispered.

"Me too," he replied, disrobing her. He observed her full breasts standing pert in the air, their little pink buds erect. He looked at her wide waist with its little love handles and her belly, which was surprisingly flat for a woman of her weight. He looked at her plump legs and her massive round backside. He looked at her triangle of fine black hair covering the part of her that brought him such unspeakable pleasure. He grabbed her backside, sensually caressing it while drawing her to him. "I'm hungry for you."

Breakfast forgotten, he buried his face in her chest, letting his tongue play. Tamara held his head encouragingly, leaned her head back and moaned in pleasure.

His fingers found the pleasure spot between her legs, slowly strumming it. Tamara closed her eyes, moving her hips to his rhythm, submitting to the wonderful feeling enveloping her. His fingers entered her, causing her to squeal with desire. She felt herself climbing higher, her body thrashing about with a mind all its own, her breathing deep and labored.

He sat her on him and entered her, hard and throbbing. Panting and moaning, she rode him like a horse at a rodeo. Together they moved in wild abandon submitting to the desires of the flesh until they fulfilled each other, climaxing together. Then they reached for each other again. They made love all morning. They could not get enough of each other.

It was midday when they finally ate breakfast. It was cold, but still delicious.

"Move in with me," she invited while munching on cold bacon. "I'm officially terminating your lease as tenant."

He smiled. "You know what that means? I no longer have to pay you rent."

She returned his smile, holding his gaze, staring into his deep brown eyes. "Yup. But as my husband, you have to pay half the mortgage and bills. That is more than rent."

"If it means waking up next to you every morning, feeling your body next to me at night, and making love to you, I can live with that."

She reached over and kissed him. "I love you."

"I love you too."

Chapter Twenty-two

Kwabena navigated the labyrinth of corridors and labs. It had been a long time since he'd been here.

"Hey, Muti," Mike greeted, laughing and pumping his hand. "Been a while. Haven't seen you around since our days of zip-disk data sharing. What brings you here?"

"Just picking up Tamara. My ride broke down so she loaned me hers."

"She's in the lab. I gave her her own project, you know. Bioinformatics. After she got the network up and running in the first few weeks, I couldn't justify keeping her. She made the system so self-sufficient, there was little she needed to do to maintain it."

"Good. How's she handling it?"

"Great. She is quick. As for statistics, she is better than my last statistician, and he had a PhD. Why didn't she finish college?"

"She followed the money. She took a networking course and ended up in Silicon Valley making more than we made for quite a few years. The tech bubble just burst on her."

They stood around talking about work, discussing data and ideas while he waited for Tamara to finish up.

"You still have that time share in St. Lucia?" Kwabena asked.

"Yup."

"Planning on using it over the holidays?"

"Nope. Saving up to take the wife and kids back to Cameroon. Haven't seen my parents for a while. Why?"

"Thought I'd do a little traveling over the Christmas break."

Mike smiled. "With whom?"

"Tamara."

Mike raised one eyebrow. "You're sleeping with her, aren't you?"

"She's my wife."

"That was not a part of your business deal."

"I know. Things changed."

"That's quite a departure. She's not like your usual."

"Man, I thought you were deeper than that."

Mike looked at Kwabena hard. "I'm not talking about the physical. I'm talking about personality. She doesn't seem like the kind who can sleep with you tonight and be casual friends tomorrow, while feigning innocence. She's one of the most open people I've dealt with in a long time."

Kwabena smiled leaning his butt against Mike's desk and looking far off. "I know. Refreshing isn't it?"

"Indeed. So what happens when you get the permanent green card?"

"We'll cross that bridge when we get to it."

"She looks happy. I hope you don't hurt her."

"I have no intention to. Sometimes you spend your life looking for something and never quite finding it. Then suddenly when you least expect it, you find it right in front of you. It had been there right in the open, but you just didn't realize it was it because it was packaged differently than you expected. That's what it's like with Tammy."

"Sounds like someone finally got the Muti man's heart," Mike teased.

Kwabena looked off dreamily, a slow smile on his face. "I'm in love with her, man. Never thought the day would come, but it did."

Chapter Twenty-three

Welcome to St. Lucia! Tamara was in awe as they traversed the tropical paradise. They stayed in a cozy cottage on the north side of the island. As an added bonus, it was walking distance from the beach and not very far from Pigeon Island.

They had arrived the day before Christmas Eve and rented a car. The first thing they did after a brief rest was sample the crystal clear waters of this tropical paradise. Tamara looked at the tiny fish swimming around in the clear blue Caribbean Sea and thought it was the most wonderful thing she had seen.

They awoke on Christmas Eve before dawn to view the sunrise from the beach. They walked along the water's edge listening to the tiny waves lap the shore. They let the warm water lick at their feet while they enjoyed the cool sea breeze, the salty air filling their nostrils.

Slowly the sun made its ascent over the horizon. It painted the sky and sea with brushstrokes of gray and orange before emerging as a big fireball in the sky, flooding the world with morning light. Tamara looked at Kwabena and smiled. He was the most romantic person she'd ever met. She was glad fate had joined them together.

When they left the beach, they drove into Castries to do a little shopping at the market. The place was a bustle of activity. Vendors in colorful skirts and blouses sat on the roadside with trays and carts of colorful flavorful fruit and vegetables. The aroma of tropical fruit filled the air. The people spoke loudly, carrying on conversations in a mixture of St. Lucian Creole or patois and broken English.

A partially enclosed market was filled with vendors peddling local crafts, colorful clothing and souvenirs. Everywhere they went the people were pleasant. It was an exciting, almost thrilling atmosphere.

Kwabena picked out a green fruit with interlocking pegs. "Try this," he said, opening it to reveal white insides.

Tamara tasted it. It was sweet with a creamy texture and little black seeds. She loved it and ate two more.

"This is sugar apple," he explained. "This place reminds me so much of my childhood. The whole market atmosphere, the loud talking, the haggling over stuff— I love it."

Kwabena seemed familiar with the culture, the foods, the roads—he drove without consulting a map or asking directions. "You been here before?" Tamara asked.

"Yup."

Tamara wanted to know who he'd been with, but she didn't ask. She was certain it must have been one of his lovers. She felt a twinge of jealousy and quickly put the thought from her mind. That was in his past. He was with her now, he loved her, and that was all that mattered. She didn't want to ruin the intimacy of this vacation by dwelling on his past affairs.

They wandered over to a strand and had a breakfast of stewed codfish, boiled eggs, and cocoa tea and passion fruit juice. It was as local as one could get.

When they returned to the cottage, they were laden

with bags of fruits and vegetables, locally baked bread, and homemade treats. The afternoon was spent lounging on the beach soaking up the sun and enjoying the warm waters of the Caribbean Sea. It was a day of beauty, rest, and wonderful lovemaking that left both Tamara and Kwabena yearning for more.

Later that night they went to Gros Islet, the Friday night party center of the island. Here fishermen grilled, fried or sautéed their catch while revelers jammed in the streets to frenzied soca rhythms or dancehall reggae belted out by loud stereos. It was a giant party that extended several blocks around the seaside village. Tamara and Kwabena dined on grilled conchs smothered in a cucumber-garlic sauce, and deep fried pot fish, a name used to describe any type of small fish caught in a fish pot. They then joined the street revelers and danced the night away. It was almost dawn when they returned to the cottage.

"Welcome, welcome. It's so good to see you," Christina St. Jean said as Tamara and Kwabena entered her living room.

Kwabena introduced Tamara as his wife to Marcel and Christina St. Jean. Christina was a fellow Ghanaian, married to a St. Lucian. Both of them had been living on the island for the past five years.

"You never told me you were married," Christina said, hugging Tamara. "You have a beautiful wife."

They were having Christmas dinner at the couple's home, which was on a hill overlooking the capital city of Castries. Christmas day was nothing like Tamara had ever before experienced. There was no early rising, no running downstairs to open presents. No all-day cooking and preparing Christmas dinner. Instead they slept in, awakening only at noon when the midday sun made the room unbearably hot. They shared a light brunch on the veranda, enjoying the cool ocean breezes, then spent the afternoon quietly at the beach. Their only commitment that day was dinner with the local couple and their family.

Dinner was beautifully prepared with all things Caribbean. From the sorrel, a red drink made from the petals of the sorrel flower, and gingerbeer, to the stewed pork over rice and pigeon peas with the fig pie and fried plantains. There was also a large ham marinated in pineapple juice and baked with pineapple slices, and a whole turkey marinated in local spices. Dessert was bread pudding with rum sauce and black cake, a treat made with wine-soaked dried fruits, darkened with caramelized sugar and doused in rum and port wine. This was eaten with homemade soursop ice cream.

It was a small gathering: just Christina, Marcel and his parents, the couple's two preteen children and Marcel's teenage son from a previous relationship, Kwabena and Tamara. As they ate, Tamara asked Marcel and Christina, "Ghana is a long way from St. Lucia. How did you guys meet?"

Christina smiled as if remembering happy times and replied, "We met in college. Marcel was Kwabena's roommate, and Kwabena and I go back a long way. We were neighbors back in Ghana, so I visited often. Then Marcel and I began to talk, and well, here we are twelve years and two kids later."

Marcel smiled. He was light skinned and about five

feet nine inches tall and appeared to Tamara to be out-going and flirtatious. Christina was quite the opposite. She was dark, slim, about an inch shorter than her husband and more reserved. "And it's been a good twelve years," Marcel remarked.

Christina did not respond.

After dinner, Marcel, Tamara and the kids sat around drinking sorrel and playing dominoes. Kwabena retired to the veranda to enjoy the cool December breeze. He sat on the concrete balustrade railing, his feet dangling over a ten-foot drop. He slowly sipped on plantain wine made by Marcel's mother while enjoying the aroma of fresh flowers from the garden below. From his perch he could see Castries laid out like a blanket. He loved that place. *Maybe someday I'll buy something here and visit often.*

Christina joined him on the veranda. "Mind if I smoke?" she asked, lighting up before Kwabena could respond.

"Thought you kicked the habit," he said in Twi.

"Thought so too. It just keeps resurfacing when things get stressful," she replied in the same language.

"Can't imagine what kind of stress you have in this little piece of paradise. Nice house on the hill, handsome husband, two beautiful children, sunshine all year round and the beach a stone's throw away."

"How about an illegitimate son six years younger than my youngest kid and another woman pregnant with my husband's child?"

"That is stressful," Kwabena agreed. "I thought Marcel had settled down."

"He did until we moved to St. Lucia. That's when all

the old girlfriends and unresolved relationships started resurfacing. It makes no difference that he's married. It seems to attract them even more."

"I'm sorry to hear that."

She was quiet for a while, looking off toward the sea, blowing a plume of smoke skyward. "I like your wife. She seems very nice. Quite opposite to what you're accustomed. How did you guys hook up?"

Kwabena smiled. "It's a long story. Suffice it to say, I met her on our wedding day, immigration was involved, but she is the person I am definitely spending the rest of my life with. She is the best thing that ever happened to me."

"What about Adeola?"

"Over. Done with. Out of the picture."

"So you finally kicked the habit?"

"Is that what you call it?"

"Oh, yeah. She is like a drug. The two of you are together, she cheats on you, you dump her; next thing I know you're back sleeping with her. She finds you with her friend, she dumps you, and then I hear you two are engaged. She runs off with some high-ranking somebody, you swear it's over this time, yet you jump back into her bed. Yes, in that respect, she is like a cocaine habit, and personally I never thought she was worth it."

"Well, I made it quite clear this time that it's over."

"Maybe in your mind, but what about in hers? The past always catches up with us. I hope you are honest and open with Tamara. Like Marcel, I can see your past relationships coming back to haunt your present one—especially Adeola." She stubbed out the butt of the cigarette. "By next year, I'm going to pack up me and my kids and return to Ghana. I've had enough of that cheating bastard!"

She walked toward the door, then turned around. "You have a nice wife. Don't blow it for her or for yourself." Then she stepped inside.

Chapter Twenty-four

The rest of the vacation was spent with lots of sightseeing and water activities in the day and quiet, romantic evenings. They visited the drive-in volcano at Soufrière and toured the rainforest. They snorkeled around shallow reefs and rode Jet Skis in the Caribbean Sea. They enjoyed fun-filled catamaran cruises from Rodney and Marigot Bay to Gros Islet. But they lived for the nights. Nights were filled with romantic dinners, long walks on the moonlit beach and beautiful, emotional lovemaking. Tamara finally knew what it was like to be loved by a man. It exceeded all her imaginations.

New Year's Eve night they attended a party at a waterfront hotel. Tamara wore a white off-the-shoulders cotton eyelet blouse and a multicolored wrap-around skirt. The party was crowded with people jamming shoulder to shoulder. They danced all night to calypso and frenzied soca music, soul-searching reggae and R&B.

Sometime before eleven, Kwabena and Tamara left the crowded dance hall and sat at an outdoor bar overlooking a nearby marina, drinking a virgin piña colada and a rum punch. It was their last night on the island, and they were enjoying every minute of it. They watched the moonlight reflecting off the surface of the water in the marina and listened to the muted sounds of the party music.

Tamara excused herself and went to the bathroom. When she returned, a slim, shapely local was sitting on her abandoned stool, openly flirting with Kwabena. Tamara observed them for a while, uncertain of how to react. Hesitantly she approached them, her face slightly red.

Kwabena looked up as she approached, placed his hand around her waist and drew her to his side. "This is the owner of that seat," he said to the girl.

The girl looked Tamara over, "Is this your friend or relative?"

"She's my wife."

The girl looked at Kwabena and Tamara and smiled cynically. She said something in Creole as she turned away.

Kwabena looked at her with steely eyes and responded to her harshly in the same language. She looked back, a horrified expression on her face.

He turned to Tamara. "Let's go."

As they headed out toward the deserted moonlit beach, Tamara asked, "Where did you learn to speak St. Lucian Creole?"

"In St. Lucia. My family lived here during my early teens and I picked up a little of the language."

Tamara smiled, relieved. At least he hadn't been here with some lover, as she'd originally assumed.

She placed her hands in his. She knew he was multilingual. She'd heard him speak in at least four languages so far. But hearing him speak Creole made her curious. "So how many languages do you speak?"

"A few," he answered vaguely as they walked hand in hand on the warm sand.

"Give me a number."

"It's not that simple. Some of the languages are considered dialects rather than official languages, depending on the perspective of the listener."

"Give it your best shot."

"My first languages are Twi, Akan and English. I speak Fante and Dagomba and a few dialects of these languages. I also speak Swahili, and I can understand a bit of Igbo, though I cannot speak it fluently. Of the European languages I speak French, Spanish, and Italian. I also speak a limited amount of St. Lucian Creole, which is considered a language by some and a dialect of French by others."

Tamara was silent as they walked along the moon-washed beach, the music of the hotel party faint in the background.

"She said something about my weight, didn't she?" Tamara questioned, glancing sideways at him.

He hesitated before answering. He knew "she" was the lady at the bar. "Yes."

He gently caressed her hand as they sauntered along the water's edge. "I know you're uncomfortable about your weight and shallow people cannot fathom us being together. But I couldn't care less what people think about our relationship."

They walked along the deserted beach until they came to a crooked almond tree with low-hanging branches. A few fishing boats, no bigger than canoes were pulled up on shore nearby; some still had nets in them. Kwabena sat on a low branch and turned to face Tamara. The moonlight bathed her face in its silver glow. "You're beautiful."

Tamara stood between his outstretched legs, leaning against him. She looked into his deep brown eyes. Just standing so close to him took her breath away. She was happy. Kwabena made her happy.

Everything was silent except for the rhythmic lapping of the small waves on the shore and the few crickets and night creatures. Kwabena broke the silence, his deep baritone like music to her ears. "I have something for you—a belated Christmas gift, early New Year's present. It's in my pocket."

"I didn't get you anything," Tamara apologized as she fished the little velvet box out of his pocket. She turned it around in her hands before opening it. From the size of it she guessed it was earrings or a small necklace.

"That's ok. This is a gift for both of us," he said softly, his heart thumping wildly. He looked at her soft brown eyes glistening with tears as she removed the pear-shaped diamond solitaire from its box. Slowly he eased himself off the branch, taking her hand in his and dropping to one knee.

"Tamara Fontaine, will you marry me—again?"

Tamara sniffled and smiled through tears, her face flushed. "Silly, we're already married!"

He slipped the ring on her finger and produced a wedding band. It was simple—no flash, no glitter; nothing like the five-thousand-dollar wedding set she had purchased for her marriage to Jared. He slipped it on her finger and raised himself to full height. "Now it's official. You're no longer Tamara Fontaine, but Mrs. Tamara Opoku."

"I like the sound of it," Tamara choked out quietly,

tears of joy flowing from her eyes. She looked up at him and for the longest while they gazed lovingly into each other's eyes. "You know how to romance a woman's pants off don't you?" she said smiling.

He smiled. "Only the one I love. I love you, Tammy."

"I love you too, Ben," she breathed.

His lips covered hers in a passionate kiss that went on forever. His hands wandered over her exposed shoulders, caressing her. Tamara melted beneath his touch, her toes curling into the soft warm sand beneath her feet. He showered her face, neck and ears with tiny wet kisses, all the while whispering terms of endearment. Tamara's breath caught in her throat; her body tingled with desire as Kwabena undid the minute buttons on her blouse. The warm tropical air caressed her exposed skin. He unhooked her bra, kissing every bit of flesh he uncovered.

"What are you doing?" Tamara rasped, her entire body ablaze.

"Making love to my wife on a deserted beach, under the full moon," he whispered huskily, kissing her neck and untying the knot that secured her wrap-around skirt.

"What if someone sees us?"

Kwabena chuckled softly, sliding her panties down her legs, ignoring her question.

He released her long enough to remove the T-shirt and cotton slacks he wore. In one fluid motion he scooped her into his arms like a baby. Tamara squealed in delight. He walked, staggering in the soft sand to the water's edge. He waded in the water with her in his arms until he was chest deep, then released her. Tamara tried to stand, but could barely keep her head above the water.

She flipped onto her back, her bare breasts pointing up to the sky, and did the backstroke away from him, heading toward shallower waters. "Catch me if you can," she challenged.

Kwabena let out a deep, throaty laugh, the sound echoing in the stillness of the night. He lunged at her, and she swam away, laughing coquettishly. He dove under the water.

Tamara flipped herself upright in waist-deep water. It was silent all around. She looked around but saw no sign of Kwabena. The water was still, not a ripple or a bubble.

"Ben?" she called softly. Silence.

"Ben, where are you?" Silence.

She began to panic. "Kwabena Opoku, stop playing around. You're scaring me. Ben, please?"

Just then the calm surface of the water broke and Kwabena emerged from below, grabbing her by the waist. Tamara squealed aloud and laughed as he drew her into his arms, her body melting against his wet, hard chest. They kissed each other passionately, touching each other, stoking the fires of desire. Tamara wrapped her legs around his hips, letting him fill her, evoking the most intense pleasure Tamara had ever felt. Kwabena moaned, rocking back and forth, plunging deeper into her as they climbed to heights of pleasure. They allowed the shallow waves to wash them to the sandy banks of the shoreline. They rode each other until they had drunk their fill of love, climaxing together.

The stillness of the night was suddenly broken by a

thunderous boom as the sky erupted in a kaleidoscope of lights and colors. Fireworks from a distant cruise ship announced the dawn of a new year. Church bells from on shore pealed loudly in the distance, welcoming the New Year.

Kwabena sighed, fulfilled, satiated, running his hands through Tamara's wet, sand-filled hair. "Happy New Year, my love."

"Happy New Year," Tamara whispered to her husband, snuggling against his naked body. It was the happiest night of her life. They were looking forward to this coming year and the rest of their lives. They had found passion, happiness and contentment in each other. They had found love.

Chapter Twenty-five

Tamara walked into the basement and slammed Kwabena's laptop shut. The room was strewn with piles and piles of papers. A laser printer on a two-drawer wooden filing cabinet spat out page after page of text and colored diagrams. Since Kwabena moved into Tamara's bedroom, he had turned his basement bedroom into an office and did most of his work there when he was home. His bedroom furniture had been used to furnish a guest bedroom upstairs.

"No more working," Tamara demanded. "This is your birthday, and we are going to do something fun, whether you want to or not!" She stood facing him, arms akimbo as he sat on the futon, surrounded by papers.

It had been almost a month since they'd spent any quality time together. Kwabena had been working on a grant application—several, in fact—and two publications. It had kept him busy, working in the lab until late in the evenings, then writing at home until the wee hours of the morning. Sometimes he would crawl into bed just before dawn. Other times he just crashed on the futon in the basement. Even when they were together he was preoccupied, mentally writing the proposals or evaluating data. The deadlines were fast approaching.

Tamara wasn't surprised at his demeanor at all. She

had seen Mike write grant proposals earlier that year. The normally easy-going, laid-back principal investigator, or PI as they all referred to him, was transformed into an angry, snapping monster. Mike harassed his postdocs for data, urging them to write up papers for publication. It was as if he were possessed. She came to understand that grants were the lifeblood of the labs. Without the funding, there could be no research, and the grants were extremely competitive. The more productive the labs were, the better the chances of the research being funded. And in this field, productivity was measured by the number of recent publications in peer-reviewed scientific journals. Fortunately, Kwabena did not react like that, at least not at home. God knows what his postdocs and technicians endured in the lab.

Her action caught Kwabena off guard, and he looked up at her in surprise. Tamara certainly had some fire. Her sudden appearance, the way she took control was certainly a turn on. He shoved the computer from his lap and pulled her down on top of him.

The action caught her by surprise, and she let out a soft scream. She was always astonished at his strength. For a lean guy, he certainly was strong. In a second he'd flipped her onto her back and pinned her to the futon, a mischievous smile on his face.

"I'm ready for fun, right here, right now. Whaddya say?" he teased, nibbling at her ears, his hand caressing her thigh.

"Not that kind of fun, you pervert," she replied blushing. She had a big surprise planned for him, a surprise she easily hid from him due to his preoccupation with work. "I was thinking more like going out, enjoying the nice spring weather."

"Oh, that kind of fun," he said in mock disappointment. He kissed her on her lips and helped her into a sitting position. "Tell you what, help me put these copies together, we'll go to FedEx and mail them out, and I'm all yours. You can do with me whatever comes to your imagination. The more erotic, the better."

She blushed. It had been months of fulfillment since the first time they made love to each other, and she still blushed anytime he talked like that. Kwabena looked at her cherry red neck and face and laughed inwardly. She really was something.

Together they assembled his grant application. Tamara was surprised to see his CV and the amount of publications he had coauthored. It was impressive. While looking at some of his preliminary data, she asked him, "Why did you analyze the data like that? You can't really draw any concrete conclusion from this as is."

He came over and looked at it. "You have a better suggestion?"

"Sure."

Together they sat down and reanalyzed the data. Tamara's way certainly made it easier to draw the conclusion he was presenting. Kwabena was impressed. He was seeing her in a new light. No wonder Mike had given her her own bioinformatics project.

"Why don't you go back to school and get your degree?" he asked her as they reprinted the pages and assembled the proposal.

"I will," she replied, packing the pages into a FedEx package. "I've begun taking a refresher course this semester and will officially enroll at UMD this coming fall."

* * *

It was midday when they joined the throngs of people enjoying the fresh spring day at the Mall in Washington, D.C. It was the height of the Cherry Blossom Festival and the cherry trees were in full bloom. Thousands of people were out celebrating this festival of nature. Bikers whizzed by, their hair blowing in the wind. Joggers ran past them. Families with children played in the warm April sun. Rollerbladers zipped by them. Tamara and Kwabena walked hand in hand around the Washington Monument and made their way along the reflecting pool toward the Lincoln Memorial.

It was the first time Kwabena had even noticed that spring had sprung. He'd been so focused on his grant writing. He was glad she insisted they go out. They took a brief tour of the Smithsonian and the Air and Space Museum. Both of them had been there numerous times, yet they were still enthralled by the exhibits.

They spread a blanket and had a picnic lunch along the Potomac River, in the shade of a blooming cherry tree. Kwabena inhaled deeply, reveling in the sweet smell of the flowers. He lay on his back, looking up at the blue skies with the sun playing peekaboo behind fluffy white clouds. Tamara sat beside him, looking down at the contented expression on his face.

"A penny for your thoughts," she said.

He smiled. "If I tell you my thoughts right at this moment, you would look like a cherry tomato."

Tamara chuckled.

Kwabena got up and held out a hand to her. "You up for a boat ride?"

They got on little paddleboats and rode down the Potomac River. They were laughing and having fun as they pedaled their boat toward the Jefferson Memorial. In the middle of the water, Kwabena stopped peddling. He reached over and kissed Tamara long and deep. She eagerly returned his kiss, oblivious to the many people on the river in boats like them. They didn't care. When they were together, nothing else mattered.

He whispered in her ear seductively, "When we get home, the things I will do to you will make a hooker blush."

"Mmmm…" she urged.

He whispered a graphic description to her, and she immediately blushed, her body tingling all over. Kwabena trailed his fingers along her reddened face and kissed her passionately. She closed her eyes and melted beneath his touch, both of them abandoning pedaling the boat. Suddenly there was a big thud. The boat had drifted with the river current and bumped into the wall adjacent to the Jefferson Memorial. They laughed and immediately resumed pedaling. This was a day they would remember for a long time to come.

Relaxed and content, Kwabena and Tamara returned home in the early evening. As they approached the house, Kwabena said, "Thanks for a wonderful birthday."

"It's not over, honey," she said. "I haven't given you your birthday gift yet."

Kwabena knew they were going to have a romantic dinner somewhere, then spend the rest of the night locked in each other's arms making delightful love. He suspected the gift was Tamara wrapped in dental floss, aka sexy lingerie. He opened the door, desiring to take her in his arms then and there. They could eat later.

"Surprise!" The lights flicked on, and crowds of Kwabena's friends shouted to him. Cameras flashed in his face, and music blasted from the stereo speakers.

Kwabena opened his mouth in disbelief. "When did you plan this?" He looked at Tamara. His friends, family and colleagues were all there celebrating his thirty-second birthday.

Tamara just laughed. Mike came up and patted him on his back. Chris and Darlene, who had been dating steadily ever since Thanksgiving, had helped coordinate the party. All the food had been prepared by the African ladies right there in Tamara's kitchen. That was the reason for the Washington, D.C. outing. Becky had baked and decorated the birthday cake.

It was an enjoyable party with great food, lots of dancing, loud music, laughter and fun. The basement recreation room was turned into a dance floor. The den and foyer were the place for those wishing to engage in meaningful conversation, though they had to shout over the music. With Mike, Chris, Edebe and Darlene coordinating the guest list, it seemed everybody who knew Kwabena was there.

"Where's that husband of yours?" Becky asked Tamara. "We're ready to cut the cake."

Tamara looked at the beautifully decorated cake. It had *Happy Birthday, Kwabena* written in English, Twi and Akan, Kwabena's native languages. "It looks almost too beautiful to cut. I hope we've got pictures of it."

"Oh yes, we do. By the way, we are lighting all thirty-two candles, so I hope he has good strong lungs. Now go find Ben. I'll try to get everyone to come upstairs."

Tamara went off looking for Kwabena. She shouldered her way around the dimly lit dance floor, getting swept up in what she could only describe as a line dance. Kwabena was nowhere to be found. She searched the den, foyer and living room, even checking in the library to see if he tried to get a moment away from the noise of the party. God knows she could do with a moment like that now. He wasn't there. Neither was he upstairs in the bedroom or the bathrooms.

She wandered into the sunroom. A few guests, seeking to hold conversations at normal voice levels were scattered about in the sunroom. She saw Chris and Darlene sitting on her wicker love seat, staring deep into each other's eyes, talking in hushed tones. He whispered something to her and she giggled. They looked happy together.

Observing them together, Tamara could tell that this relationship was more than Darlene's customary short flings. She recalled Darlene's frantic call the Saturday after Thanksgiving. She was supposed to meet him that night for a date and she'd misplaced his number. She then proceeded to question Tamara and Kwabena about Christopher. Christopher was equally enamored with Darlene. He couldn't stop talking about her and had inundated Kwabena with questions, describing her as "the one." Since then, they seemed inseparable.

When Tamara had returned from St. Lucia, Darlene had called her excited but scared. Christopher had invited her to Tanzania to meet his family. It was the first time any man had invited her to meet his family and she didn't know what to do. Consequently, Darlene had immersed herself in all things Tanzanian. She read and watched every documentary she could find about the country, the customs, the culture and the people. When she returned from Tanzania last month, Chris and his family was all she could talk about. Darlene had finally found the love of her life.

Tamara sauntered over to them, smiling inwardly. She was happy that Darlene had finally found her knight in shining armor and Chris had found his fair damsel. "Sorry to interrupt you lovebirds," Tamara said, "but have you seen Ben?"

Neither of them had seen Kwabena.

Finally Tamara wandered out onto the deserted deck. Though it had been a warm day, the moment the sun set, the temperature plummeted. It was chilly. Tamara never expected to see anyone outside tonight, but there he was, at the farthest darkest corner, leaning against the railing talking to a medium-built woman with a beautiful figure in traditional African dress.

Tamara observed them for a moment before alerting them to her presence. They were standing in the same spot where Tamara and Kwabena had shared their first kiss six months ago. She felt a twinge of jealousy. Though she could hear snippets of their conversation, she could not understand a word. It was all done in a dialect of Twi. But looking at the way the woman stood with folded arms, her lips pouting, her head raised defiantly looking afar off, Tamara could tell that their conversation had been anything but casual.

Tamara cleared her throat loudly and announced, "Ahm, we're ready to cut the cake."

Kwabena looked up, momentarily startled, before regaining his usual unperturbed demeanor. The girl flipped her long braids and sashayed toward the door. As she passed Tamara, she gave her a cold stare and rolled her eyes.

Though Kwabena took Tamara's hand in his as they

headed inside, Tamara had a sinking feeling that something was terribly wrong. For the first time since becoming intimate, she questioned his fidelity.

As they entered the noisy family room, Becky brought out the large cake with thirty-two lit candles. A jovial roar went up as everybody wished Kwabena happy birthday. Chris, Edebe and Mike surrounded him with well shaken bottles of champagne, waiting to pop the cork. Everyone else had a glass of champagne in hand ready to toast Kwabena's birthday.

Kwabena, laughing easily, took center stage as guys teased, betting each other loudly about his ability to blow out all thirty-two candles in one shot. With one breath he had all the candles out. He called Tamara up to him and cut the cake with her, feeding her with a small slice. Tamara tried to enjoy the moment and be happy, but it was hard putting that girl, who had now left the party, out of her mind.

As soon as the cake was cut, Mike did a toast. The guys popped the champagne corks, sending a spray of bubbly in the air that soaked Kwabena, Tamara and all in close proximity. There was lots of laughter and loud chatter before the music resumed and the revelers returned to the basement to dance.

Chapter Twenty-six

Tamara wandered off by herself and sat on the private balcony outside the master suite, hugging a blanket around her shoulders. It was the quiet time she needed away from the noise of the party. Judging by the parties she'd attended with Kwabena, it would be almost morning before they could get to bed.

She heard a quiet knock and Jordan came onto the balcony. He sat in the Pier 1 papasan chair next to her and asked, "Are you ok?"

"I'm fine," she answered, taking a long sip of her apple cider.

"You don't look fine, and you didn't look fine cutting the cake."

"I'm ok. I'm just a little tired, that's all. It's been a long day. We went to D.C. and had a lot of physical activity before coming to the party. A good night's sleep and I'll be good as new."

"Tamara, you've never lied to me before. Don't start now."

Tamara laughed uneasily. There was nothing about her that Jordan missed. The first time she and Kwabena had made love, she didn't have to tell Jordan what happened. He looked at her face and simply asked, "How was it?" He knew. That was what she liked most about having a best friend/brother like Jordan, he knew her inside and out. And there was nothing she couldn't tell him. Becky understood that. Kwabena was beginning to understand it.

Tamara sighed. "I don't know…I feel like an outsider among Kwabena's friends. It's as if there is this circle of trust that I'll never be able to penetrate."

"That usually happens when there is a tight group of people of similar culture living in a foreign land. They become mistrustful of anyone outside of the group. But I know that's not the only thing bothering you."

She remained silent for a while, looking at the darkened woods in the distance. Jordan was right; that was not the only thing bothering her. There were other more pressing issues and concerns.

Tamara sighed and said softly, "Ben disappeared tonight just before we cut the cake. When I finally found him, he was out on the deck with a woman. They weren't in any compromising position or anything, but just their demeanor had me wondering if there was something between them. Do you think he may be still running around?"

"Ask him."

"I can't. He'll think I'm jealous or I don't trust him."

"Truth is, Tammy, if you trusted him, we wouldn't be having this conversation. If I've learned one thing about marriage or any relationship in general it's that you've got to communicate. If your relationship to his friends is bothering you, talk to him about it. If you think there is something between him and this woman, ask him about it. Give him the opportunity to explain."

She sat quietly for a while. "I bet you've never had to deal with that situation."

He laughed. "I have. When Becky and I first became serious, she thought something was up between me and you because we spent so much time on the phone. But she refused to tell me what was bothering her. Instead, she let it fester until we were on the brink of a breakup when in anger she blurted it out. Only after she finally admitted to me that she had an issue with our friendship, I was able to address the problem. That's why we visited you in LA. I figured if she got to know you and see the way we related to each other, she would understand the nature of our relationship. And she did. Now she gets more time with you than I do."

Surprised, she exclaimed, "How come you never told me about that?"

"If I did, you would have backed off, because you wouldn't want to get between Becky and me."

She could only smile. He was right. He certainly knew and understood her. She wondered if Kwabena thought the same thing about her and Jordan. *Ah never.* "I guess I have no choice but to ask him."

It was just after three in the morning when the party ended and Tamara and Kwabena crawled into bed. In all the excitement and fun of the party she had forgotten about his birthday gift. She'd bought him a watch and cologne. She also bought sexy lingerie and had all intentions of wearing it to bed tonight and seeing his mouth water as he imagined what lay beneath it. But the mood was no longer there. Not only was she tired, she was feeling insecure about their relationship. Tamara could not ignore the beautiful women who surrounded and openly flirted with Kwabena. Many of them were much more sophisticated and polished than she ever could be. Seeing him on the deck tonight with that very attractive woman brought many of her insecurities back to the surface. What if he still desired slim, shapely women? What if she wasn't attractive enough for him? The girl at the hotel in St. Lucia certainly thought so. Furthermore, she had no idea how to even broach the topic.

She lay on her back, looking up at the ceiling, her hands resting beneath her head. She prayed for the courage to ask Kwabena the questions that were burning her, but she didn't know how.

Kwabena reached over and held her. Tamara stiffened. He kissed her. She responded without enthusiasm, without feeling. Kwabena lay in silence. He had never seen her that cold or unresponsive. He knew something was bothering her.

"Tamara, talk to me. What's bothering you?"

"I'm ok," she responded hesitantly. "Maybe I'm reading more into things or I'm imagining things, but I don't think your friends really like me very much."

"I don't think that's the case at all. Though you and Edebe got off to a rocky start, he respects and likes you. Chris likes you a lot, especially as he credits you for introducing him to the love of his life. And Mike adores you."

"I'm not talking about your inner circle. I'm talking more specifically about your female friends."

"What makes you think so?"

"They are very cold and aloof when I'm around, even when they come to my...our house."

"It's probably because they see you as an outsider. Some African women tend to be like that...cold and aloof when dealing with people of different culture and background. Some of them don't trust Americans. It's not just you."

"But they liked me just fine before they knew we were married."

Kwabena was silent for a long time. He didn't like the direction the conversation was heading, but he could do little to steer it otherwise. He tried humor.

Chuckling softly, he said, "Well, I'm off the market… bought and paid for by an American woman."

Tamara was in no mood to joke. "How many of them did you date?"

Kwabena didn't respond.

"Let me rephrase that…How many of them did you sleep with?"

Kwabena sighed. "I don't like this conversation. I think we should just stop now."

"Ok," Tamara responded. She felt tears stinging her eyes, but she refused to cry. She turned her back to him and lay silent.

Kwabena looked over at Tamara. He knew she was hurting inside. He wanted to be open with her, but he wasn't certain how much she could handle. He didn't want to hurt her, yet he felt obligated to answer.

"A few," he responded softly.

"And they are still your friends?"

He knew she wouldn't understand the way things were. Yet he wanted her to understand. With Tamara's lack of a sexual past, she could make the most chaste person sound like a whore—and God knows he wasn't chaste.

"A few years ago, I was engaged. Things didn't work out and I decided that I didn't want another long-term committed relationship. So I just had casual noncommitted sexual relationships with people I've remained friends with."

"And that lady on the deck, was she one of your friends with benefits?"

Kwabena sighed. He and Imari had been together just before the arranged marriage with Tamara. It was a discrete relationship that no one knew about. They both preferred it that way. He'd ended it about a month prior to his marriage, but they remained friends. Unfortunately, she had found out about his marriage like most of his friends: when Tamara had drunkenly announced it at the party the week before Thanksgiving. Needless to say, Imari was very hurt, partly because she had U.S. citizenship and would have been willing to marry him had he asked. At that time, he never intended to have a real marriage and he didn't want to hurt any of his friends by marrying them for a green card.

"Yes, but we ended the relationship prior to our marriage. Tamara you probably won't understand. Monogamy never came easy for me. It's not something I'm proud of, but I can't pretend to have lived a chaste lifestyle. However, I never used women. Anyone I was with knew exactly what kind of relationship and level of commitment that we had—and it was mutual."

"So what makes you think, monogamy will come easy to you now?"

He lay quiet for a few minutes before answering. "Because I love you and I don't want anyone but you. That's the difference. Come here," he whispered, drawing her close to him. "You don't have anything to worry about. I promise to be faithful to you always, Tammy."

Yet Tamara still worried. Long after they'd made love and Kwabena had fallen asleep, Tamara lay awake, her mind racing. She mentally examined the girls in Kwabena's little circle...his friends with benefits. They all had one thing in common: they were pretty. That girl on the deck earlier was a cross between Halle Berry and Nia Long. She was beautiful, with high cheekbones, long lashes, full lips and a body that most women would die for. All Tamara had was two hundred and twenty pounds of loose flesh with cellulite and stretch marks on her legs and dimples in her bottom. How could she compete?

As Tamara lay in the dark listening to Kwabena's rhythmic breathing, she knew what she had to do. By hook or by crook she was going to lose the weight. She was going to keep her husband.

Chapter Twenty-seven

"Wake up, honey!" Kwabena shook Tamara.

It was Saturday evening and Tamara had been asleep on the couch since early afternoon. Tamara opened her eyes slowly, shifted position and promptly went back to sleep.

"Wake up!" He shook her even harder. "We're going to be late, and you know your mother hates lateness."

Tamara's mother had been in New York on business and had driven down to be with them that night. They, along with Leticia, Ebony and her boyfriend, Darlene and Chris, and Afie and her husband were supposed to have dinner at an Ethiopian restaurant in Washington, D.C.

"Come on, Tammy. Get up." If he didn't know better, he would have thought she was pregnant, the way she'd been sleeping lately. He shook her again.

Finally, Tamara opened her eyes and stretched lethargically. "I'm just so tired," she whispered, dragging her body off the sofa. Her face was pale. She looked exhausted. Her skin sagged.

"You're sure you're not pregnant?"

"How many damned sticks do I have to pee on to convince you I'm not pregnant!" she snapped.

Kwabena was taken aback by the vehemence in her tone. It reminded him of the Tamara he had first met— the perpetually angry version.

"I'm sorry," she said. "I've been really busy at work these last few weeks and with the classes, I've just been drained."

Kwabena didn't respond. He knew she worked hard, but there was nothing out of the ordinary that would put such a strain on her. Plus, it was Mike who had first alerted him to Tamara's lack of energy. He'd told him she'd been dozing quite a bit at work and he was worried about her. That's when Kwabena first insisted she take the pregnancy test, though she assured him she couldn't be. They had always used protection.

Kwabena did not pursue the issue further. "I brought you this," he said, handing her a plastic bag.

She opened the bag and smiled. In the bag was an authentic African dress made by Kwabena's aunt in Ghana. She had made it based on measurements they had taken last month. "Thanks, Ben," Tamara said without enthusiasm.

"Go ahead, try it on. I want you to wear it tonight."

She removed her clothes and stepped into the dress. The dress sagged on her. He'd noticed that she lost a little weight, but it was only looking at her in the droopy dress tailored to her size that he realized how much smaller she was.

"How much weight have you lost?" he asked, finding it hard to believe her change in size.

"I haven't really been checking," she answered vaguely.

He knew Tamara and he knew she had been recently obsessed about her weight. She was on the scale almost daily.

"How much?" he demanded sternly, upset that she would blatantly lie to him.

"Thirty pounds," she responded hesitantly.

"Thirty pounds in three weeks? That is way too rapid. What have you been using?"

She knew how he felt about diet pills or anything artificial. "Nothing. I've just been eating less and cutting down on the chocolate chip cookies and ice cream."

"It's not healthy to lose weight that fast. No wonder you're always tired. Maybe you should see a doctor."

"Believe me, Ben, I'm ok."

Leyoca took one look at her daughter and immediately knew something was wrong. Tamara was all decked out in her African attire, complete with matching headdress, quite appropriate for dinner at the Ethiopian restaurant. She smiled brightly when she greeted Leyoca and kept up interesting conversation with the rest of the party, yet she looked haggard. Leyoca could tell that Tamara had lost weight, but it was more than that. She was pale and she looked tired and she was jittery. The most obvious change was Tamara's lack of appetite. She hardly touched her food, and Leyoca knew Tamara had love affairs with food—any kind of food. She ate when she was depressed; she ate when she was happy. She ate when she was lonely; she ate when she was surrounded by friends. Tamara always ate.

As soon as dinner was over, Leyoca drew Tamara aside. "Tammy, you don't look well. Are you ok?"

"I'm ok. I'm just tired."

"Are you pregnant?"

Tamara exploded, "Why the hell does everyone think I'm pregnant! Good grief, Mommy, when I get pregnant I will let you know!"

Leyoca looked at her daughter, stunned. Of all the reactions, she never expected this. Something was definitely wrong. "Why the anger? Did you and Ben have a fight or something?"

Tamara sighed. "No, we didn't have a fight. I'm just tired. I've been working full time, and I'm taking classes. I guess I'm just lacking sleep."

Leyoca considered giving her a lecture on the many years she spent working full time, taking care of a child and going to school, but she decided against it. She would ask Kwabena as soon as she had the opportunity.

The opportunity presented itself the next day as she prepared to return to New York. Tamara was upstairs sleeping, though it was already noon. Kwabena was outside, preparing the pool for the coming summer season. Leyoca walked outside, looking at him whistle as he worked.

"Hey," he said.

"I wanted to talk to you about Tamara," she said, taking a few steps toward him. "I notice she is not herself lately. Is everything ok?"

Kwabena stopped what he was doing and responded, "I wish I knew. I've tried asking her, but she just snapped my head off."

"Yup, that's exactly what happened when I asked her. But she looks sick."

"I suggested that she see a doctor, but she insists that she's fine and her weight loss is by choice. I was hoping you would help me convince her to see a doctor. You know how stubborn she can be."

"I thought maybe something was wrong between the

two of you," Leyoca said, carefully observing Kwabena to see his reaction.

"Well, if there is, I am not aware of it. With the exception of her temper, we've been getting along great." There was nothing in his tone or body language that indicated dishonesty.

Kwabena gave Leyoca a hug. He said, "Tamara and I may not have had a conventional marriage initially, but things changed, and I do care about her deeply. I promise you Ley, I will take good care of Tamara."

It was almost two P.M. when Kwabena finished his work in the yard. He went upstairs to check on Tamara. He was worried. She'd had a hard time falling asleep last night when they got back from dinner and had slept until long past noon today. As he entered the room, he heard her slam the drawer of the nightstand shut.

"Hey, sleeping beauty," he said. "You're finally awake."

She looked up at him nervously. "I'm just going to take a shower and prepare lunch. Where's Mommy?"

"She already left. She had to be back in New York to catch her flight this evening."

Tamara grabbed her robe and lumbered like an old lady to the bathroom. Kwabena waited until he heard the shower running, then eased open the nightstand drawer. He was not a snoop, but he was worried. Tamara's rapid weight loss, her mean-spirited temper, the sleeplessness at nights and the tiredness during the day had him concerned. Plus she'd become secretive overnight.

Then he saw them. Buried beneath her lingerie were two giant bottles of extra-strength diet pills. They were both three-month supplies. One was still unopened, the other almost empty.

She had lied to him. Anger burned within him. He grabbed both bottles and stormed into the bathroom. Tamara had just exited the shower and was toweling dry. Her once smooth breasts and butt were nothing but sagging flesh.

"What are these?" he demanded, his voice hard, his tone harsh and angry.

She looked up at him guiltily and quickly wrapped a terry robe around herself.

"Diet pills," she answered testily and snatched them out of his hands.

"Are you crazy, woman?" he bellowed. "You've used a three-month supply in three weeks. Are you trying to kill yourself? Give them to me."

"No," she responded. "They are mine and if I want to take them to lose weight, I will."

"So why the hell did you lie to me?" he roared.

Kwabena tried snatching them away from her, but she moved them behind her back. He grabbed her roughly around her waist and wrestled the bottles away from her.

"Give them back," she cried.

He took both bottles and emptied them into the toilet bowl, then flushed. He angrily threw the empty bottles across the room.

He grabbed her and turned her toward the mirror. "Look at yourself!" he screamed. "Look at what you're doing to yourself. I don't give a damn whether you're fat or thin. I won't sit back and let you kill yourself!"

Tamara felt tears stinging her eyes. She had never seen him angry like this. His eyes were blazing mad, and it scared her. Tamara ran out of the bath and across the hall into the guest room. She locked the door and threw herself across the bed. She let the tears flow.

Kwabena picked up the two empty containers and walked into the master bedroom. He sank onto the bed. He turned the bottles over in his hands. They were the same ones that were surrounded by controversy. A consumer advocacy group was pushing for their recall, but the FDA insisted there was not enough scientific data to warrant removing them from the shelf. He didn't mean to get angry like that. He hated that he'd lost his temper, something he rarely ever did. He just couldn't let her kill herself with those stupid pills. He loved her too much to lose her like that. When would she ever understand that he loved her just the way she was?

He heard the sobs coming through the thin walls of the guest bedroom and knew she was hurt. He put his head in his hands, trying to think of a way to rectify the situation.

He knocked on the door. Tamara did not respond. He could hear her sobs, and it was tearing away at his heart. He turned the knob, but it was locked.

He knocked on the door again. "Tamara," he called softly, "open the door."

"Go away," she yelled, sniffling.

"Tammy, I'm sorry. Please open the door."

She didn't respond. He felt around atop the doorway for the flimsy key and unlocked the door. She was lying diagonally across the bed, her shoulders heaving as she sobbed.

He walked over to her and placed his hand on her back.

"I said leave me alone," she cried.

"I'm sorry, Tammy." He pulled her upright and cradled her in his arms.

Her eyes were red, her cheeks tearstained. He wanted to kiss away her tears to make everything right.

They remained like that until the sobbing subsided. "It's only diet pills…harmless diet pills. I'm only trying to lose a little weight."

"Tammy, those diet pills are not harmless," Kwabena whispered softly, stroking her hair. "My first year in college I had a classmate who was the first American on campus to make me feel welcome, and not like an outsider. We became very close friends. She always obsessed about her weight. No matter how good I told her she looked, she always thought I said so only to make her feel better about herself. She wanted to lose weight, to be slim like most of the others on campus. I saw her using diet pills. I never said anything. I saw her become skeletal thin, yet each time she looked in the mirror, she thought she was fat. I didn't say anything. Ultimately, she had a heart attack. A healthy nineteen-year-old woman with no signs or history of heart disease had died of a massive heart attack. That was the effect of the diet pills. Tammy, when I saw you using those pills, I just lost it. I cannot bear the thought of losing you too."

Tamara reached up and touched his face. "I'm sorry about your friend."

"Tammy, I want you to know I love you as you are. When I met you, you were big, and I still found you attractive, I still found you sexy, and I fell in love with you. It's not your size that makes you. Please don't feel you have to lose weight for me. I love you, and I think you are beautiful no matter your size."

Tamara wiped at her tears. "But, Ben, look at the women you dated. They are all slim, shapely and attractive. People look at us and they can't believe you and I are even together. I see the way your friends look at me. To the guys I'm the one keeping you away from their women and they are thankful. To the women, they all think it's only a matter of time before you come to your senses and put me out to pasture. Look at me. What do you even see in me?"

"I see you: a beautiful person. A loving, kindhearted, open and honest person with more integrity and honor than anyone I've ever met. I see the most wonderful woman in the world." He added with a smile, "And those double-D breasts feel really good in my hands."

Tamara chuckled softly, then looked away from him. "When I saw you with that girl on the deck at the party, I got really scared. I thought maybe you were having an affair with her. I could see there was some attraction between you. Ben, what happens when the honeymoon is over—when the novelty of me wears off and you desire a beautiful sexy person? I can't compete with these people. Not like this. Not in this body."

"Tamara, I don't know what you see when you look into the mirror, but when I look at you, I see a beautiful, desirable woman. If not, I wouldn't have fought so hard to make you mine. I love you, Tammy. I really love you, regardless of your weight. You are everything to me."

She smiled and looked up at him. His eyes communicated sincerity. "I still need to lose the weight. I need to do this for myself, for my health. Obesity kills."

"So do diet pills. Tammy, if you need to lose weight, you don't have to do it in one day. The safe way to lose weight is to lose one to two pounds per week."

"Oh gosh, Ben, you don't know how many years I've struggled with my weight. I've tried every diet. Only the pills work. They worked two years ago when I tried to slim down for my wedding."

"And you gained it back and then some. If you really want to lose weight and keep it off, we can make some lifestyle changes. I'll help you. We will eat healthier and exercise together. I promise I'll help you through it. But please promise me: no more diet pills or crash diets."

"I promise," she said with a sigh, glad he loved her.

Chapter Twenty-eight

True to his word, Kwabena did help Tamara with her weight loss, though some of his methods were unconventional. He shocked her when he first suggested that she eat all the chocolate-chip cookies and ice cream left in the kitchen in one day. She thought he was crazy, but eventually she understood the logic. By the time she was finished, she was so sick of chocolate-chip cookies and ice cream she had no desire to eat them for months to come.

They made a lot of lifestyle changes. They cooked healthier meals, ate smaller portions. It was frustrating at first, as Tamara's weight did not change much in the first few weeks. Eventually the pounds began to drop.

Then they added exercise, something she wasn't accustomed to doing, but he made it fun. They went on brisk walks in the early mornings. Several days a week, they played tennis on the community courts or racquetball at the community club. Eventually he introduced her to the treadmill, the elliptical machine and the weights in his homemade gym.

Even though Tamara was not a lover of physical activity, Kwabena made it something to look forward to. It was never the same. He enjoyed it as much as she did. And after a heavy workout, they would relax in the Jacuzzi together, making passionate love among the bubbles.

Once while working out in the gym Tamara asked, "Why do you really need to work out so hard? You don't have an ounce of fat on you."

"Let's say I have the opposite problem as you. You have to work out to lose weight, I have to work out to maintain my weight. If I don't, I lose weight and I am just too scrawny. I have an extremely high metabolism."

"I envy you."

He took an old photo from his wallet and showed her. There he was like a string bean, a cross between Steve Erkel and Screech from *Saved by the Bell*. Tamara laughed. She could not believe that this nubian god standing before her, with the ripped muscles and the chiseled body was the same guy in the photo.

"Believe it or not, this photo was taken ten years ago. This is me without body-building exercise."

"Ok, let's pump some iron!" she laughed. She'd already lost an extra ten pounds in the six weeks since they'd started the exercise program, bringing her down to one hundred and eighty pounds. Her skin had a healthy glow, and her body was firmer and a lot more muscular than the loose fat of before. Yes, she still had the cellulite and the dimples on her butt. Exercise, creams and massages performed by her own personal sexy masseuse husband would eventually bring them down. She could hardly wait to wear her bathing suit at the pool party they were hosting this coming Independence Day.

* * *

"Where is Tammy?" Leyoca asked Leticia, dropping her bags at the bottom of the stairs. Leyoca had flown in just in time for the barbecue and pool party Tamara hosted for Independence Day.

"Somewhere around the pool," Leticia responded.

Leyoca drifted past Kwabena manning the giant charcoal grill and past their many guests on the deck and stone patio before she saw Tamara at the poolside.

"Oh my God, Tammy, you look great!" Leyoca exclaimed, turning Tamara around for a better look.

Tamara wore a one-piece hot pink bathing suit covered by a sarong. Her skin was glowing. She looked like a bundle of energy—she looked healthy.

"Thanks, Mommy. You look good yourself," Tamara responded, hugging her mother.

Tamara not only looked good, she felt good. She was now down to one hundred and seventy-five pounds, still big by most people's standard, but model thin for her. She was a size fourteen. It had been years since she was a size fourteen. Her double chin and her love handles were gone. Her flab was firm, harder muscle. For once, she felt comfortable enough to wear a bathing suit around the crowds of people at the party today. Moreover, she felt less threatened by Kwabena's former girlfriends than she'd ever felt before.

It had taken a lot of effort, especially the last ten pounds. The brisk walks had evolved into power walks and then into jogs. In addition to tennis and racquetball, she'd joined the softball team at Independent Labs. She was not good at it, but neither were the academics on the team. Then Kwabena kept increasing the weights as she progressed. He was a great personal trainer. As the weather got warmer, Tamara added swimming to her regimen. At first one lap had her panting, gasping for breath. Now she had enough energy to go six laps nonstop. The hardest part was the eating. As she lost weight, she had to decrease her portion size to maintain the new weight and lose more, so she filled the gap with high-fiber low-calorie foods. It was a tough few months, but the effort paid off.

"I was really worried about you back in April when I last saw you."

Tamara smiled. "Yeah, I know. Ben was too. I tried losing weight too fast with diet pills. Ben finally knocked some sense into my head and became my personal trainer."

"He did a good job. You seem happier, healthier, more confident."

"I am happy. We've also been talking about starting a family sometime in the near future, so brace yourself."

"Now you gonna go make me a grandmother, huh? Well, at least I guess I'm old enough for that now. You know, Tammy, I'm really happy for you. I'm glad you didn't follow my advice and sell this place when I told you to."

"See, I was thinking ahead," Tamara joked, pointing at her head. "I predicted the future...that there would be a husband and children, and who knows, maybe grandchildren."

Leyoca laughed. She looked at Darlene and Chris frolicking in the water. She looked around at the children playing with their super soakers. She looked at Tamara's radiant glow and her contented smile. She was happy that Tamara found love with a man who had integrity, who loved, respected and took good care of her.

Kwabena came over and joined them. He hugged Leyoca and kissed Tamara on her lips. "Looks like you guys are having more fun than the cook."

He handed them both plates of barbecued chicken.

"Mmmmm, delicious," Tamara said, biting into the succulent chicken.

"You know how to flatter a man, don't you," Kwabena teased.

Just then she heard a group of guys behind her whistle. Tamara looked back and followed their eyes as they ogled. Walking along the side of the pool in a skimpy white bikini was Adeola. She sashayed slowly, seductively, her broad hips and narrow waist and long slim, shapely legs moving rhythmically to inaudible music. As she passed, she flashed Kwabena a seductive smile. He uneasily returned her smile, his eyes following her until she slithered catlike onto an Adirondack deck chair.

"Who's that girl?" Leyoca asked, eyeing Kwabena suspiciously.

"That's Adeola," Kwabena replied distractedly.

"Friend of yours?" Leyoca pressed on.

"You can say that. Well, I'd better get back to the grill," Kwabena said uncomfortably.

Tamara looked at Kwabena as he left. She felt a twinge of jealousy. She had no idea if Adeola was one of Kwabena's friends with benefits, but she had her suspicions. The effect Adeola had on him was unmistakable.

Chapter Twenty-nine

It was mid-August. Tamara lay on the Adirondack deck chair on the pool patio enjoying the last days of summer. The warm air felt good. The mild breeze coming from the woods and the creek behind her house felt wonderful. She looked at the reddened sky. A few rays of the setting sun filtered between the leaves of the trees and gently kissed her skin. She listened to the birds chirp peacefully as they settled in for the night. A few flew in V-formation back and forth in undulating waves before finding a tree to roost in for the night. Peaceful. At last she could now read the romance novel she'd been intending to read all summer.

It had been a hectic summer. Tamara knew Kwabena was social, but didn't realize how much until this summer. There was never a free weekend where they could relax and do nothing. His friends were always at the house. If they weren't hosting a party or some informal gathering, they were attending a party or some function. Several times he had flown out to conferences and invited her along. Other times, he'd gone alone. When he returned, Tamara would greet him, freshly showered and in a robe concealing some new tantalizing lingerie. She relished the look on his face when she slowly, seductively peeled off the robe.

Several times they'd had Kayla and Katanya over. They took the girls to the zoo, to amusement parks, to the Baltimore aquarium and other fun places. Tamara loved seeing Kwabena with children. From the way he related to Kayla, Katanya and Jordan's kids, she knew he would make a good father someday. And that topic had come up several times in the past month.

However, starting a family would have to be put on hold. In a few weeks, she would be officially enrolled in the University of Maryland computer engineering program while working full time. She would not have time to take care of a baby—at least not yet. As for reading romance novels, that would be a thing of the past...at least until the semester was over.

Tamara was deep into her historical novel, a romance between a freedman's daughter and a plantation owner's son. She was a few chapters from the end; a few chapters from finding out if the hero would sacrifice everything to marry the woman he loved or would bow to the societal pressures and marry the woman from the right family handpicked by his racist, elitist father. She could hardly wait to find out.

Tamara saw a long shadow over her. She raised her eyes and looked directly into Kwabena's handsome face. She smiled and lowered her eyes onto the printed pages, refusing to leave her book or her make-believe world of romance. She ignored him.

"Hey," Kwabena called. "This is family time. Let's put away that silly romance novel and make one of our own."

Tamara ignored him and kept on reading. Nothing was going to keep her from getting to the end of that book. He tried snatching the book. She moved it out of his grasp and continued reading.

Kwabena disappeared into the sunroom and emerged

with two glasses of ice cold lemonade. "Come on, Tammy," he tempted. "Just think of this cool drink on your tongue, quenching your thirst…Mmmmm, refreshing." He rolled the glass around on his face, licking his lips seductively.

Tamara still ignored him, her head buried deep in her novel.

He placed the drinks on the ceramic top table and took her barefoot in his hand. He ran his fingers along the soles of her size-six feet. The sensation tickled, and Tamara jumped, her foot kicking involuntarily in the air. The sudden movement knocked Kwabena off balance and he fell fully clothed into the swimming pool with a big splash.

"Oh my God, I'm sorry," Tamara cried, jumping up from the chair. She placed the wet book on the table beside the drinks and extended a hand to Kwabena. "Here, let me help you out."

Kwabena, laughing, took hold of her hand and pulled her into the water with him. She fell into the deep end, fully clothed. She let out a squeal as she hit the water, then laughed.

"You little devil," she said. "You just wanted to get me in here, didn't you?"

Kwabena laughed in return. "And now that I've got your attention…"

Before he could finish, Tamara swam off toward the shallow end of the pool. Kwabena swam behind her. She'd gone two lengths before he caught up with her. She certainly enjoyed her newfound energy and athleticism.

Laughing, he cornered her at the side of the pool. "Take it off," he urged, removing his wet clothes.

"You're nuts. The neighbors will see us."

He laughed. "That's why I put that seven-foot fence and planted that thick hedge."

"You are quite devious, aren't you?" she replied, letting him remove her wet shorts and T-shirt.

His lips covered hers, his tongue darting into her mouth, tasting the sweetness of her hidden treasures. Tamara returned his kiss, her tongue curling around his, taking his breath away. He released her and stared longingly into her eyes.

"I've got good news," he whispered breathlessly.

Tamara searched his eyes, waiting anxiously for the good news.

"We've got a date. My permanent green card, we've got a date!"

"We've got a date..." Tamara repeated, suddenly fearful of what that meant. They hadn't discussed what would happen when he got his green card, or the verbal agreement they had initially made to divorce soon after. They had always said they would cross that bridge when they got there. Well, the bridge was looming ahead of them like a mammoth in the middle of the road.

"You don't sound too ecstatic," Kwabena observed. He could hardly contain his excitement.

"I'm happy for you. I...I just...never expected it to be so soon."

"I know, but I'm just so happy it's finally coming through."

"Ben," Tamara asked hesitantly, "what about our initial agreement? What happens now?

"Mrs. Tamara Opoku, do you love me?"

"Of course I love you, Dr. Kwabena Opoku."

"Then nothing happens. Nothing changes, except maybe a couple of kids down the road."

"Oh, Ben." Tammy clung to him. She kissed him passionately. Every hair on her body stood at attention. He kissed her face, ears and neck, his lips and tongue licking, nibbling and teasing the hollow of her throat. His hands caressed her legs and bottom, drawing her close to him. His mouth sought her breast, as his tongue eagerly licked and teased at her erect nipples.

Tammy gasped, feeling his hard arousal pressing into her. She let her hands grasp his bottom, feeling his muscles. She arched her back invitingly against the side of the pool as he stroked her, making her moist.

"Oh, Tammy," Kwabena breathed against her wet skin. "I'd never dream of leaving you."

He placed his hand beneath the crook of her knees, gently spreading her legs, and entered her. He closed his eyes, feeling her warm moisture envelope his manhood. Slowly they moved against each other, stoking the embers of their desire. Soon passion overwhelmed them, and Kwabena plunged deeper into her. Rapidly grinding against each other, they moaned, grunted and groaned as they soared to heights of pleasure. With a burst of fulfillment, their names rolling off each other's tongues, they climaxed together. They held each other at the edge of the pool, the sunlight fading into darkness, the warm water washing away the sweat of their passion, their naked bodies crushed against each other. They were satiated. They both knew there was a lifetime of love ahead of them.

Chapter Thirty

Adeola extended one long shapely leg out of the car and onto the pavement. The workmen across the parking lot whistled. It was a reaction she expected and loved. She was beautiful, and she knew it. She slid her curvaceous body out of her car and glided across the parking lot. She ignored the catcalls. Another day, she might have allowed herself to feel flattered, but not today. Today she was on a mission to get what rightfully belonged to her.

She walked through the maze of corridors leading to Independent Laboratories. She smiled as guys ogled at her and women watched her with envy, wishing they could look like her. Her straight skirt ended just above the knees and was just long and loose enough to be businesslike, yet short and fitted enough to tantalize men with her long legs. She strutted like a model on the catwalk, though her reign as Miss Nigeria ended almost a decade ago.

"Hello," she said to an administrative assistant. "Where can I find Mrs. Opoku?"

The lady looked at her blankly. "Pardon me, ma'am?" she responded politely.

"I'm looking for Tamara Opoku."

"Oh, Tammy," the lady exclaimed. "Nobody uses last names here at the labs. She's in room 426…two doors down on the left."

Adeola thanked the lady and sashayed off. As she entered the room, all heads turned. Men—whether they were Chinese, Korean, Indian, black or white—looked at her lustfully. She felt like telling them to wipe the drool from their mouths. Yet she reveled in the attention. It was such a shame the person she wanted that attention from wasn't giving it…at least not right now. But that would change very soon.

"Hi, Tamara," Adeola said in her deep, throaty, thick Nigerian accent.

Tammy was sitting behind a bank of computers and deep in concentration. She had been reading an e-mail from Kwabena. He'd arrived at the conference in Pasadena, California, safely and was preparing to give a talk sometime later that evening. She looked up, startled. "Oh, hi, Adeola. Mike is out to lunch right now. He should be back shortly."

"I'm not looking for Mike. I'm looking for you."

Tamara looked at her puzzled. "Me?"

"I was in the area and I thought I'd stop by and maybe we can do lunch?"

"Lunch?" Tamara asked dumbfounded. Of all Kwabena's female friends, Adeola had been the coldest toward her. Tamara had met her only a few times: that night at the party at Chris's house, twice when she dropped by the lab to see Mike, at a few of the parties they'd attended during the summer and Independence Day, when she'd made her grand entrance at the pool party. Each time Adeola had been cold and aloof toward her. *Maybe she's finally beginning to accept me,* Tamara thought hopefully.

"Ok, I see you're busy. I'll take a raincheck. Maybe we can do this some other time when I return from California."

"Oh, no. No, it's ok. I can do lunch now. I was just a little surprised to see you here. Where would you like to go?"

"How about the café downstairs?"

"Sure." Tamara grabbed her purse and followed Adeola's lead. Tamara observed Adeola's stunning beauty and the effect she had on men with a tiny twinge of envy. Heads turned as she glided gracefully along, just a step ahead of Tamara. Men tripped over themselves opening doors for her. Beside her, Tamara felt diminutive.

They sat outside at a small table and made small talk while eating chef's salads. All the while Tamara wondered what the purpose of the visit was. Finally, unable to contain herself Tamara asked, "You work near here?"

"Oh no. I work in Washington, D.C. I just thought we'd have a little celebratory lunch, you know."

Tamara was perplexed. "What are we celebrating?"

"Kwabena's permanent green card. The wait is over. That is worth celebrating, isn't it?"

"Who told you he got it?" As far as Tamara knew, only Chris, Edebe and Mike knew he'd received the green card.

Adeola smiled sweetly. "Why, Kwabena told me, of course." She sighed. "Aren't you relieved? Now you can get your divorce and go on with your life."

"Divorce?" Tamara's antenna went up. Something did not feel right about this conversation. "Who said we're getting a divorce?"

"Kwabena. That was part of the agreement, wasn't it? Now he can get on with his life and you can go back to yours. I'm just so happy that it finally came through. It's been a long year."

Tamara was annoyed. "I have no idea what you are talking about, but Ben and I are not getting a divorce."

"Really? That's not what he told me." She slipped an envelope out of her bag and pushed it across the table toward Tamara. Tamara opened the envelope and her heart sank. In it were divorce papers. The only things missing were the dates and the signatures.

Tamara swallowed the lump in her throat. "What's in it for you?" she asked quietly.

Adeola smiled sweetly. "He didn't tell you, did he? We're engaged. We've been for a while."

She held out her left hand, showing Tamara the large pear-shaped diamond. It was almost identical to the one he'd given her, except for the size—it was twice as large. Adeola removed the ring, and like she would a friend, showed Tamara the inscription: *Kwabena* ♥ *Adeola*.

Tamara knew Kwabena had been engaged sometime in the past, but he never told her it was Adeola. She looked at Adeola's physical appearance, her confidence and sophisticated poise, and Tamara's heart sank. How could she ever measure up? Was that why he never told her about Adeola? Was it because he never ended the relationship? Was it because he still found her attractive? But then, who wouldn't?

Tamara's mind was in turmoil. She remembered him saying that he and his fiancée didn't work out, which was why he'd had uncommitted relationships, and for a brief moment, she felt comforted. "Our marriage may have started out as a marriage of convenience, but it changed. We have a real marriage."

Adeola laughed her throaty laugh. "Tammy, I'm sorry you had to be caught up in this, but it's never over between Ben and me. In fact, it was my idea that he marry for the green card. You see, dear, I work for the Nigerian government at the embassy. I've been in this country for a long time, and I have no way of becoming a U.S. citizen except maybe through marriage. But you know how fickle African governments can be…One party's in power, a coup and another is in power…then I'll be out of a job. I really do not want to go back to Nigeria. So we figured Ben would get his green card and then marry me and I get mine that way. When that little incident with his mentor happened, we realized we had to get it quickly. Marriage to a citizen was the only option. I was with him all the while. Who do you think answered the phone when you called to tell him about the interview? We just never anticipated that whole temporary green card issue and him having to move in with you. And I certainly didn't expect you to seduce him."

"What! I never seduced him. I was a virgin when we married."

"Oh yes, we all know that. Do you think for one minute I thought your dirty dancing after announcing your virginity to everybody at the party was an accident? You planned it quite carefully, didn't you? What man could resist deflowering a twenty-six-year-old virgin?"

Tamara bit back tears. All her insecurities of the past resurfaced. How could Kwabena make love to her, tell her he loved her and promise to be with her forever when he had plans to marry another woman? How could he make people believe that she seduced him? She should have known that a man like Kwabena could not really love her. No matter how much weight she lost, she could not compare with the women he dated in the past. She wasn't tall, slim, or long-legged. She didn't have a face or body that turned heads and made men drool. She didn't dress in sophisticated designer clothes or glide around gracefully.

"Look, Tammy, Kwabena is a man, and as you must know by now, he has a voracious sexual appetite," Adeola said to Tamera's silence. "That's why in some parts of our country we still practice polygamy. I wasn't ok with him messing around, especially when I caught him in bed with my friend. I wasn't ok with him sleeping with you. That was not a part of the plan. But when you love somebody, you learn to forgive and overlook their indiscretions. We've been together over eight years now. But you know what? Each time he strayed, he came right back to me. You know why? Because we love and understand each other."

Tamara was quiet for a long time. Jared's deceit and ultimate betrayal came fresh to her mind. She'd thought Kwabena was different. She had trusted him. To have him use her like Jared had was more than she could bear. "I have to go back to work now," she said quietly. She was not going to let this woman see her cry.

"By the way," Adeola said with a smile. "I love your home, especially the master suite. Pink satin sheets are a little feminine for a man, don't you think?"

Tamara's jaw dropped. She felt faint. "You...you were in my house...in my bed?"

Adeola smiled triumphantly. She got up and looked at her watch. "I'd love to stay and chat some more, but I've got a plane to catch. I'm heading to Pasadena for the weekend."

Tamara dragged herself upstairs, locked herself in the restroom and cried her eyes out. A while later she popped her head into Mike's office. She was supposed to meet with him after lunch to go over some data she was presenting for the lab meeting next Tuesday.

"Mike," she said hoarsely, "can we reschedule our meeting for Monday? I'm not feeling very well."

He looked up at her. "Sure," he replied, hiding his shock at her pale appearance. "Besides a lunch seminar at Johns Hopkins, I'm wide open on Monday. Take the rest of the day off. You can take tomorrow if you need to."

"Thanks," she said. Then she added, "How long was Ben engaged to Adeola?"

Mike, who had already returned to the paperwork on his desk, answered distractedly without looking up, "Three, maybe four years."

Tamara drove home like a madwoman, tears streaming down her face. *How could he do this to me? How could he? How could he use me like that?*

She wished Jordan was there for her to call, but he and his family had gone to Jamaica for a three-week vacation. She didn't want to talk to her mother or any other member of her family.

She lay on the bed and cried. Then with a sudden burst of energy, she began removing his clothes from her closet and dumping them into garbage bags. With each item of clothing she removed, she cursed Kwabena in a language not even a drunken sailor would use. She knew exactly what she had to do. Jared had taken her money, but Kwabena had robbed her of her soul.

Chapter Thirty-one

Kwabena's heart beat wildly in anticipation as he unlocked the front door. Oh, how he'd missed Tamara! He could only imagine what she was wearing now. The last time he'd returned from a conference, she had greeted him in an outfit that was nothing short of dental floss. Her thong had more in common with a slingshot than an undergarment. That time, they'd never made it past the stairs. Right now he wanted to hold her, touch her and taste her. He could hardly wait.

"Honey, I'm home," he called loudly. Instead of Tamara dressed in a satin robe, he was greeted by boxes piled up in the foyer. His voice echoed in the large room. He looked around perplexed. *What in the world is going on here?* "Tammy?"

He heard low voices coming from the library. He strode briskly to the library, worried. There was a strange foreboding—a little voice telling him something was desperately wrong. As he opened the door, he saw Tamara and a young African-American woman sitting at her desk, deep in discussion.

They both stood as he entered. "This is Janelle Jackson," Tamara said coldly. "She is a lawyer, and she will be handling our divorce."

Kwabena looked at her, surprised. "This is a joke, right?" he asked. But from the steely expression on Tamara's face, he knew she was serious.

"No, it's not a joke. This was part of our agreement, and I'm just keeping my end of the bargain. Your stuff is already packed. I want you out of my house today."

Janelle Jackson showed him some papers and began going over the information with him. Kwabena did not hear a word she said. He did not understand what was up with Tamara or why she was acting this cold. He looked at her, but she refused to make eye contact.

"Miss Jackson, I need a moment with my wife please…alone."

Janelle looked at them, nodded and left the library. As soon as she stepped out, Kwabena asked, "Tammy, what is this all about?"

"It's about the marriage of convenience we had. You've now gotten your green card and it's time to move on. I won't keep you from your life any longer."

"What are you talking about? I thought we agreed that our marriage was more than one of convenience? What's gotten into you, Tammy?"

"Nothing. You need your freedom to get along with your life, and I'm giving it to you. Now please sign the papers, give me my money and leave."

"Tammy?" he called. That was not the Tamara he knew. Even in the worst of times she was never cold or calculating. She was always passionate, be it in anger or in desire. "Talk to me. We promised to be open and honest with each other. Tell me what's bothering you. You can't make a drastic decision like this without first talking to me."

"Honest? Open? Do you even know the meaning of those words? Just take your things and go back to your Nigerian beauty queen. Adeola's waiting for you. You knew we never had a chance in hell."

He knew he should have told her earlier about Adeola and their past relationship, but he wanted to protect her. He'd recognized early on that Tamara was insecure about her physical appearance and he didn't want her to feel threatened by his ex-fiancée. He didn't want her comparing herself to Adeola or anyone else for that matter. Yes, Adeola was physically attractive, but Tamara was twice the woman she could ever be. He took a deep breath and walked toward his wife. He just wanted to hold her in his arms. "Tammy, Adeola and I are ancient history. We were engaged a long time ago, and it's over between us."

"Is that why you slept with her in my house?" It took every ounce of energy she had to hold back the tears welling in her eyes. As much as she wanted to keep her cool, she couldn't. "How could you, Ben? How could you? You knew how I felt about you. You knew I trusted you. How could you?"

"Tammy, that happened before our relationship changed." Kwabena was not a person to cry, but he felt tears stinging his eyes. He was losing the one person he loved, and he knew no amount of explaining would convince her to stay. His world was turning upside down and there was little he could do change that.

"Tamara, I'm not signing those papers. Not as long as I think there is a chance for us."

"There is no chance, Ben. We had an agreement, and I'm sticking to it. I want a divorce. I want out of this marriage."

"Tamara, if you can look me in the eyes and tell me this marriage was nothing more than a business deal, if you honestly can tell me you don't love me, I'll sign the papers."

Tamara swallowed. She knew this was the hardest thing she would ever do in her life. She concentrated on a spot somewhere behind his shoulder and spoke, "Kwabena, I don't love you, Muti man—Yes, I finally figured out the meaning, you're the stud aren't you? Now just give me my damned money and go."

Kwabena swallowed hard. How could she even say that? He knew she was lying, yet he was crushed. He called Janelle back into the library and asked for the papers. Slowly, painfully, he signed all the designated pages. It would be an uncontested divorce. No strings, no alimony, no division of property.

He turned to her as he exited the library, his hands clenching and unclenching in an effort to hold back tears. "I'll be back for my stuff tomorrow. I…I…never mind." He turned on his heel and left.

Tamara stood quietly until she heard his car pull out of the driveway. Then she broke down in tears. Janelle held her, letting her cry on her shoulder until Tamara was spent. As she packed up her stuff to leave, she handed Tamara the signed divorce papers.

"Maybe you should hang on to these instead of filing them until you think it through. You guys don't need a divorce. You need marital counseling."

Chapter Thirty-two

It was a month since Kwabena had signed the divorce papers. Tamara had never felt more alone. The house felt big and empty. Her footsteps on the ceramic floor of the kitchen echoed cavernously. Her bed was cold and unwelcoming. Her den was lifeless and empty. She missed Kwabena and the void he filled in her life. It seemed his six-foot-four frame filled the house while he was there. His deep baritone filled the space. His laughter brought warmth and sunshine and made her house a home. Now that he was gone, it was just empty space. She was depressed. Yet she trudged on. She had her job and her classes. Her mother, Aunt Leticia, Darlene and Ebony all wanted to know what happened between Kwabena and her. Her answer was always the same: "He got his green card and I got my money." Simple.

But there was nothing simple about Tamara's life. Her period was late—six weeks late. She had always had irregular periods, but had never missed one for so long. With trembling hands she held up the digital pregnancy test.

"Oh God, no," she cried. "This can't be."

She closed her eyes and screamed silently. She knew exactly when it happened. It was that day in the pool in August. Everything had been spontaneous. They had always been careful about birth control. But that evening in the swimming pool they had let their passions guide them.

She looked at the test and stared hopelessly at the floor. For the first time in her life she felt lost and out of control. She had no idea what to do.

Kwabena sat at the bar in Chili's drinking tequila. He had carefully chosen this bar, because he did not want to run into any of his friends. He didn't feel very social tonight—hadn't felt social for the past month. It had been the worst month of his life. He missed Tamara so much. He tried to fill the void with work. It made for a very productive career, but a very achy heart. He tried so hard to get her out of his mind, but he couldn't. He thought of her night and day. He wondered how she was doing. He called a few times, but she never picked up the phone or returned his messages.

A woman came and sat next to him on the bar stool. "Hey, handsome," she said seductively. Kwabena looked at her. She was easy on the eyes, but he had no interest—and he sure didn't even feel like talking.

He nodded distractedly and looked away.

She didn't get the hint. She continued, talking and flirting. He wished she would just shut up and leave. Instead she invited him to some club she was attending later.

"I'm married," he said just to get her to leave him alone. It was not quite true, but it wasn't a lie either. His divorce to Tamara wasn't final. For some reason the papers were never filed. Yet Tamara refused to speak to him or have anything to do with him.

The lady was undeterred. "I don't see a wedding ring.

Plus," she swirled her drink with her finger, licking it seductively, "your wife doesn't have to know."

Kwabena sighed, silently wishing her away. Just then he heard a child's voice. "Hi, Uncle Ben."

He looked down and there was Devon standing by his stool. *Saved by the kid.* "Hello, big man." Kwabena smiled, scooping him up in a giant bear hug. From the corner of his eye he could see the woman slither off her stool, drink in hand, and move to the other side of the bar. He breathed a sigh of relief.

"Why don't you live with Auntie Tammy anymore?"

He smiled. "You ask too many questions. Where are your parents?"

Jordan and the whole brood joined him. They greeted each other stiffly.

"How are you doing?" Kwabena asked Jordan.

"Everything's fine." Jordan looked at him uncomfortably for a while. Since Tamara had told him what happened, he had lost respect for Kwabena.

"How's Tammy doing?"

Becky looked at Jordan. She knew he was angry at Kwabena. When they returned from Jamaica, a very distraught and broken Tamara had told Jordan and Becky about the affair and the divorce. It left Jordan so irate, Becky had to remind him that every coin had two sides. Becky said, "I'll take the kids to the car. Why don't you two catch up on old times?"

As soon as Becky left, Jordan responded coldly, "She's doing fine."

"Be honest with me, Jordan. How is she really doing? Does she need anything?"

"If you're so concerned about her well-being, why don't you call her and ask her how she's doing?"

"I've tried. She never returns my calls."

"And justifiably so."

"What did she tell you?"

"Exactly what happened."

"Jordan, maybe I deserve what happened, but I still at least should be given a chance to explain things to her."

"What do you want me to do?"

"Talk to her for me."

"If you are asking me to be a mediator between you and Tammy, don't expect me to be impartial. Tammy and I grew up together. When I came to this country scrawny and ugly, the butt of every discriminatory joke, Tammy became my friend when no one else would. She is a sister to me. If I have to choose sides, I'll be sitting ringside as Tammy's manager, if not in the ring fighting right beside her."

Kwabena looked at him. "I understand and I'm not asking you to mediate anything. I just want to talk to her."

"What for? To hurt her again? For a highly intelligent man, you are the biggest ass I've ever met. How could you trade in what you had with Tammy for a piece of tail? When you are married, you have to learn to keep your pants zipped. Regardless of how attractive Adeola may be or what history you had together, you had no right sleeping with her while married to Tammy."

"You don't understand."

"What's there to understand?

"Adeola and I have had a very complex relationship—one where fidelity on either side was not often a top priority. Things didn't work out between us. My career wasn't taking off fast enough, I didn't have the kind of status she wanted, so she left. That was three years ago. A year later she moved to Washington, D.C. and we started dating noncommitally. Yes, it continued for a short time after the green card marriage, but, Jordan, once Tammy and I decided to pursue a relationship, I ended it with Adeola. Anything that happened between me and Adeola happened before Tammy and I became intimate."

Jordan studied him for a long time. He appeared to be telling the truth. He'd never known Kwabena to be a liar, but Kwabena was not an open book. As Tamara described him, he was honest, not open. Jordan shook his head. "I could speak to her, but don't expect miracles. You hurt her really badly."

Kwabena nodded. "I know, man, and I wish I didn't."

Jordan shook Kwabena's hand. "Peace," he said and left.

"Tammy!" Jordan called, entering the foyer. He had rung her doorbell multiple times but got no answer, so he'd used his key. He knew she was home because her Lexus was parked in the driveway.

He was concerned. He knew Tamara was depressed and hoped she didn't do something stupid to harm herself. He rushed up the stairs two at a time to the master bedroom. As he opened the door, he saw Tamara sitting on the edge of the bed, staring in shock at three pregnancy test sticks.

"Tammy," he called softly, "are you ok?" He sat on the edge of the bed beside her.

She nodded forlornly. "I'm pregnant," she whispered, sobbing.

"Are you sure?"

"All these sticks can't be wrong," she said.

"Well, you certainly have it covered," he teased, holding her comfortingly. He let her cry on his shoulder, handing her a tissue to dry her eyes when she regained control of herself.

"I don't know what to do. I don't know if I can even handle a baby alone."

"Tammy, you don't have to have this baby alone. I'm sure Ben will help you take care of it…Ben is the father, right?"

Tamara gave him a dirty look. He smiled sheepishly. "Just checking. Some people do crazy things when they're hurt."

"I can't tell Ben. What would I do? Walk up to him and say, 'Hey, honey I divorced you, but now I'm having your baby'?"

Jordan laughed. Even in pain Tamara had a sense of humor. "I saw Kwabena today. Tammy, he still loves you, and he wants you back."

"He cheated on me. He and Adeola belong together. We only had a business deal that went bad when I fell in love with him. Jordan, he used me when he didn't have to."

"Tammy, Kwabena didn't use you. Adeola lied to you." He explained Ben's story.

Tamara looked away. "Jordan, I can't tell Ben about this baby. Promise me you won't tell him please."

"Why? He has a right to know if he's going to be a father."

"You don't understand. If I tell him, he will want to do what is right. He will come back for the sake of the baby. We will have another marriage of convenience.

Jordan, I don't want to be married because of a green card or money or a baby. They are all the wrong reasons. I want to be married because he loves me and wants to spend the rest of his life with me. Please, Jordan, promise me you won't tell him."

Jordan sighed. Even though he thought she was being idiotic, he understood her logic. "Look, Tammy, I think you're making a huge mistake. You and Kwabena belong together. He deserves to know about his kid. But I will respect your wishes and I won't tell him. However, I'll harass you until you do."

Tamara smiled. She knew she could count on Jordan.

Chapter Thirty-three

Leyoca looked at her daughter fussing about the kitchen. She had gained a few pounds since she'd last seen her, but Tamara was still much smaller than a year ago. She looked good physically: glowing skin tone, thicker hair. But her eyes were sad. Leyoca shook her head. She wanted her daughter to be happy, not pretend to be having a ball preparing a huge Thanksgiving dinner for a few people. Leyoca had invited her daughter to San Diego for Thanksgiving this year. It would have been only the two of them, since Carl was in West Africa shooting a documentary. But Tamara had resisted, insisting that Leyoca come to Maryland for Thanksgiving.

This year was nothing like last year. The weather was unseasonably warm and the guests were few. Only Leticia, Ebony, her boyfriend and the kids, Darlene and Chris, Leyoca and Tamara were there for Thanksgiving. Jordan and his brood were off visiting Becky's family in North Carolina.

It was a nice dinner, with all American food, except fried plantains, which Tamara's unborn baby craved. Besides Jordan, she'd told no one she was pregnant. Compared to last Thanksgiving with the snow storm and the blackout and dramatic turn of events, this year was uneventful. Everyone reminisced fondly about last year's Thanksgiving. For Tamara it was a painful reminder of what she would forever miss.

The only life-changing event that evening occurred just as dessert was served. Chris got up, looked fondly at Darlene and then addressed the family.

"Last Thanksgiving, I had a little accident," he said, smiling fondly. "I literally bumped into Darlene and lost my heart. Since then I have grown to love Darlene with all my heart. It was the best thing that ever happened to me."

Tamara smiled, remembering the huge mess in her kitchen. Darlene looked at him with starry eyes.

Christopher looked at Darlene tenderly. "Darlene, you've shown me what it's like to be loved and I can't imagine what life would be like without you. You are the star that I wish upon at night. You are the voice of love in my heart. You are the whisper of the breeze in the trees. You are the silver moon glistening on the ocean. You are the words to the song that I sing. You are everything to me."

A lone tear slid down Darlene's cheek as Chris moved from the table, took her hand and got down on one knee. He continued speaking in a soft, melodious tone. "Darlene, I love you and I want to spend the rest of my life with you. With your family's blessing, Darlene, will you marry me?"

Darlene smiled through tears, holding her hand over her heart. In an almost inaudible voice filled with emotion, Darlene whispered, "Yes, Chris, oh yes!"

Tamara felt tears well up in her eyes. She wasn't certain whether they were tears of joy or sorrow. She was happy for them, but she couldn't deny the ache in her heart or the yearning for Kwabena to be there at this moment. It was a moment she felt they should have shared together.

After everyone left, Tamara retired to her room, but could not sleep. She heard her mother next door packing for her flight the next day. Quietly she slipped through the French doors and out onto the balcony. She looked at the darkened woods beyond her backyard and the myriad stars twinkling silently in the sky. Tears came to her eyes. How many nights had she and Kwabena sat in those same papasan chairs and talked, or just silently held each other while listening to the night creatures.

She sipped some herbal tea left over from Kwabena's batch so many months ago. She ached for him. Scenes of last year's Thanksgiving flitted through her mind. She remembered how they sat with his arms around her by the fireplace while his parents told Anansi stories. She remembered when he walked out of the bathroom, and she'd seen him naked for the first time and had been thankful that the dimness of the candlelight hid her embarrassed blushing. She remembered how he touched her hair and braided it; his hands were so soft and gentle. She smiled as she recalled how she dressed up in her sexy nightgown for him only to find him asleep. It was going to be a hard year.

"You miss him, don't you?"

Tamara looked up and saw her mother standing in the doorway. She wore a terry robe over flannel pajamas, and very comfy slippers. Her mother stepped out onto the balcony. "The holidays and anniversaries are always the hardest," she continued.

Tamara smiled and sipped on her tea. "No use crying over spilled milk, right?"

"Not when you can do something about it. Do you still love him?"

Tammy nodded in response.

"Go to him. Tell him how you feel."

"I can't go back, Mommy. We had a deal and it's over."

"I'm not buying that. What you had was a real marriage. And I know Ben still loves you and wants you. You're just not giving him the chance."

"And how would you know that?"

"I had dinner with him last night," Leyoca answered, measuring her words carefully.

She knew Tamara hated when she meddled in her life, but she felt Tamara wasn't telling her the truth about the divorce, so she had Kwabena pick her up at the airport and they went to dinner. Leyoca, as usual, wasted no time in getting to the point. She'd asked him what happened between him and Tamara. He had given the same answer about the business-deal nonsense, which she told him was crap. That's when he admitted he screwed up. Leyoca always knew, once a man admitted he screwed up it involved another woman. "Is it the lady in the white bathing suit from the barbecue?" she'd asked, remembering the feeling she'd gotten after seeing his reaction to her. He nodded yes. Then he explained their history and the reason Tamara kicked him out. She finally asked him if he still loved her daughter. He looked her in the eyes and said, "I never stopped loving Tammy. I don't think I know how."

Tamara looked up at her mother, who leaned against the banister. "Did he tell you he cheated on me?"

"Tamara, the two of you weren't involved at the time, even if you were legally married. I'd hardly call that cheating."

Tamara sucked in her breath. "I know. But that's not the whole story. They didn't end their relationship after we became intimate, Mommy. She told me that their relationship never ended."

"Tamara, have you considered for one moment that this girl was lying to you, manipulating you so that you would drive him right into her open arms?"

Tamara looked over at the woods. It was as if the weight of the earth crushed her. She had thrown away her marriage because she didn't trust Kwabena enough. She sighed deeply, letting the crisp air sting her nostrils. "It's too late now. I didn't believe him when he tried to explain it to me. I just didn't trust him anymore. You know what sucks big time, Mommy? I'm pregnant. I'm alone and pregnant."

"Is it Kwabena's?"

Tamara shot her mother a dirty look. Like Jordan, Leyoca backtracked immediately. "Tammy, people do irrational things when they feel hurt and betrayed— like jumping in bed with another man."

"Well, I didn't, nor did I have the desire to. Mommy, I'm so scared."

Her mother went over and hugged her. "It's going to be alright. Does Kwabena know?"

Tamara shook her head.

"You have to tell him. You have to make him a part of the baby's life."

"Mommy, I can't tell him. I can't. I'll just raise my baby alone."

"Tammy, don't be irrational. Being a single parent is

the most difficult thing for a person. I'm not thinking just about for you, but for the baby."

"Granny did it, you did it, Auntie Let did it, Jordan's mother did it, Ebony is doing it."

"Tammy, we did it because we had no choice in the matter. Momma was a single mother because Pa died when we were little. Leticia did it because Darlene and Ebony's father landed in prison. As for Ebony, if single motherhood was her choice, she wouldn't have La'Mont in court so often for child support."

"What about you Mommy? What's your story?"

Leyoca looked away. A pained expression came over her face. She swallowed hard and spoke, her voice barely above a whisper. "I was not a single mom by choice. During our teens, Let and I were as different as night and day. She was vivacious, promiscuous and full of life. I was strictly academic—best in my class, on the debating team, you name it. In regards to sex, I took the moral high ground: no sex before marriage. I even led a group that used that as our mantra—celibate by choice. But then I met Charles. He was not some little school-boy. He was a college man—a senior at Georgetown University, a member of the debating society. He had light skin with straight hair, as close as one could come to being white without being white. He came from a family with enough money to send him to Georgetown University. I fell for him hook, line and sinker. When Momma met him and told me he was too mature for me, I got angry with her. I was in love. Then I invited him to my junior prom. I was so excited. I had my hand-some, though short, college man. After the prom he took me back to his fraternity for a party. Everything was going well until he took me up to his bedroom. He wanted me to have sex with him. At first I said no, but when he was finished telling me how much he loved me, how much this act would complete us and make us one, I was willing to do anything he asked. So I willingly tossed aside my convictions and I made love to him. A month later when I discovered I was pregnant, I told him, certain he would marry me and we'd live happily ever after. He gave me some money and told me to get rid of it. He didn't want anything to do with me or a baby. That's when I discovered he was engaged to a woman who, in his words 'could help him get along in life.'"

"Oh, Mommy, I'm so sorry you had to go through that," Tamara whispered, becoming the comforter now.

"I was so ashamed, I quit school. I couldn't face my friends. I only told Momma what had happened to me a few days before she died. You were already two years old then."

"Where is he now? Charles."

"He's your congressman, in Washington, D.C."

Tamara held her mother's hand comfortingly. She finally understood why she was so mistrustful of men. No wonder Carl had pursued her for so many years before she finally agreed to marry him.

Leyoca looked Tamara straight in the eyes. "Tamara, don't think for a moment it is easy being a single mother, even if you have help. Momma died thinking she failed us because we both got pregnant and dropped out of high school. On her deathbed she told Leticia and me that even though we made mistakes in life, we could still go on to accomplish whatever we wanted to and be good mothers. Leticia and I interpreted it differently. I sacrificed spending time with you and got an education and financial security. Let sacrificed financial security to spend time with her children. I failed you as a mother, because though I provided for you, I was never there in person for you." She squeezed Tamara's hand. "Please, Tammy, let Ben be a part of his child's life."

"Oh, Mommy, I don't know if I can. But please, don't tell him. This is something I have to do myself, when I'm comfortable with it. I'm afraid if I tell him, he'll come back strictly for the sake of the baby and not because he loves me. I can't do another marriage of convenience."

Chapter Thirty-four

Kwabena sat in a darkened corner at the far side of the bar. Tonight he wanted to get drunk. He wanted to drown his memories in a bottle of wine; no, make that scotch. He wanted to forget how she looked, how she felt in his arms, the strawberry scent of her hair. He wanted to forget what happened a year ago today. He wanted to forget the song they danced to beneath the tropical plants of the indoor garden. He wanted to forget the sound of the Jacuzzi bubbling invitingly, or the sound of Kenny G's saxophone, or the scent of the lavender votive candles. He wanted to forget how she felt lying in his arms as they'd made love. He wanted to forget what happened this time last year when Tamara gave herself to him.

He indicated to the bartender to replenish his drink. "Scotch straight up."

Thanksgiving had been tough. He spent it at Mike's house, but his mind was elsewhere. All the talk turned to last year and the snow storm, the blackout and impromptu sleepover. He had taken it in stride, smiling, laughing as if it didn't bother him. But deep down the memories were painful, because he knew he would never have that feeling again. Today, the Saturday after Thanksgiving, was worst. The memories were all too vivid, the loneliness too painful.

"That bad, huh?"

"Uh huh," he responded without looking up. He didn't have to. He smelled her before he saw her: her signature scent—Elizabeth Taylor's White Diamonds. Seemed she bathed in it.

"Anniversaries and holidays are always the hardest," she said, slipping onto the stool next to him. She ordered a strawberry daiquiri. "Make it a virgin."

"What are you doing here, Adeola?" Kwabena asked.

"I guess misery loves company," she responded in her throaty voice.

He ordered another scotch. "What do you know about misery, besides how to inflict it?" He downed the scotch in one gulp and ordered another.

"I guess I know what it feels like to want something really bad and know that I can't have it, because I didn't appreciate it enough to protect it when I had it."

He shrugged, drained his glass and signaled the bartender for another drink.

"You must be quite ecstatic," he said, slurring his words slightly. "It happened just as you predicted, or is it orchestrated? I'm free, I'm single, I'm disengaged. You must be quite proud of your handiwork."

"I like you better when you're sober. You're a miserable drunk.

"So what?" He signaled the bartender again.

Adeola waved the bartender away. "He's had enough." She asked the bartender for the check and got up from her stool. "Come on, let's get you home. You drink any more, you'll die of alcohol poisoning."

Kwabena slapped down a bill on the bar, got up unsteadily and reached for his car keys. Adeola snatched them out of his grasp. "I'll drive you home. Friends don't let friends drink and drive."

"What do I do with my car?"

"I'll give you a ride back tomorrow to get your car. Let's go."

The first thing Kwabena did when he got home was fix himself a stiff drink. Adeola came up to him and removed the drink from his hands. She poured it down the sink and fixed him a cup of strong coffee.

"You think you're my mother, do you?" he asked.

Adeola smiled. She didn't need him drunk for what she wanted. Tipsy maybe, but definitely not drunk. "I'll go freshen up," she said and slipped into his bedroom.

Kwabena leaned against the couch, sipping his coffee. *Maybe drinking is not the answer. It certainly didn't make me forget anything.* He was still standing there when Adeola stepped out of the bedroom dressed in red lacy boy-shorts thong panties and a matching bra.

She walked up to him slowly, sensually, smiling seductively and placed a long shapely leg between his thighs. Without a word, she unbuttoned his shirt, dropping it on the couch behind him. She reached up and kissed him, caressing his chest in the process.

Maybe this is what I need, Kwabena thought. There's nothing like a hot, sexy woman to take your mind off another.

He returned her kiss hungrily, grabbing her exposed backside and pulling her close to him. It had been a long time since he'd been with a woman. Three months to be exact. Even though he'd had more than his fair share of willing women throw themselves at him, he didn't have the desire. All he could think of was Tamara and how lonely she must have been without him. Hell, he had more friends than he could count, and he was lonely without her. He sighed. He wished Tamara had at least returned one of his calls or e-mails. Well, he rationalized, it's not like we're together anymore.

"Mmmmmmm," he moaned as Adeola took his hand and led him to the bedroom.

Tamara drove slowly, uncertain how she was going to do this. She had decided since talking to her mother that she would tell Kwabena, and whatever the consequences were she would live with it. She mentally rehearsed what she was going to say to him. She would admit that she had misjudged him and allowed herself to be manipulated. She would admit that she'd been wrong in not giving him a chance to explain himself. She would apologize for mistrusting him and ask his forgiveness, ask for a second chance. If he was willing to give her a chance to work things out between them, she would tell him about the baby; but only if he gave her a second chance.

She pulled onto the little two-lane road lined with leafless oaks. Her heart raced as she approached his condo. She scanned the neatly parked cars at the side of the road for Kwabena's Civic but didn't see it. The only car parked in his assigned space was a red Acura Integra with a Nigerian flag hanging on the rearview mirror. Maybe he's not home.

She double parked next to the Integra and waited, deciding what to do. Though his car was absent, his bedroom and living room lights were on. Then she saw him through the partially open blinds, standing in the middle of his living room, sipping from a cup. Tamara's heartbeat quickened. She felt her face flush. She prayed for the courage to do what she needed to do.

Tamara closed her eyes. When she opened them, she

saw the almost naked woman approach him. Adeola! She saw them kiss and walk toward the bedroom. Tamara's heart sank. She was crushed. Any hope she'd had of reconciling with Ben was gone. She had allowed Adeola to manipulate her and strip her of the man she loved.

She took one last look at the empty living room and made her decision. She would be a single mother, no matter the consequences. If Kwabena wanted to be with Adeola, there was nothing she could do about it. But she sure as hell was not letting that woman anywhere close to her child, even if it meant that her child may never know his or her father. Tamara did an illegal U-turn in the middle of the street and headed home, tears running down her face.

Kwabena looked at the naked woman lying before him. Not a spot or blemish was on her body. Every curve was perfect, everything in the right proportion. Yet he couldn't get aroused. All he could think of was Tamara.

Adeola kissed his body, letting her tongue play along his chest. Her hands touched all the places that at one time would have had him moaning with pleasure, but it just wasn't working. He wanted to. He needed to. He needed to move on. He needed to desire another, but all he could think of was Tamara.

"Oh, Tammy," he whispered softly.

Adeola froze. She looked down at Kwabena lying still on his back, his eyes closed. "The name's Ade," she snapped. "I'll attribute that to the liquor talking." She resumed touching him. Kwabena remained unresponsive.

"I'm sorry, Ade," he whispered. "I can't do this."

Adeola got up from the bed, and began dressing. Never once in her life had her sexual advances ever been rejected by a man, especially Kwabena. She knew him. She knew his body. She knew what brought him up and what sent him down. Yet he'd chosen a fat, short woman over her.

"Where are you going?" Kwabena asked.

"Home," she answered in frustration, adjusting her bra straps.

"Listen Ade, I'm really sorry. It's not you, it's me."

"Save it." She dressed rapidly, replacing her skintight pants and low-cut sweater. "I tried, but now it's time to admit what I should have admitted a long time ago. I'll never get your heart. Even if I use all the trickery and deceit in the world, you'll never look at me the way you look at Tamara."

She grabbed her purse, leaving him lying naked on the bed. She turned to face him. "Go to her, Kwabena. Go to Tamara. It's clear you love her. I'm the one who pushed her to divorce you. I'm the one who gave her the impression that we were still a couple and that you were using her only for the green card. I wanted you, Kwabena. I really did. But not like this. Go back to her." With that, she left.

Chapter Thirty-five

The dreaded party: Independent Labs's Christmas party. Tamara was reluctant to attend, but knew she had little choice. Mike expected all his lab members to be there. She knew Kwabena would be there, most likely with his Nigerian beauty queen. So she'd worn her finest: a red empire-waist dress with molded cups that hung loosely in front but clung close enough to the back to accentuate her rounded behind. The low-cut top molded to her perfectly round breasts, accentuating her now triple-D cleavage. Below her breasts was a rhinestone clasp that held a red satin sash. The sash hung loosely, concealing her growing bump. The dress highlighted all the right curves and concealed what she didn't want others to see. She wore her hair in tiny curly twists. She knew she looked good, but for her own comfort, she had dragged along Jordan.

This year the party was held at a cocktail lounge in Annapolis. The place was elegantly decorated with crystal chandeliers and mirrors all over the spacious hall. There were multiple balconies overlooking the famed Annapolis Harbor. A live band played cocktail music as guests mingled. It was a semiformal shindig, with current and potential investors in suits sipping wine and champagne with the PIs of the individual labs. Beneath the soft music and dimmed lights, business transactions that determined the direction of Independent Laboratories were being conducted. Pledges for the support of scientific endeavors were being solicited.

Tamara stood talking to Jordan, sipping cranberry juice and munching on a delicate shrimp cocktail.

"I think your ex just made his grand entrance," Jordan observed.

Tamara's eyes turned to the door, her heart attacking her sternum with a vengeance. Kwabena stepped in, wearing a dark gray suit and striped tie, his tall frame filling the entire doorway. His presence filled the room as he greeted the guests with his ever-present, ever-pleasant smile and firm handshakes. Tamara observed him silently, her heart doing somersaults, as several people gathered around him. His presence seemed to attract others—and he looked good. A few seconds later, Adeola walked in, decked out in her most elegant African finery. She stood next to him as he met and greeted guests, oftentimes introducing her to them. Even Tamara had to admit, they looked good together. Tamara turned back to Jordan. A twinge of jealousy shook Tamara's soul. She should have been at Kwabena's side.

Tamara walked around, mingling with the guests. Fortunately she knew most of the postdoctoral fellows, staff scientists and technicians and some of the graduate students at the party. She was talking to a Japanese postdoc when she felt herself being watched. She looked over her shoulder and her eyes locked with Kwabena's. He smiled brightly, revealing his beautiful, even white teeth, and waved at her. She smiled timidly and waved back. Kwabena strode toward her, but was waylaid by Mike and a few potential investors. Soon he was whisked off in another direction to attend to business.

For the next few hours, Kwabena, Mike and several of the PIs were busy courting investors. Jordan had taken the opportunity to network, pitching his business to many potential clients. Tamara hung around with her coworkers, wishing the party was over.

By ten, most of the suits and the family men were gone. According to ten-to-whenever happy-hour winers, this was when the real party began. Champagne and wine were disappearing off the waiters' trays faster than they could be replenished. The open bar got more frequent visits. The dance floor was finally put to use. The music changed in tempo, the conversations got louder, the laughter grew more raucous.

Tamara was talking to a Korean staff scientist from one of the affiliate labs when she saw Kwabena for the first time in hours. He was headed for the dance floor with none other than Adeola. Tamara's heart sank once more. She tried keeping up the conversation with her colleague, but couldn't concentrate. It didn't help that his English was poor.

"I'll go get a drink," she said to her colleague and walked off before he could respond.

She stood at the punch bowl, ladle in hand, about to pour the peach-colored punch into her glass when she heard, "Maybe I should taste it first, make sure it is no spiked. We wouldn't want any tabletop dirty dancing tonight would we?"

Tamara's heart flipped at the sound of Kwabena's accented baritone voice. Despite the calm tone, she could tell he was as nervous as she was. His accent deepened considerably when he was nervous or anxious. Right now he sounded as if he just stepped off the plane from Ghana. She smiled and looked up at him. He stood, observing her, his glass outstretched, waiting for her to pour him the drink, a flirtatious smile on his lips.

"Hi, Ben," Tamara said softly, pouring the drink into his glass.

He tasted the drink. "All clear."

Tamara laughed nervously and poured herself some of the fruit punch.

"So how have you been doing?" Kwabena asked, looking her over. She looked wonderful. From the soft rise of her chest, to the glowing smoothness of her delicate golden skin, to her soft curly twisted hair, she looked good. He could see she had been able to maintain her weight. Whatever she'd gained back was minimal and seemed to be seated on her breasts and backside. He felt a twinge as he thought about her breasts and butt and all the parts of her he had enjoyed just four months ago. He tried not to stare.

"I've been fine. Classes are going well. I do some of my work out of the lab at College Park. That way I can take daytime classes. It's been all good."

"You look good," Kwabena responded. "In fact, you look absolutely gorgeous tonight. I like your dress."

"Thanks." Tamara blushed.

Kwabena smiled. He loved it when she blushed. "So any plans for the holidays?"

"Not really. I've been toying with the idea of going to San Diego, but I haven't made up my mind as yet. Why?"

"Maybe I was planning to ask you out."

Tamara smiled coyly. "And maybe I would say yes."

"Even if that date involved a trip to Vegas?"

Tamara smiled and met his eyes. "Not as exotic as St. Lucia, but it beats the cold and the quiet."

Kwabena laughed. They began chatting easily, like they had so many times in the past. They spoke about Chris and Darlene's engagement and their plans to wed next September. They reminisced about last holidays and the famed Thanksgiving dinner. They reminisced about St. Lucia. Just talking to him felt right. It felt like coming home.

Just then the band began to play "Lady in Red." Kwabena extended his hand. "May I have this dance m'lady?"

Tamara placed her hand in his and they walked hand in hand to the dance floor. They danced together slowly in the dim light. Tamara laid her head on his chest as she had done so many times before. She closed her eyes inhaling deeply. She loved his masculine scent: fresh Irish Spring mixed with Obsession, the cologne she had bought him for his birthday—or was it their anniversary? She had missed him so much. She wanted to hold him forever.

Kwabena leaned his cheek on her head. He loved the scent of her hair: the smell of fresh strawberries and some other fruit, which he knew came from her shampoo and the moisturizer she used at night. He closed his eyes and pictured her standing before the mirror brushing her hair, performing her nightly ritual. He loved the feel of her in his arms moving slowly against his body. He knew without a doubt, he wanted her back in his life. He wanted to wake up next to her every day. Tonight was his chance to win her back, and he was going to do anything in his power to win her back, even if it meant groveling at her feet.

The song ended, but they remained on the dance floor, swaying slowly to imaginary music. Kwabena gently kissed the top of her head. Instead of bolting, she looked up at him and smiled. Their eyes met and held, their hearts beating in unison. Tamara slowly released the breath she was holding.

Kwabena sighed. "It's getting kind of hot in here. Why don't we go outside for some fresh air?"

Tamara followed Kwabena's lead out the glass doors onto the balcony. It was chilly, but they didn't mind. They leaned against the railing, observing the crescent moon shining on the calm waters of the harbor. Millions of stars twinkled in the night sky. Behind them the muted sounds of the band playing oldies love songs filled the air. Neither of them said a word. Each waited nervously for the other to talk.

Kwabena ran his hand through her hair. It felt soft and beautiful through his fingers. He liked the way the moon light highlighted her cheek bones. He liked the soft look of her lips and longed to feel them against his.

"Did I tell you how lovely you look tonight?" he asked, breaking the silence with his deep voice.

Tamara smiled and looked up at him. "Only about a hundred times."

He smiled and looked away. "So are you seeing anyone?"

She shook her head. Kwabena couldn't hide his relief. Here he was with the woman he loved. He had so much he wanted to say to her, but the words evaded him. He had to admit, he didn't expect this. He expected a fight. He expected anger. Their relationship had never been one of gentle flirting and coy statements, but one of open expression.

Oh, hell with it. I may as well get to the point. "I missed you, Tammy," he said. "I want you back in my life."

Tamara closed her eyes. When she opened them, he was staring at her, waiting for a response.

"Why, Ben? Why?"

"Because I still love you. I never stopped loving you."

Tamara turned to face him. "I love you too, Ben, but is that enough? Is love enough? What about honesty and openness and fidelity and trust? What about Adeola?"

His voice was impassioned when he spoke. "Tamara, I know you think that I was unfaithful to you, and I know I hurt you. I'm just asking you to give me a chance to explain what happened." He paused for a short while. "Adeola and I were engaged a long time ago, but that committed relationship ended years ago. There was never a future for Ade and me. When I met you, what Ade and I had was a noncommitted relationship. But the minute you and I became a couple, the minute I started feeling what I felt for you and still feel now, I ended it between us. Yes, things happened between Ade and me while you and I were legally married, and yes, I brought her into your house, into the basement when I was your tenant. And for that I am very sorry. I should have exercised more common sense and never subjected you to that. But I never had any relations with her or anyone else once you and I became intimate. Tammy, I love you, and if I knew that we would have developed the kind of relationship that we developed, I would never have done that. I'm sorry, Tammy. I'm just asking you to forgive me and come back to me. I need you in my life. I need you as my wife."

Tamara took a deep breath. "When Adeola came to me and told me you were a couple waiting to resume your relationship, when she showed me the divorce papers you had drafted, her engagement ring...when she described my bedroom even down to the color of the sheets, I believed her." Tamara swallowed as she felt tears sting her eyes. "I believed her because I never knew she was your ex-fiancée. I believed her because she sounded honest. I believed her because I didn't trust you enough. And when she implied that she was meeting you in Pasadena, I was crushed. I..."

Kwabena drew her into his arms. "Adeola never met me in Pasadena. She and some friends went to Vegas for the weekend. And those divorce papers were drafted a week before our initial INS interview."

"Ben, I was such a fool, and now I've sent you running right back to her."

"Ade and I are not together. We just happened to arrive at the party the same time tonight. I'm not with her."

Tamara stepped away from him and looked out across the waters. She spoke slowly, quietly. "The Saturday after Thanksgiving, I went to your house. I wanted to see you, to talk to you, to ask your forgiveness for misjudging you...to ask you for a second chance. But you were with her. I saw you the two of you at the condo, and I knew it was all over."

"I'm sorry you had to witness that, Tammy. I wanted to move on. I wanted to get over you. I wanted so badly to forget what we had because I thought there was no chance for us. So when Ade approached me, I responded. But I couldn't. I couldn't do it. All I could think of was you and how much I missed and wanted you. Nothing happened between us that night, Tammy. There hasn't been anyone since you were gone."

"Oh, Ben," she whispered, entering his open embrace. "I want you back in my life."

He kissed her gently, tenderly. She enjoyed the beautiful feel of his full lips against hers. He closed his eyes, reveling in the soft sweetness of her kiss, almost forgetting to breathe. He released her slowly, searching her eyes and seeing happiness. He kissed her again, this time with unbridled passion. Every nerve was ignited with passion. Her breathing slow and raspy, her eyes closed, her heart beating wildly, her being filled with love.

When he released her this time, Tamara was shivering…not because of the cold but because of all the deeply buried emotions that surfaced like a tidal wave.

"I want you, Tamara," he said and whispered something in her ear. Tamara blushed and nodded her response. "Let's go home."

Tamara looked at him, a coy smile on her lips. "I thought I'd never live to say this: your place or mine?"

He laughed, a light laugh of a man imbued with happiness. "Ours."

They walked hand in hand into the reception hall and said their good-byes.

The ride home seemed interminable. They held hands all the way. They were happy. As they entered the foyer, Kwabena drew Tamara into his arms and kissed her passionately, caressing her through her clothing. He looked at her and smiled. Then he lifted her gently in his arms and took her to the bedroom he knew so well.

Slowly they undressed each other, hungrily kissing

every inch of exposed flesh. Kwabena laid Tamara naked on the bed. He kissed her eyelids, her cheeks, her chin, her ears, her lips. He kissed her shoulders and neck, letting his tongue linger in the hollow of her throat. He knew that would send her wild, and it did. She gasped, a soft purring sound escaping her lips.

He gently caressed her breasts, feeling her nipples grow hard and erect beneath his fingers. He took each firm, dark nipple into his mouth, kissing, tasting, teasing. Slowly he trailed feathery kisses down her belly to her navel.

Tamara moaned softly, parting her legs in anticipation. She was hot and wet and ready. Kwabena always knew how to use his mouth and tongue to set her on fire. He kissed her rounded belly his tongue darting into her protruding navel. Then he froze.

Hard round belly? Protruding navel? Is this what I think it is? Even when Tamara weighed more than two hundred pounds, she did not have a high belly. There was no mistaking the signs: her darkened nipples, the protruding belly button, but most of all, the telltale dark line that began just above her navel and extended down toward her pubic triangle.

Kwabena brought his face next to Tamara's. He looked her in the eyes. "Tammy, are you pregnant?"

Tamara swallowed and went rigid with fear. She knew he would be angry at her for keeping it from him. She closed her eyes and nodded, yes.

"How far along are you?"

"Twenty weeks."

He did a quick mental calculation, then smiled in relief. It was his baby. And he knew exactly when it happened. It was last August in the swimming pool. They had been spontaneous, unprepared and unprotected. They'd had careless, carefree sex, the kind that made babies without anyone expecting it to happen. And he should have known. It had been two weeks after her menstrual period.

He looked at her, exhaling slowly. "Why didn't you tell me?"

Tamara looked into his eyes. "And what would you have done had I told you?"

He thought for a while. "I would have found you, destroyed those divorce papers and pounded some sense into your head. I'd never abandon my child."

"Exactly. I was afraid if I told you, you would come back to me, not because you loved me and wanted to spend the rest of your life with me, but because of the baby. We would have a marriage of convenience again. Ben, I don't want a marriage of convenience with you, be it for green card, money or a baby. I want a real marriage of love with you."

"Honey, what do I have to do to prove that I love you, whether there is a baby or not?"

Tamara smiled, "Finish what we started."

He laughed softly. He kissed her and worked his way down until he got to her belly. He kissed her belly, caressing it possessively when he felt the baby kick. He stopped. "I'm gonna be a daddy," he said excitedly. "I'm gonna be a daddy! *I'm gonna be a daddy!* Oh, Mama and Papa will be sooooooo happy." He put his ear to her belly. "You know what that means? We've gotta get married. We'll have a traditional African wedding. No, we'll have a Christian wedding. We'll…"

"Ben, we're already married. I never filed the divorce papers."

"Yeah, but that was a civil wedding. I want a real wedding, with a minister to bless our marriage. I want a marriage that is true in the eyes of God. We will have a wedding—a big wedding. We'll have bridesmaids and flower girls, and…"

"Ben…"

"We'll have it in a church. That church you go to on Sundays—and I'll start going with you. No, we'll have it on the lawn."

"Ben…"

"And my family will come over. I know Mama and Papa will come. So will my uncles and aunts. Mike could be my best man, or maybe Chris…"

"Ben?"

"Yes?"

"It's been four months. Shut up and make love to me."

Kwabena smiled, taking Tamara into his arms and making love to her, fulfilling their longing, fulfilling their passion, fulfilling their love for each other.

Epilogue

It was a perfect day for a wedding. Blue skies with nary a cloud, a warm gentle breeze wafting through the oak and willow trees, verdant grass and blooming May flowers: spring filled the air. A trellis with pink and red roses stood on one end of the grassy lawn. The stone pathway, covered with red carpeting led the way from the pool on one end to the gazebo on the other end. Hanging baskets overflowing with pink, white, blue, purple, and red flowers decorated the gazebo. The walkway was lined with baskets of fresh flowers picked from Tamara and Kwabena's well-tended garden, and green potted plants. The large willow close to the gazebo provided shade from the warm May sun. Rented chairs covered with cream fabric and tied with organza bows provided seating for the two hundred-plus guests. Rented tables with beautiful pathos ivy centerpieces nicely wrapped in gold ribbons converted the poolside patio into an elegant outdoor dining room. The pool was decorated with a million floating candles, each giving off a light lavender scent adding to the dreamlike atmosphere. A buffet table under a portable gazebo sported dozens of silver chafing dishes containing a mixture of Caribbean, African and American food. A DJ and a live Ghanaian drumming ensemble provided music for the event.

The guest list was four times the size of Tamara's wedding two years earlier, yet she spent almost nothing. The lovely African dresses for the bride and her bridal party were made of authentic Ghanaian handwoven cloth with intricate embroidery and custom made by Kwabena's aunt. The wedding cake, a five-tiered confection with staircases leading to other smaller cakes, was prepared by Becky. The flowers were all picked from Tamara's garden, which was well tended by Kwabena. Tamara had learned pretty quickly that Kwabena had a knack for gardening and a very green thumb. It began with the privacy hedges and ended with a garden as beautiful as those profiled on television shows. The perfectly presented food was prepared by the African women and Jordan's mother, potluck style. All in all, Tamara paid next to nothing for her wedding. Even the professional photographer and videographer gave their services free. It had been arranged by Leyoca, a part of a promotion for the photographer's work. All the rented chairs and tables were provided by Edebe, who ran a bridal and limousine service.

With everything from the weather to the planning all cooperating wonderfully, it should have been perfect. But as with all things in Tamara's life, arriving at this day was anything but simple. The wedding should have taken place since February, a long time away from her due date. But that was not to be. Kwabena's family wanted to attend. By the time they had obtained visas it was almost May, a few weeks from her due date.

The greatest holdup was Kwabena's great uncle Kofi, his mother's maternal uncle. For reasons beyond Tamara's comprehension, nothing happened in that family without his approval. Kwame and Akwape only married with his approval, as had Afie and her husband. However, since Tamara was American and her roots could neither be traced back to Asante, Fante or Akan heritage, he was uncomfortable giving his blessing to the marriage. So he insisted on coming to America to meet Tamara before approving the marriage. Unfortunately, he had neither a passport or visa. When he finally obtained them, it was the beginning of May. The wedding date was set a week after he bestowed his blessing. Tamara was thirty-eight weeks pregnant.

When Tamara met him, she expected a big, tall person. She was surprised to see a very small shriveled old man with a shy smile. He looked a hundred years old. Tamara wondered how someone as small and quaint as this man could be the commander in chief of this large family. All that changed when he opened his mouth. He had a voice that bellowed deep and loud and strong. His voice was as commanding as James Earl Jones as Mufasa in *The Lion King*. Everyone deferred to him, and Tamara finally understood why. Kwabena and Akwape wanted a Christian wedding; Uncle Kofi wanted a traditional African wedding. Eventually they compromised on an African-American wedding. The style was Christian with a minister presiding over the exchange of vows, but the dress, the cuisine, and some of the rituals were traditional African.

"Ready?" Jordan asked, taking her hand in his.

Tamara smiled up at him. "I've been ready for two years now."

The bridal party, all dressed in traditional African dresses, preceded them as Jordan escorted a very pregnant Tamara from the deck and down the aisle. She was the epitome of radiant beauty. Her neatly braided hair was elaborately wrapped in a gold head piece. She wore a cream dress of Adinkra cloth with elaborate gold hardanger-styled embroidery, the loosely fitted sash effectively concealing her super-sized low-riding belly. The embroidered design: a crescent moon and star, Osram ne Nsoroma, represented loyalty, faithfulness, harmony and love. She was an African queen.

As Tamara walked slowly, smiling at the many guests assembled for her wedding, she felt a cramp in her lower abdomen and back. She stiffened on Jordan's arms.

"Are you ok?" he whispered in her ear.

"Just some Braxton-Hicks," she whispered in response and continued walking. "False contractions."

They continued up the aisle where Leyoca, decked out in a beautiful brown and gold Ghanaian dress with a matching headpiece, joined them in the walk to meet Kwabena. It was a dress fit for the mother of the bride and Leyoca wore it with regal bearing. With a bow, both Jordan and Leyoca handed Tamara over to Kwabena.

Tamara looked up at Kwabena and smiled. Boy was she happy she'd worn five-inch platform sandals. Everyone had told her flats was the way to go in that dress, but with Kwabena's height, she needed to balance out things a bit. Her pregnancy and her slightly swollen feet did not permit her favorite stilettos, but the platforms were beautiful. Thank goodness they were back in fashion.

Kwabena stood tall and proud, in a brown and gold robe with sash and matching kofia and sandaled feet.

He was freshly shaven, his coffee-cream skin glistening. He looked like royalty.

Kwabena smiled down at Tamara, his heart racing in anticipation. She was beautiful, the most beautiful person present. Her face was radiant. He couldn't believe he'd almost lost her. He was happy to be here, to let the whole world know that he was committing and would remain committed to his beautiful wife forever.

"You look wonderful," he whispered as he bowed and kissed her hand.

Tamara felt her lower back and abdomen contract once more, this time lasting a few seconds. She dismissed it again. After all, she was a full two weeks from her due date, and everyone had told her, first babies are always long in coming. Plus, she'd been to the altar before without exchanging vows. Nothing was going to prevent her from exchanging these wedding vows with Kwabena today—not even a baby. The contraction caused her to grip Kwabena's hand like a vise. When she released him, the blood was drained from his hands.

He looked at her quizzically. She smiled reassuringly. They'd been through the Braxton-Hicks and the baby kicks before. In fact, sometimes the baby kicked so hard it distended her belly like an alien.

They looked in each other's eyes as they exchanged the traditional Christian vows to honor, obey, love and respect each other till death. Finally, after a lengthy ceremony, the minister announced, "I now pronounce you man and wife. You may kiss the bride."

Tamara and Kwabena kissed passionately, and walked back down the aisle amid the cheers of friends and family. As they greeted the guests, another contraction froze Tamara. Kwabena, busy smiling, laughing and greeting friends and family did not notice.

At the reception, Kwabena and Tamara opened the floor with their song, "Lady in Red." It was the song they danced to the night of their first union. It was the song they danced to the night of their reunion. It was the song they were dancing to the night of their wedding.

"Ben," Tamara whispered as they danced to a series of love songs while their friends and relatives swirled around them, "I think it's…"

Tamara felt a tap on her shoulder and swung around to face Darlene. "Time to cut the cake, guys," Darlene said and whisked them over to the table with the enormous cake.

Tamara went through the motions of cutting the cake and feeding Kwabena, but she was worried. The contractions were coming too frequently to be Braxton-Hicks. But before she could say anything to Kwabena, she was whisked off to throw the bouquet, which Ebony caught with ease.

Within minutes, Tamara was seated on a chair in the center of the room, while men urged Kwabena to remove her garter. The guys were all chanting, "Use your mouth. Use your mouth," encouraging Kwabena to remove the garter with his teeth rather than his hands.

As Kwabena raised Tamara's skirt, she felt a contraction so long and hard she wanted to scream. "Ben, I think the baby's coming," Tamara whispered frantically.

Kwabena could not hear above the din of the chants

and proceeded to remove the garter from her leg with his teeth. Suddenly Tamara felt a gush of warm water escape her. Her skirt was wet, her legs were wet. Her water had broken.

Kwabena stood up staggering slightly, a panicked expression on his face. He was happy, excited and scared all at the same time. Despite his normally cool and calm demeanor, Kwabena froze. Tamara was having his baby, and she was having it now.

They had barely made it up to the master bedroom when another contraction hit. This one was barely a minute behind the first one and was accompanied by a second gush of amniotic fluid.

Tamara got to the bed, just as Kwabena's mother entered the room.

"Let me examine you," Akwape said.

"Hell, no!" Tamara responded emphatically before another long contraction hit. The contractions were now coming one on top of the other.

"Tammy, Mama is a midwife. She knows what she's doing. I'll call Dr. Falcon, and we'll meet him at the hospital."

Tamara reluctantly allowed Akwape to examine her. Akwape looked at Kwabena. "Forget about hospital. We aren't going anywhere. The baby is crowning."

Akwape immediately took charge, barking orders to the women who had accompanied them upstairs. In the meantime, the party downstairs resumed under the direction of Darlene and Chris. The music, a mixture of West African drumming, soukous, R&B, hip-hop and jazz could be heard through the open French doors of the master bedroom.

Kwabena stood by the bed, holding Tamara's hand. Akwape looked at him. "Get out!" she barked in heavily accented English. "Childbirth is a women's affair. Men have no duty here."

Kwabena looked at his mother and responded firmly but respectfully, "No Mama, my place is here. I put that baby in there and I want to see it come out."

Akwape shouted to him sharply in Akan. Kwabena answered back in the same language, carefully keeping his tone reverent, but maintaining his position.

Leyoca looked at the exchange before butting in, "In Ghanaian tradition, it may be taboo for men to witness childbirth, but this is America. You don't know how reassuring it is to see a man willing to take responsibility for his child from birth. Akwape, this is the first chance he will get to really bond with his baby. Let him stay if he so desires."

Akwape looked at Tamara, silently questioning her desire for Kwabena to witness the birth. Tamara looked at her and took a deep breath. "Mama, it's ok. I want Ben in here with me." She looked at Ben as he lovingly wiped her sweat-drenched brow with a handkerchief.

"Ok, push," Akwape instructed her.

Tamara pushed with all her might. Perspiration soaked her wedding dress. She squeezed on Kwabena's hand until it went numb.

"Push!"

Tamara pushed with all her might, then lay back exhausted. Suddenly she heard the cries of a baby.

"It's a boy," Akwape said excitedly. She called to Kwabena. "You can cut the cord."

Kwabena smiled and left his station by Tamara's bedside, gently cutting the umbilical cord with sewing scissors, sterilized by boiling water and rubbing alcohol.

Akwape cleaned the baby as best she could and placed the crying infant in Tamara's arms. Tamara looked at her tiny son, and tears came to her eyes. Kwabena could hardly hold back the tears of joy as he looked at his little baby.

Leyoca came over to them and smiled happily. "You broke the trend," she observed.

Tamara looked at her confused. "Single motherhood?"

"No, daughters. My grandmother had one girl, my mother had two girls, Leticia had two girls, I had a girl and Ebony had two girls. You have a baby boy."

Tamara smiled and looked down at her baby boy. She looked up at her husband and their eyes held. She never felt this loved before in her life. She was complete.

In his wildest dreams Kwabena never imagined his life taking this turn, but he couldn't be happier. In the distance, he could hear the sound of the ambulance coming to take Tamara and his baby to the hospital. He could hear the revelers outside partying. He looked down at Tamara.

"What shall we name him?"

Tamara smiled. "Let's call him Kwabena."

Kwabena shook his head. "Kwabena means born on a Tuesday. Today is Saturday."

"How about Benjamin?"

"Benjamin junior." He smiled. "I love the name. His second name can be Kwame. That means born on Saturday. It will make Papa very happy."

Tamara looked down at the tiny infant sleeping peacefully in her arms, then looked up at her loving husband. "He looks like a Kwame. Benjamin Kwame Opoku, I love that name."

"I love you, Tammy."

"I love you too, Ben."

They looked at each other and knew they had found love, they had found home, they had a family, they were complete.

The holidays aren't so festive when you're
celebrating by yourself. But with a little luck and
a lot of love, three single women find their soul
mates and get the holiday weddings of their dreams.

Holiday Brides

"NO ORDINARY GIFT" FARRAH ROCHON

They had the start of something real, but one of them got
scared. Now that a special Kwanzaa celebration has thrown
them together again, he's determined not to let go until she
says, "I do."

"HEAVENSENT.COM" STEFANIE WORTH

Can an online dating site and two guardian angels change
one career woman's mind before the clock strikes midnight
on New Year's Eve?

"FROM SKB WITH LOVE" JEWEL AMETHYST

A whirlwind affair on the tropical island of St. Kitts would
lead to a romance to remember and a Christmas morning
ceremony on the sparkling white sands.

ISBN 13: 978-0-8439-6319-

To order a book or to request a catalog call:
1-800-481-9191
Our books are also available at your local bookstore, or you
can check out our Web site **www.dorchesterpub.com**
where you can look up your favorite authors, read excerpts,
glance at our discussion forum, and check out our digital
content. Many of our books are now available as e-books!

Deborah MacGillivray

Trevelyn Sinclair Mershan is…

A WOLF IN WOLF'S CLOTHING

Revenge—that was Trev's goal when he first set his sights on Raven. And a delicious revenge it would be. He and his two brothers had each selected a Montgomerie sister to systematically seduce and destroy, and this quiet granddaughter of his enemy was perfect. She lived simply in a cottage in the English countryside, a painter, and socialized only with gypsies and a menagerie of misfits: her fat orange tabby, her one-legged seagull and midget pony. And in addition to beauty, Raven had a delicious vulnerability begging to be exploited. Trev was happy to oblige. In fact, it felt like destiny.

"What makes MacGillivray's romance so special are the eccentric characters…."
—*Booklist* on *The Invasion of Falgannon Isle*

Magic and fate have brought a self-proclaimed wolf to Colford Hall. He's dressed in a designer suit, drives a Lamborghini Murciélago and apologizes for nothing. And though Trev doesn't realize it, wolves mate for life.

ISBN 13: 978-0-505-52781-3

COLLEEN THOMPSON

"[Thompson] more than holds her own in territory blazed by Tami Hoag and Tess Gerritsen."

—*Publishers Weekly*

In Deep Water

Ruby Monroe knows she's way out of her depth the minute she lays eyes on Sam McCoy. She's been warned to steer clear of this neighbor, the sexy bad boy with a criminal past. But with her four-year-old daughter missing, her home incinerated and her own life threatened by a tattooed gunman, where else can she turn? Drowning in the flood of emotion unleashed by their mind-blowing encounters, Ruby is horrified to learn an unidentified body has been dredged up, the local sheriff is somehow involved, and Sam hasn't told her all he knows. Has she put her trust in the wrong man and jeopardized her very survival by uncovering the secrets...

BENEATH BONE LAKE

ISBN 13: 978-0-8439-6243-7

FARRAH ROCHON

"Rochon presents a stellar story that thoroughly entertains."
—*Romantic Times BOOKreviews* on *Release Me*

Rescue Me

Sometimes love needs a little push...

His two younger brothers have both taken the plunge, and now the entire Holmes clan has their sights set on him. But Alexander Holmes is no fool for love. He's been there, done that, and all he has to show for it is a whole lot of scars and one beautiful little girl. Unfortunately, his precious angel has become a terror in the classroom, so Alex has no choice but to trade in his tool belt for a text book.

And sometimes it needs a big shove...

When Renee Moore sees the new parent volunteer waging war against the school copy machine, she can't help admiring his obvious...assets. After all, there's nothing sexier than a parent who's involved—especially when he has a rock-solid body and a voice that makes her weak in the knees. Even more important, underneath that hot exterior is a man she knows she can trust and respect. All she has to do is convince him to give love a second chance.

ISBN 13: 978-0-8439-6224-6

"Kate Angell is to baseball as Susan Elizabeth Phillips
is to football. Wonderful!"
— *USA Today* Bestselling Author Sandra Hill

KATE ANGELL

WHO'D BEEN SLEEPING IN KASON RHODES'S BED?

The left fielder for the Richmond Rogues had returned
from six weeks of spring training in Florida to find someone
had moved into his mobile home. That person was presently
in his shower. And no matter how sexy the squatter might be,
Kason wanted her out.

He had his trusty dobie, Cimarron; he didn't need anyone
else in his life. Not even a stubborn tomboy who roused all
kinds of wild reactions in him, then soothed his soul with
peace offerings of macaroni & cheese and rainbow Jell-O.
The bad boy of baseball was ready to play hardball if need be,
but with Dayne Sheridan firmly planted between his sheets,
he found himself . . .

SLIDING
HOME

ISBN 13: 978-0-505-52808-7

A Taste of Magic

Tracy Madison

"Fun, quirky and delicious!"
—Annette Blair, National Bestselling Author
of *Never Been Witched*

MIXING IT UP

Today is Elizabeth Stevens's birthday, and not only is it the one-year anniversary of her husband leaving her, it's also the day her bakery is required to make a cake—for her ex's next wedding. If there's a bitter taste in her mouth, no one can blame her.

But today, Liz is about to receive a gift. Her Grandma Verda isn't just wacky; she's a little witchy. An ancient gypsy magic has been passed through the family bloodline for generations, and it's Liz's turn to be empowered. Henceforth, everything she bakes will have a dash of delight and a pinch of wishes-can-come-true. From her hunky policeman neighbor, to her gorgeous personal trainer, to her bum of an ex-husband, everyone Liz knows is going to taste her power. Revenge is sweet…and it's only the first dish to be served.

ISBN 13: 978-0-505-52810-0

JOY NASH

When a girl with no family meets a guy with too much...

For Tori Morgan, family's a blessing the universe hasn't sent her way. Her parents are long gone, her chance of having a baby is slipping away, and the only thing she can call her own is a neglected old house. What she wants more than anything is a place where she belongs...and a big, noisy clan to share her life.

For Nick Santangelo, family's more like a curse. His *nonna* is a closet kleptomaniac, his mom's a menopausal time bomb and his motherless daughter is headed for serious boy trouble. The last thing Nick needs is another female making demands on his time.

But summer on the Jersey shore can be an enchanted season, when life's hurts are soothed by the ebb and flow of the tides and love can bring together the most unlikely prospects. A hard-headed contractor and a lonely reader of tarot cards and crystal prisms? All it takes is...

A Little Light Magic

ISBN 13: 978-0-505-52693-9